RESISTANCE WAS FUTILE

Remain calm, Lacy told herself. Above all else, remain calm. "Where are your clothes?" she asked him.

"Body heat, Miss Garder. It was the only way to warm you up."

"And I suppose *underwear* wasn't a consideration?"

"Clothing is meant to keep body heat in. Hardly a benefit when attempting to share."

His fingers were making tantalizing little circles on her back, and she sucked in a startled breath. "Hey. We hate each other, remember?"

He slid his big hand down the curve of her bottom. She had to make a conscious effort not to groan.

"Yeah," he said softly. "We hate each other all to pieces."

Books by Suzanne Elizabeth

When Destiny Calls
Fan the Flame
Kiley's Storm
Destined to Love
Destiny Awaits
Till the End of Time
Destiny's Embrace
*Destiny in Disguise**

Published by HarperPaperbacks
*coming soon

Destiny's Embrace

⊱ SUZANNE ELIZABETH ⊰

HarperPaperbacks
A Division of HarperCollinsPublishers

HarperPaperbacks

A Division of HarperCollins*Publishers*
10 East 53rd Street, New York, N.Y. 10022-5299

This is a work of fiction. The characters, incidents, and
dialogues are products of the author's imagination and are not to
be construed as real. Any resemblance to actual events or
persons, living or dead, is entirely coincidental.

ISBN 0-06-108341-0

HarperCollins®, ®, HarperPaperbacks™, and
HarperMonogram® are trademarks of HarperCollins*Publishers* Inc.

Cover illustration by Vittorio

First printing: October 1996

Printed in the United States of America

Visit HarperPaperbacks on the World Wide Web at
http://www.harpercollins.com/paperbacks

❖ 10 9 8 7 6 5 4 3 2 1

For little Suzie, who spent her life searching people, places—things—for her happiness . . . only to discover that she'd been in possession of it all along.

Destiny's Embrace

Prologue

The business of fulfilling destinies is a tricky and by no means unerring science. Stella had spent her entire custodial career reminding herself and others of that. When dealing with the unpredictable and sometimes irrational dispositions of human beings, there simply were no guarantees, only honest to goodness best intentions.

And sometimes even heaven made mistakes.

Occasionally an earthbound soul was born in the wrong place or even in the wrong time, something other than what was contractually agreed. Thus placement hearings were not uncommon in the Department of Spiritual Affairs. And every guide without something pressing to deal with attended—not only out of curiosity, but to be sure that their clients weren't affected by the outcome.

This day was no different. The Celestial Auditorium was packed to overflowing with eager, apprehensive angels as Stella stood twiddling her thumbs to keep herself calm. Maximillian, the Director of Spiritual Affairs, brought the meeting to order from behind his

high, white bench and Stella struggled to hide her
anxiety. She'd defended at several of these hearings
during her long, illustrious career, but this would be
her toughest case yet. For the sake of her floundering
client, she had to persuade Maximillian to see things
her way.

"Stella," the director greeted with a nod.

She smiled politely and tried to put some meaning
to his casual tone, give herself some shred of hope
that he might be on her side in this matter. But, as
usual, his regal expression was unreadable.

"I understand you've put in for a promotion to
management," he continued.

"Yes. Yes I have."

"Your record is impeccable. I'm sure you'd make a
superb guidance supervisor."

"Thank you, sir. I hope you'll keep that in mind
while deciding this case." She wanted this hearing
over and done with as quickly as possible. Frankly,
she was afraid to leave her client alone down on earth
any longer than was absolutely necessary.

"Is this woman your last assignment?" Maximillian
asked.

"Yes, sir, she is." And thank heaven for that, Stella
added to herself. After dealing with Lacey Garder for
the past three years she was due for a long vacation at
the very least.

Maximillian smiled. "Nothing like going out with a
bang, is there?"

The representative of the opposing side smacked his
hands down onto the disputer's table and stood. "This is
all very interesting, but if we could please get on with—"

"Sit down, Nelson," Maximillian directed, frowning at the young angel. "I'm fully aware of the
urgency concerning this little problem."

The tall, cleft-chinned angel smiled wryly. "I beg your pardon, sir, but calling Miss Lacey Garder a little problem is a rather large understatement."

Maximillian's frown darkened, and Nelson promptly sat back down in his chair. "How are things in San Diego, Stella?" the director continued.

Stella blanched at the question, and with all her heart she wished she still had the human capacity to lie. "Things?" she repeated. "I'm, um, I'm afraid they're not so . . . so good, sir."

"Then you're still not seeing any signs of spiritual progress?"

"No. Not yet," she was quick to add.

"Not *yet*?" Nelson echoed, standing again. "Sir, Stella has been hoping for progress for three long years now, keeping the rest of your guides teetering on the edges of their seats, so to speak, wondering whether or not this spiritual catastrophe of hers is going to be set loose on their clients in the nineteenth century. In my opinion there is no hope. Miss Lacey Garder is irredeemable."

"*Irredeemable*!" Stella burst out. "And what gives you the authority to make such an offensive supposition?"

"The woman has no conscience—"

"She wouldn't hurt a fly!" Stella defended.

"I agree. She'd be far too busy stealing the poor insect's wallet!"

The auditorium broke into muffled laughter, but Maximillian cleared his throat, and that was all it took to bring things back to order. He looked straight at Nelson, who paled visibly. "I will not stand for this sort of inflammatory display. You are not the only disputer in this department, and if you cannot stick to the facts and control your opinions then I can easily have you removed from this case."

Nelson smiled grimly. "I apologize," he muttered, and sank back down into his chair.

Stella was relieved to note that Maximillian's expression softened when he settled his attention back on her. "I understand you're here to request a relocation."

"Yes," she said confidently. "I feel the time has come."

Nelson made a grumbling sound and Maximillian turned his attention to the disputer's table. "And obviously you are here to dispute it?"

"Yes, sir," Nelson replied. "That's correct, sir."

"Then let us proceed. Stella, you may state your case."

Stella took a deep breath. "Thank you." Maximillian hated long-winded speeches, so she knew her best bet was to make her point as quickly and concisely as possible. She'd been rehearsing it for hours. "My case is very simple," she began. "As is standard, my client received a valid contract from us before leaving to begin her temporal life. She agreed to certain terms, and we agreed to certain terms. However, the moment her placement error occurred, the very second she was born in the twentieth century instead of the nineteenth, we failed to live up to our end of the bargain. Why, then, should we expect her to be living up to her end?"

That said, Stella sat down in her chair behind the defender's table and took another deep, calming breath. Maximillian simply had to agree to a relocation. If he didn't, she wasn't sure she'd be able to save her client from certain spiritual disaster.

Maximillian nodded thoughtfully at her, and then he turned to Nelson. "You may now proceed."

"And proceed I will, sir," the angel replied, rising

dramatically from his chair. "Why then, Stella asks, should her client be expected to live up to her end of the bargain? Why? Because she's been given a conscience like everyone else. Because she's been given morals like everyone else. Because she knows the difference between right and wrong, good and bad, and yet chooses—*chooses, mind you*—to live this lovely little scoundrel's life that she's carved out for herself. And now her faithful spiritual guide wishes for us to place her back into the century where she rightfully belongs, hoping that this will magically correct the woman's poor values. Well I say, what about the others? What about the clients of all the noteworthy guides in attendance here today who will be directly affected by Miss Garder's nefarious presence? Don't we have contracts with them as well? Weren't they promised certain ways of life and liberties? Frankly," he added, chuckling, "I'm surprised by Stella's single-mindedness in this matter. One might think she's lost her perspective after all these years."

Stella glared at Nelson as he sat back down in his chair.

Maximillian leaned back and sighed. "Stella, I have read your reports on this young woman, and find I can understand why you've taken this case so much to heart. Because of this placement error, your client's life thus far has been an unfortunate one. Still, she has displayed a consistency toward making unfavorable choices, and I hesitate to place such an unpredictable presence in the midst of others who are struggling to walk the straight and narrow."

"But her mission!" Stella interjected. "The happiness of others is at stake if she isn't relocated."

"Stella, you know as well as I that many times missions can be accomplished in other ways, and with almost precise accuracy. Relocations are rarely ever imperative for anyone but the client."

Stella's hopes began to slip. She thought of Lacey Garder, of her inability to trust and to love, and shook her head sadly. "Refusing this relocation would be very tragic, sir."

"I agree. And you must understand that I want to give this woman a chance. But the opportunity for her to do something destructive is so vast—"

"Not if I'm allowed to intervene."

The director blinked at her in surprise.

"Objection!" Nelson cried, jumping to his feet as the entire auditorium erupted. "Intervening is forbidden! *Strictly* forbidden by Section 23 of the Code of Guardians. I absolutely protest!"

"What basis do you have for making such an extraordinary request?" Maximillian asked of her.

"You've read my reports," Stella replied. "This is a most extraordinary situation. If I'm allowed to intervene when necessary, to remind Miss Garder of her innate goodness, then perhaps she will begin to recognize it on her own. She's been either abused or abandoned by every person in her life, sir, and none of them has bothered to offer her a moment of productive guidance. Allow her this one final opportunity to turn her life around."

"Sir," Nelson pleaded, "agree to this proposterousness and you will be making a serious mistake. Relocating this woman could cause irreparable harm to those she'll come into contact with. I've said it before, and I'll say it again: This woman is *irredeemable*."

Maximillian sighed. "Nelson," he began slowly, "you haven't been with us long, so allow me to remind you of something. It isn't for us to judge them, it is

simply our job to guide them. This woman may yet
surprise us all."

"And if she doesn't, sir? If she continues on this
path of duplicity and begins to destroy the lives of
others who have been promised things as well?"

Maximillian nodded slowly. "That is why I'm going
to grant Stella's request to intervene."

"But, sir!—"

Maximillian held up a silencing hand. "Stella, you
may relocate your client and inform her of her mission, which she will be expected to complete to the
very best of her ability within one week. If she shows
no true signs of doing so, or if she interferes in any
detrimental way with the lives of the others in her
midst, you are to return her to the twentieth century
and to the circumstances in which you found her."

"Yes, sir," Stella said, relieved beyond description
and yet hoping one week would be enough time.

"Is that satisfactory, Nelson?"

"Can I say no?" Nelson replied testily.

Maximillian glowered. "No. You cannot."

"Well, then, there it is."

1

San Diego, 1996

Lacey Garder stared dispassionately at the man sitting across the table from her in the attorney conferencing room. He was a typical-looking public defender: thin and watery-eyed, with a choirboy haircut and a little too much cologne. He didn't exactly inspire confidence, but she was considering how lucky she was to have him as she assessed his cheap blue suit. The more helpless she appeared in court, the better her chances were of beating this rap and getting the hell out of town.

"How do you intend to plead?" Paul F. Baker asked in a monotone that suggested he'd already posed the question a hundred times that day.

Lacey ignored his question and glanced up toward the ceiling. Bright floodlights were placed in three-foot intervals above her head, adding to the stark reality of the room. She imagined that most people who sat where she was now probably felt like rats under glass, but she'd done this dance so many times before it was like a walk in the park to her.

"May I make a suggestion?" her tireless public defender asked. He leaned back in his metal folding chair until it creaked. "Plead guilty."

Lacey still didn't respond. She chewed her gum and stared at him, at his thin lips, his chinless face and tiny blue eyes, and waited for him to explain— because she knew he was dying to.

"It'll save the city the cost and hassle of a trial," he continued, "and the judge may take that into consideration during your sentencing. Trust me. Plead guilty."

Possibly a suggestion for someone with a little less determination to avoid a prison term, but Lacey was a bit more motivated than that. What had this man been thinking when he'd been handed her extensive file? That he'd be defending a half-witted idiot?

"Frankly," he added, with a faint chuckle, "I'm stumped at what you could hope to gain by pleading innocent."

Uh-oh. Perry Mason was stumped. "Exactly how long have you been practicing?" she asked.

He blinked, probably more surprised that she'd dare to question his impeccable credentials than that she'd finally opened her mouth and spoken.

"Two years."

"Two years?" She leaned back in her chair and folded her arms. "Well, Mr. Baker, two years ago I was being brought up on charges for my fifteenth misdemeanor. Which would suggest that I've spent more time in a courtroom than you."

He smirked at her. "That's not exactly a point to brag about, Miss Garder."

"I agree. I'm certainly not proud of being caught so many times."

She knew she'd shocked him by the way his small

eyes narrowed, and it was her turn to smirk. Ever since the age of seven, when she'd lifted her first wallet, her chosen occupation had been a life of crime. And remorse was something she'd never felt. Hell, to ask her to feel bad about what she did for a living would be like asking Mr. Baker here to repent for taking the bar exam.

He cleared his throat and leaned forward, placing his elbows on the table. "Miss Garder, just exactly what do you intend your plea to be?"

Lacey sighed and began her standard speech. "I was born to a heroin addict, and spent the first five years of my life in and out of hospitals—until my loving mother was finally charged with child abuse. I was then shuffled back and forth between a countless number of foster homes before being labeled unmanageable. I landed in a youth home when I was thirteen, and remained there until I turned eighteen. I am without means, without prospects, and I'm only trying to survive in this dark, dangerous world the best way I know how. My crimes are nonviolent, do not involve children, are basically unimportant compared to the rest of the judge's docket, and putting me in jail for any significant amount of time would be cruel and unusual punishment." She finished by punctuating her statement with a tight smile.

"You intend to tell the judge all that, do you?"

"No, Mr. Baker, that's your job. My job is to wear something unassuming, and cry at all the right moments."

He frowned and casually looked her over as if reassessing his initial opinion. Then he turned his attention to the thick file resting on the table in front of him and thumbed up the top page. "I take it this tactic has worked for you in the past?"

George gave him a bolstering clap on the shoulder. "I know you will, son." Then he broke into a smile. "That is, if Miss Lacey Garder doesn't kill ya first."

Matthew rolled his eyes at the reminder that he had more than stolen bank money to worry about. "Maybe I'll get lucky and in the morning Miss Lacey Garder will have vanished as mysteriously as she arrived."

George chuckled. "I wouldn't count on it. That's the kinda woman sent by the good lord to keep men like you and me in line."

As if on cue, Hazel called from the front room, "George? What are ya doin' in there, roastin' a turkey? Bring the pie and some plates when you come back."

"I hear ya, honey," he called. He gave Matthew a direct look. "See what I mean?" He gathered up some plates from the cupboard, scooped up the tin of pie on the counter, and turned for the hallway. "Buck up, son. Unless the young lady plans to knife ya in your sleep tonight, you oughta survive just fine till mornin'."

By the light of a kerosene lamp on the night table, Lacey found a fresh nightgown hanging in the armoire and quickly put it on. There was a biting chill in the room, and she hurried to the bed and snatched up a small quilt to wrap herself in. Then she dropped down on the edge of the feather mattress and reached for her purse.

She needed a reality check.

She unzipped the soft suede, and pulled out her wallet. It was full of twentieth-century money that was useless to her now. She popped open the side flap and stared at her driver's license. Yes, she was Lacey Garder. Yes, she was born in 1976. Yes, she was completely sane.

She heaved a heavy sigh and put the wallet back into her purse beside her small canister of pepper spray. Then she tucked the purse under the bed out of sight. Yawning, she leaned back on the bed and checked out her room.

Besides the armoire, there was a short dresser against the far wall with a porcelain pitcher and washbowl resting on top of it. Lacey stared at the washbowl, with its lacquered, painted rose design, and figured it was pretty safe to assume that she was staring at her sink. The latrine itself would be outside somewhere, well out of smelling range of the house, meaning she'd have to trudge through a blizzard to reach it. Considering how much water she had drunk at dinner, she figured it was best not to think about that at the moment.

The bed beneath her creaked. It was the old-fashioned wrought-iron type with a half-moon head-board and springs supporting the lone mattress. The two fluffy pillows beside her looked very inviting, as did the bed's mound of thick blankets, but Lacey resisted the urge to lie down. She had too much to work through, and couldn't afford to rest.

She had to find that little woman. That spiritual guide, as she'd called herself. And what was that, anyway? Some sort of angel? And how in the world did a person get in touch with one? By calling 1-800-ST. PETER?

A soft knock came at her door. "Lacey, honey? Did you find everything all right?"

It was Hazel Martin. She was a nice woman. A bit doting, but nice.

"Lacey?"

"Just a minute," Lacey called back. She checked to be sure her purse was out of sight, and then shrugged off the quilt and went to the door. Hazel was standing on the other side, smiling. "I found everything fine, thank you," Lacey said.

"Then come on into the parlor and have some pie and clotted cream with us."

She followed Hazel into the parlor where the fire in the hearth was still going full blast. The leather chair that Lacey had been sitting in all afternoon had been moved back to its position across from the couch, and Hazel sat down in it to serve from a tin of pie resting on the coffee table. George Martin was sitting on a stool next to the fire. The marshal was sitting on the couch, and his dark gaze swung toward her as she entered the room.

"Any permanent damage, Miss Garder?" George asked, as his wife handed him a piece of pie.

"No," Lacey replied. But she intended to stay a good five feet from that hearth at all times.

"Did Hazel tell ya about the time she singed her hiney over a brandin' fire?"

"It was mentioned, George," Hazel retorted. She turned to Lacey. "Have a seat, dear," and handed over a small plate of pie.

"The missus couldn't sit down for a week straight," George continued. "All she did was whine about how much her feet hurt from havin' to stand all the time. That wasn't the worst of it, though. She had to let the air get at the burns for 'em to heal properly, so I'd come home from a hard day's work and find her lyin' face first on the bed. Yep, the sight that greeted me each and every night was a backside as red as a radish—"

A glob of cream went flying through the air and hit George right between the eyes. Hazel burst into laughter, and Lacey had to bite her bottom lip to keep from doing the same. "Goodness, George," Hazel said. "It looks as if you've been bombarded by a large seabird."

"More like an old hen, my love," he retorted, and wiped the mess from his forehead.

Hazel looked over at Lacey. "Sit. Sit," she commanded.

But the only place left to sit was beside the marshal on the couch, and Lacey felt just a tad uncomfortable plopping herself down beside him after she'd stomped his toe, punched him in the stomach, and then kicked him in the face. Not to mention the fact that he kept glowering at her.

"Go on," Hazel prompted. "Cream, Matthew?"

"No, thank you," he said, and Hazel handed him a plate of pie.

Lacey realized that her apprehensions about the marshal were beginning to show. She figured she shouldn't blame him for being ticked about her karate-kicking him in the nose, but the least he could do was cut her a little slack considering she'd been ablaze at the time.

She steadied her nerves and sat down beside him with her plate of pie in her hand, and heaved an inner sigh of relief when he propped his ankle up on his knee and, for all intents and purposes, ignored her.

"So, Lacey, how long are ya intendin' to stay in our quiet little town?" Hazel asked, serving herself some pie. "Dare I hope that you might be plannin' to make it your permanent residence?"

Lacey could have sworn she actually saw the marshal's ears perk. She chewed the bite of apple pie in her mouth and swallowed. "I haven't decided yet," she answered. Let him gnaw on *that* for a while, she thought spitefully.

"Lord knows we could use a few more women around here," Hazel put in.

"Yep," George said. "It just might tame the lumberjacks down a bit if there were a few more to go around."

"Who's talkin' about the lumberjacks?" Hazel retorted. "I could always use another female ear to jabber off. And Lacey's got spunk. Not like our newest female citizen. That Amanda Simmons is the sweetest little thing, Lacey, but I swear she's got the constitution of a bunny rabbit. How she'll survive through one single winter here, I just don't know—" George cleared his throat, and Hazel suddenly shot a startled look at the marshal, as if she'd forgotten that he was in the room.

Lacey angled the lawman a curious look and found his expression downright morose. Just what was this Amanda Simmons to him?

Hazel quickly tried to recover whatever blunder she'd obviously just made. "That . . . that is to say . . . she's such a—a tenderhearted young woman. Such a gentle soul— How are things goin' between the two of you, Matthew?"

"Fine," the marshal answered curtly.

"Matthew says he might be makin' an announcement soon," George piped up, grinning.

"Really?" Hazel looked surprised.

"Maybe in a while," the marshal replied.

"An announcement about what?" Lacey asked.

George's grin broadened. "Matthew, here's, been courtin' the town schoolteacher. He's workin' up the courage to propose."

"Really. Congratulations—or my deepest sympathies, whichever you feel best applies."

"I take it you have a problem with marriage," the marshal replied. "Or does it only have a problem with you?"

"I just don't understand why women get so excited about the idea, when all it really means is that the man they're involved with is tired of doing his own cooking and cleaning."

Hazel snickered, and she and Lacey shared a conspiratorial smile.

"And what it means for a woman, Miss Garder," the marshal answered, "is security, protection, and support."

"I provide all those things for myself."

"Is that why you were out lost in a snowstorm?" he asked. "Is that why you're now relying on the kindness of strangers? If you were my wife, I'd blister your backside for wandering off alone."

"If I was your wife," Lacey retorted, "my wandering would have been intentional."

"Now, you two," Hazel said in a chiding tone. "Matthew, I expect you to bring Amanda for supper on Saturday." She picked up the pie tin from the coffee table. "I'll just run these dishes into the kitchen and then we can discuss the particulars."

"Oh, here," Lacey said, standing. "Let me get those. You've been on your feet all evening." She hadn't seen the poor woman sit down for anything other than dinner since she'd arrived.

Hazel thanked her, and Lacey took the dishes into the kitchen. She set them in the dry sink, and then turned, only to catch what she thought was movement against the far wall. "Little lady?" she whispered, moving across the room. "Hello?" She crept around the table. "Little lady? Is that you? Jesus, I have no idea what I'm doing—"

"Neither do I."

Lacey started, and spun around. The marshal was standing by the counter, staring at her as if she'd lost her mind. "What are you doing in here?" she demanded.

He held up his dirty plate, and then set it in the dry sink. "Didn't mean to interrupt."

"Like hell you didn't."

"Just exactly what were you doing?"

"Looking around. Is curiosity a crime in these here parts, Marshal?" she drawled, circling the table toward him.

"Should I make it one, Miss Garder? I could call it . . . the Lacey Law."

"That's very cute."

"I thought so."

"But then you'd have to arrest yourself, or has your ravenous curiosity about me finally been satisfied?"

"Now, how could it be when you haven't given me the tiniest bit of information? A curious man can find no satisfaction in your presence."

"Don't take it too hard. An intelligent woman can find none in yours."

"You're very good at that."

"Thank you."

"You must get bored when there's no one around to insult. Or do your loved ones play stand-in?"

"Am I mistaken, Marshal, or did you just toss in another fishing line? You know, I hate to disappoint you, but this pond is off limits to the public."

"Not to mention frozen solid." He punctuated that remark with a tight smile.

"Oooh, very witty. Have you been practicing that one all night, or did it suddenly come to you in a rare moment of insight?"

"You know, we could go on like this all night, Miss Garder, trading insults like a pair of adolescents, or we could finally get to the meat of this matter between us once and for all."

"And that would be?"

"I know you from somewhere."

Lacey blinked, stunned by his admission.

"And it's only a matter of time before I figure out exactly where that somewhere is," he added.

"That sounds just a tad paranoid."

"The circles I've traveled in have been large, but distinctive, Miss Garder. If you've traveled them, then I've got good reason to be paranoid."

"Your assumptions about me have been wrong from the very beginning."

"My daddy used to say that if it looks like a duck, walks like a duck, and quacks like a duck, it's a pretty safe guess that what you've got there is a duck. And my best guess on you is that you're about as straight as a mountain road."

"And what if you're right," she replied, hating that he could read her so well. "Just what the hell do you intend to do about it?"

He leaned closer, until she could see the tiny gray flecks of color in his green eyes, and whispered, "The second you cross the line in this town . . . will be your last second of freedom for a very long time."

His gaze drifted over her face for a moment, and then he turned and exited the kitchen, leaving Lacey with her eyes narrowed on his departing back. The man was a walking menace—and with a loaded weapon, no less. For some strange reason he'd made her his next crime-fighting target, and she was pretty well sick of it.

Hazel Martin came bustling into the kitchen. "Me and the mister are headin' for bed, Lacey," she announced. "We'll see ya in the mornin'."

Lacey frowned. "But it's seven o'clock."

"I know," Hazel said, chuckling. "We don't usually stay up this late, but we've enjoyed you and Matthew so much tonight that we hated for the evenin' to end. See you bright and early."

Bright and early? Lacey never went to bed before one, and never woke before ten.

"And be sure to turn the lantern off when you leave the kitchen." With one final smile, Hazel headed off down the hallway.

Lacey shook her head in shock as she heard the loud thud of George and Hazel's door closing. Bed before prime time? She reached for the lantern on the counter and turned its small metal dial until it went out, sending the kitchen into darkness. Then she followed the light in the hallway back to the front room. The marshal was standing with his back to the fire, and his eyes rose to hers as she paused in the archway. "Are you staying up?" she asked.

"For a little while."

"Then I'm going to bed." She turned for her room.

"I'll be sleeping on the couch, Miss Garder . . ." he called after her.

"Congratulations," she grumbled to herself.

". . . just in case you decide to go lurking around in the middle of the night."

Lacey paused and turned back to him, not liking the insinuation in his voice. Did he actually think she might steal from these two nice people?

"And don't get any bright ideas about throwing the

covers over your head in the morning and sleeping in. The Martins are going to need help shoveling the snow off the porch."

"Oh, I wouldn't dream of it," she retorted, although hiding in bed was precisely what she intended to do.

"Don't dream of getting any peace while you're in town either. I plan to stick to you like sap on a bear's furry butt. I guarantee you're not going to like the kind of attention I plan to give you."

"Why, Marshal. Don't you know by now that I wouldn't like any kind of attention you'd care to give me?"

"Then we both know where we stand."

"Vividly." She turned and went into her room where she barely kept herself from slamming the door shut behind her. "Self-righteous bastard," she muttered.

"Hello, Miss Garder."

Lacey gasped at the unexpected greeting, and looked across the room to see the little angel lady sitting on the edge of the bed. "Well, it's about time," she stated, striding toward her. "Just who the hell do you think you are?"

"Young lady, if you are going to be difficult—"

"Difficult? I'd say difficult was being abandoned in a snowstorm to freeze to death!"

"You didn't freeze to death."

"I certainly could have."

The woman sighed. "Destiny, Miss Garder, is a very complicated yet simple thing: What is, is. What isn't, was never meant to be."

"Just tell me what the hell I'm doing here?"

"We all have our destinies, our missions in life, and you are now finally in the midst of yours."

"Terrific. Well, we've all had our fun, now when do I go back?"

"You don't."

Lacey leaned closer. "I'm sorry?"

"Unless you wish to go back to the exact place where I found you."

"Are you saying that you'd put me back in jail?"

"If you return to the twentieth century then you will have to live with the life you have created for yourself."

"So my choices are life in prison, or life in the nineteenth century? That's a bit like asking somebody whether they'd rather be shot or stabbed!"

"Come now, Miss Garder. Granted this place is a little antiquated—"

"A *little* antiquated? We're talking pre–Abbott and Costello, here!"

"But it is certainly better than prison."

"Come on. How am I supposed to survive in this place?"

"*I* am here to help you."

"Oh, there's a great comfort," she grumbled. "My own personal Jiminy Cricket."

"I will be watching you very closely, Miss Garder. You are going to have to prove to me that you deserve this second chance, and that you will use it wisely."

"Great. I'm supposed to *earn* my way into hell? And if I refuse to jump through hoops for you?"

The woman gave her an intent look. "Then you go back. No other chances."

"How sweet."

Lacey was beginning to feel a tad panicked by this whole situation, and suddenly the woman reached out to take her hand. Lacey instantly flinched away.

A look of sympathy and understanding came over the woman's small face. "I'm sorry," she said softly. "I forgot for a moment that you don't like to be touched. It's a very reasonable reaction considering what you went through as a child."

"Oh, if you'll forgive me, I don't really care to hear your armchair analysis of my childhood."

"You must let that pain go, Miss Garder. You must overcome your fears."

"Here, we go. Ladies and gentlemen, Doctor Joyce Brothers."

"You are no longer a child, you are a woman in control, a woman with choices. You have within you the same capacity to love that exists in all of us. But you have built a wall of protection so high and so thick around yourself that nothing can get in or out."

"Lovely. Well, if I'm so pathetic, how 'bout you forgive me my transgressions and send me back to good old 1996 so I can get on with my life?"

The woman shook her head. "The moment you knew the difference between right and wrong you were held accountable. Nothing and no one has forced you to do the things you've done. You've chosen to be dishonest, and if you return to 1996 you will have to pay the price for that decision.

"And yet you're willing to let me stay here."

"I am correcting a wrong by putting you back where you belong in the fabric of time. Consider yourself lucky to have this opportunity."

"I guess the gratitude comes later?" Lacey retorted.

"As I said, you will have to prove to me that you deserve this second chance."

"And what, exactly, do you expect me to do?"

"Fulfill your mission."

"My mission?"

"Every human being has one. Some complete them by simply being born. Others by accomplishing greatness in their lives."

"And mine?"

"Yours is somewhere in between. Do you remember me telling you that the town of Tranquility went bankrupt in 1879?"

"You said that in the attorney conference room."

"Yes, well, the reason behind its bankruptcy is you, Miss Garder. You weren't here to save it. Originally you were to be born in Chicago, Illinois, in 1853, and migrate here with your family in 1876."

"I save a whole town?" Lacey replied.

"In a roundabout way."

Now there was an evasive answer if Lacey had ever heard one. "How roundabout?"

"The problem, Miss Garder, arose when you weren't here to help the person who was intended to save Tranquility."

"And that person would be?"

"Now please remain calm. I know—"

"Who?" Lacey demanded.

The woman paused, and then sighed. "Matthew Brady."

"No *way*, lady. Not on your life! Not on *my* life!"

"Not even on your life in prison?"

"Oh, that's dirty pool. I never thought I'd see the day when I'd be blackmailed by an angel!"

"If Mr. Brady doesn't find the money that the Rawlins brothers stole from the city bank, he will lose his job. Lawlessness will reign in this town, no new citizens will settle here, and when the loggers move on to find other timber there will be nothing left but a few ramshackle buildings and a stray dog here and there."

"And what's your point?" Lacey said dryly.

"My point, Miss Garder, is this: Do it for this town or do it for yourself, but you will help Mr. Brady find that stolen money. He will not be able to recover it without you. You accomplish this within one week, without any major mishaps, and I will allow you to stay here. You create problems, and you will go back to jail."

"Wonderful."

"If you simply lower your guard a bit, and stop trying to aggravate the man so much, you might actually be surprised by the results."

Lacey laughed. "Oh, I don't think so."

The woman sighed and stood up from the bed. "Get some rest, Miss Garder. I hope you'll feel better about all this in the morning."

"And where will you be?"

"I have other duties, but I will be checking up on you frequently."

"Probation all over again."

"Just keep in mind that things could be worse. Much worse." And with that, the woman vanished.

Lacey dropped down onto the edge of the bed. "Terrific," she muttered. It seemed this was one situation she would not be wriggling out of.

She thought of Matthew Brady, the man whose job she had to help save. The man who had become the bane of her existence. "I don't want to help him," she grumbled.

And she didn't exactly get a big picture of him being thrilled with the idea either. Chances were they'd kill each other before her great "mission" was even fulfilled.

But it was either help him or go to prison. And nothing and no one stood in the way of Lacey

Garder and her freedom. Not even a dangerously handsome, annoyingly overconfident man with a Colt .45.

5

Lacey opened her eyes the next morning and found herself buried beneath a layer of thick blankets instead of the one cool sheet she was used to. She stared groggily at the far window, at the light just beginning to glow through the lace curtains, and tried to remember which hotel she'd checked into the night before. Whichever one it was, they needed to have a serious look at their air-conditioning system—the room was *freezing*.

And then her gaze landed on the kerosene lantern resting on the night table beside her bed, and it all came back to her in a flash: the angel, the Martins— the marshal. She groaned and pressed her face down into her feather pillow. Why couldn't it have all been just a nightmare?

The house seemed quiet, and she frowned, wondering what had awakened her. But it was barely dawn, so she burrowed deeper into the soft mattress beneath her, determined to drift back off to sleep.

And then suddenly, she had a sense that someone was in the room with her. Her heart pounding in her ears, she held perfectly still and carefully scanned the area around her. The back of her neck started to tingle. She slowly rolled to her left, and found herself staring up into the one face she didn't care to see first thing that morning.

"What are you doing in here?" she demanded in a sleepy rasp.

"Time to get up, Miss Garder."

Lacey propped herself up on her elbows and glared at the marshal. "How long have you been in here?"

"Long enough to know you snore."

"Get out."

"The rooster crowed fifteen minutes ago."

"Screw the rooster." She dropped back down onto the bed and closed her eyes. She'd get up when she was damn good and ready, and not a moment before.

The heavy blankets covering her were torn back, and she was exposed to the frigid air in the room. She let out a shocked cry and bolted upright. "You *bastard*! Give me those!"

He was standing at the foot of the bed with her blankets clutched in his hand. "It's time to get up," he insisted.

"I don't *want* to get up yet!" She scrambled to her knees to keep her feet warm beneath her nightgown. "I want to sleep until noon! I want to lounge around in this bed—the only luxury left to me—until I'm damn good and ready to face reality! Now, give—them—*back*!"

"It's nice to see your lungs made it through the night," he remarked. "Too bad your hair didn't fare so well."

She glared at him, and fought an annoying urge to smooth down the coppery locks that were no doubt sticking up in knots upon the top of her head. She wanted to slug him, she wanted to kick him, she wanted to beat the living daylights out of him for being her "mission" in this godforsaken place!

With a cool smile, she reached behind her for a pillow.

"I'm going to ask you one more time to give me back my blankets and get out of my room."

"And I'm gonna tell you one more time to get your lazy butt out of bed."

With a cry of outrage, she brought her arm around and flung her pillow at him. It shot through the air and hit him full in the face with a loud *whop!* and she smiled in satisfaction.

She was met by his steely eyed glare. "That was a mistake," he stated.

She let out a cry of alarm as he lunged for her. But she scrambled from his reach and grabbed up the other pillow. She jumped to her feet in the bed, and when he reached for her again, she walloped him on the side of the head.

"You stay away from me!" she shouted, dancing in the center of the mattress.

"You hit me with that thing one more time, lady, and God *Himself* won't be able to protect you!"

"Haven't you ever heard the theory that God's a *she*! And that on the day *she* created rodents *men* just sort of snuck into the mix!"

He pointed a finger at her. "You're pushing your luck!" She sneered at him, and then knocked his hand aside with one swing of her pillow.

"That's it." He bent down and retrieved the pillow she'd thrown at him earlier. "You want a fight, lady. You got one." He swung out with his pillow and clipped her on the side of the head with it.

Fuming, Lacey pushed the hair back out of her

face and clenched her teeth. "Prepare to die, *law-boy*."

She jumped down from the bed and pillows began to collide . . . with arms, with backs, with heads—with each other. Lacey finally gave up trying to see where her hits were landing, and concentrated on putting every ounce of strength she had behind each of her swings. The marshal was getting in quite a few good hits himself, but she refused to let a slight jarring of the head stop her from beating the tar out of him.

Feathers were soon scattered throughout the room, on the bed, the floor, floating through the air, and Lacey started coughing as she breathed in the dust.

"Had enough?" the marshal demanded as his pillow once again connected with her head.

"Are you dead yet?" she retorted, landing a good one against his stomach.

"You're acting like a child," he said, grunting as he swung his weapon.

"And you're not?"

They both kept swinging until their arms and pillows finally dropped to their sides, leaving them standing there, nose to nose, breathing hard.

"Get out of my room!" she threw into his face.

"Been here one day and already it belongs to you?"

"You have no right to come in here and wake me up like this!"

"I should have used a bucket of cold water."

She clenched her jaw, glaring maliciously into his eyes, and they stood there like that for what seemed like minutes, neither one of them willing to back down. And then the strangest thing happened. His stare suddenly dropped from her eyes to her lips, and Lacey's heart actually skipped a beat. "What are you doing?" she demanded.

"Nothing," he replied. But his attention was still latched firmly on her mouth.

She couldn't have something stuck in her teeth because she hadn't even eaten anything yet that morning. Then what the hell was he staring at?

His lips parted slightly, and she suddenly recognized the posture. To some strange passerby the man might have actually looked as if he were about to kiss her.

"You so much as lay one lip on me, buddy, and you'll find it rolling in the dust at your feet."

His eyes shot back to hers. "Kissing you is the furthest thing from my mind."

He stepped back from her, but Lacey wasn't buying it. Something told her that kissing her had been exactly his intent, although *why* she couldn't even begin to fathom. They could never in a million *years* be attracted to one another. Not when they obviously hated each other so much.

"Oh, my stars!"

Lacey looked past his shoulder, toward the doorway, and found Hazel standing there staring at the feathers scattered all over the floor. "What in tarnation happened in here?"

"A mess," Lacey said. "One I'll be cleaning up right away."

Hazel frowned at her. "You look a little flushed, Lacey, honey. Didn't you sleep well?"

"I slept just fine, thank you."

"Well, maybe the next time you and Matthew decide to go nose to nose you should have a little something to eat first. There's some hot coffee on the stove, so feel free to help yourself." She turned and left the room, adding, "George and I'll be out in the barn seein' to the animals."

"Get dressed," the marshal said. "We've got work to do."

Lacey threw him a glare as he headed for the door. "I'm not going out in that frigid air to push around some snow that'll probably only start falling from the sky again the moment we're finished, so you can just think again. I plan to spend the morning by the fire, drinking tankards of hot coffee."

"You'll be outside in five minutes or I'll be coming in here and dragging you out dressed as you are."

A heated retort danced on the tip of Lacey's tongue, however she knew he was very capable of carrying out exactly what he was threatening. And the humiliation of being carted outside and dumped in the snow, not to mention the cold, was enough to make her hold back and go for a more sensible argument. "I don't have any clothes to wear out in the snow," she told him, "so I'm afraid you're going to have to shovel it all by yourself."

He strode over to the dresser and started pulling open drawers. Lacey watched, holding her breath, but he hit gold in the bottom drawer. She groaned as he began tossing out clothes: a dingy white pair of winter underwear, some canvas pants, a green flannel shirt. A pair of wool socks hit her in the face, and she caught them before they dropped to the floor and threw them furiously to the bed.

"Put them on," he said. He headed out of the room, but turned back just beyond the threshold. "I expect you out of that room in five minutes or else."

"You try carting me outside, you swaggering jackass, and you'll get a snow shovel crammed down your throat."

"Don't tempt me."

"Oh, I wouldn't *dream* of it," Lacey replied

smoothly. "Not when actions speak so much louder than words!" And with that, she slammed the door in his face.

"Five minutes," she heard him call through the door.

"*Five minutes,*" Lacey mimicked. She picked up the long underwear from the clothes pile on her bed. "These aren't going to be warm enough!" she shouted for the marshal's benefit. "I'm gonna need an insulated space suit to survive out there in that cold for more than two minutes!" She knew he wouldn't understand that statement, and congratulated herself all the more for thinking of it.

With a bitter attitude, she yanked off her nightgown, and dressed in the stiff clothes. She rolled the long sleeves of the shirt up to her elbows, leaving just the winter underwear to cover her forearms, and then cuffed the bottom of the pants about six times before she could finally see her feet. Everything was about three sizes too big, and, without a belt at her disposal, she had to tie the tails of the shirt through the side belt loops to keep them up. When she was finished dressing she looked down at herself and didn't need a mirror to know she looked ridiculous.

She pulled on the thick, itchy socks, cursing Marshal Matthew Brady with every single one of her brain cells—and then she caught sight of her shoes peeking out from under the bed where she'd dropped them the day before. The sun couldn't have rivaled her responding smile. The marshal would probably be able to come up with a coat for her to wear, but shoes? Sure she could manage with Hazel's old clothes, but Hazel was a big woman, and probably wore a size twelve *double wide* shoe. Lacey couldn't possibly be expected to go outside without something on her feet. Praise the lord, she was saved!

She left her bedroom for the entryway. The marshal was in the front room, and he came toward her wearing his trusty hat. He stopped in front of her and looked her over, with his hands poised behind his back, and she thought she saw the slightest twitch of his lips. So he found the way she looked humorous, did he? Well, she'd be getting the last laugh.

"You're going to have to shovel that snow by yourself after all," she told him.

"I thought we'd settled this."

She smiled tightly at him. "I don't have any shoes to wear."

He matched her smile, and produced a pair of scuffed-up leather boots from behind his back. "I stuffed rags in the toes."

Lacey gritted her teeth and snatched them from his hands. "You're going to pay for this, Brady," she muttered. She sat down in the middle of the floor and pulled the boots onto her feet. "I'll have blisters on top of blisters."

"You'll survive." He reached down to help her to her feet, but she lurched away from him and stood up on her own. "Don't I at least get a cup of coffee before being put to work out in the freezing cold?"

"The porch needs to be cleared before someone breaks their neck on it."

"And that'll probably be me with these twin tuna boats on my feet."

"It's a pity you lost your luggage in the storm. You did have luggage, didn't you?"

"Why would I travel without it?" she said evasively, sensing another interrogation coming on.

"Know anyone who could send you some more clothes?"

"Nope."

He gave her a steady look from beneath his hat brim. "Then I suggest you buy yourself some as soon as you get into town, Miss Garder. One strong gust of wind and the ones you're wearing are liable to fly right off you." He walked over and opened the wooden door. "Let's get to work."

"Yes, master," she grumbled.

He pushed on the screen, but it stuck at the bottom and bounced right back into place. He gave it another strong shove on its metal frame, but it wasn't budging.

Lacey smiled. Luck was on her side after all. "Guess we're stuck inside. Where's that coffee—"

"Not so fast. We'll go out the back door and circle around."

"Well, you're just full of bright ideas this morning, aren't you?"

He strode off down the hallway, and she followed him into the kitchen and out the back door. They walked beneath a wooden lean-to sheltering stacks of cut wood, and out into the dull light of another overcast day. "Hasn't the sun been invented around here yet?" she grumbled to herself.

"What's that?" he asked, marching a path for her through the calf-deep snow.

She ignored his question as a cold chill crept through her. "You know, if I die out here I'm holding you personally responsible."

"You'll be warm enough once we get to work."

They passed between the house and the barn, and headed toward the walkway leading to the porch. It wasn't long before Lacey understood the problem with the screen door. Snow and ice had blown up against it and frozen it in place.

The marshal picked up one of two shovels leaning against the porch railing and handed it to Lacey. "I trust this won't come anywhere near my mouth."

She smirked at him. "Trust is a hard thing to come by."

"So is a meal in my jail."

Understanding the meaning behind his veiled threat, she snatched the shovel from his hands and turned toward the door. She drove the sharp edge against the base of the blockage but didn't even make a dent. "We could be here all day."

"You had something better to do?" he asked sarcastically. He picked up the other shovel and took a turn at the snow pack, only to have the same meager results.

"I could think of a few things more exciting than this, yeah." She struck at it again, and this time broke off a few chunks.

"Got friends in town?" he asked, taking his turn, and making some headway.

"Not a one."

"I guess that's not too surprising."

"Yes, I imagine you can relate."

They were working at a rhythm now, each trying to knock off a bigger chunk than the other, and they were beginning to clear the ice away.

"Got a telegraph office in town if you need to contact anyone to let them know where you are."

"That won't be necessary."

"Nobody cares, huh?"

"Only you." She knocked off most of the blockage with her next strike and the screen door shuddered. "Hallelujah," she muttered. She reached for the door handle, but so did the marshal. And neither one of them were willing to let go.

"Stand back and let me try giving it a good pull," he told her.

"You stand back and let *me* try giving it a pull."

They glared at each other, and then they both pulled. However, the door was no longer blocked, and it flew open with no problem at all. They both did a little dance on the slippery compact snow beneath them, grabbing at each other for support, but finally went crashing down to the snow-covered porch.

When Lacey opened her eyes again she was sprawled over him. And he had a tight, steady grip on her butt. "Get your hands off me," she ordered, not liking the rapid beating of her heart.

She was about to tell him she'd chop off his hands if he didn't move them, and that's when she heard the snort of a horse behind her.

The marshal's gaze darted past her shoulder. He sighed, and closed his eyes, and Lacey looked back to see three mounted men staring down at them, grinning from ear to ear.

"Mornin', boss. Need some help?"

Matthew had been in some suggestive situations before, but this one really took the cake. And with Larry, Gene, and Bill as witnesses, it was bound to be spreading through town like a Texas wildfire before either he or Miss Garder had a chance to get back on their feet.

"Wipe those stupid grins off your faces and help the lady up," he ordered irritably. There wasn't anything improper going on here, he added to himself. He'd simply grabbed what was necessary, and that *necessary* had just happened to be Miss Garder's shapely backside. It was as plain and as simple as that. However, he was now having a hard time letting go of it. It just fit so damn neatly in his hands.

Before any of his deputies could dismount and help her to her feet, Miss Garder climbed off him and stood back. Matthew's sense of relief could have literally been measured, and his first impulse was to climb to his feet and deny any wrongdoing to his men. But a hasty action like that might just imply some sort of guilt on his part, so he lay back in the snow and pretended to be disgruntled by the whole situation.

"We, uh, hurried on out here this mornin' 'cause we thought you might be in some sorta trouble, boss," Larry Dover said. "But you seem to have the situation well in hand." The other two deputies broke into chuckles.

"Looked like a hand *full* to me," Gene Peers added, laughing harder.

Bill Booth leaned forward in his saddle and grinned at Miss Garder. "Mind if I try my hand?"

Lacey Garder crossed her arms and eyed the men's horses. "You know, I've heard a man often compensates for a small penis by choosing a powerful mode of transportation."

Matthew groaned and closed his eyes. Where the hell had she come up with the nerve to say something like that to three armed men?

There was a tense moment of silence, and then Larry said in a slow, stunned drawl, "I beg your pardon, ma'am?"

"The larger the mode, the smaller the load," she added with a shrug.

Matthew sat up, only to see his deputies' beard-stubbled faces turning hot-pepper red. These men had followed him into rattlesnake dens, knife brawls, and gunfights without ever showing a hint of fear.

And Miss Lacey Garder had just laid them all low with one quick lash of her tongue.

"Now, what the hell kinda remark is that?" Larry Dover demanded.

"An honest one?" she replied.

"You can't just go around sayin' things like that to a feller," Gene Peers declared. "Can she, Larry?" he added cautiously.

"Well, you certainly had no problem insulting *me*."

"That was dif'ernt," Bill Booth protested.

"Different why? Because I'm a woman and only men can make lewd remarks?"

"Women ain't s'pose ta . . . Well, they don't just . . . Aw, you tell her Larry."

"Women ain't supposed to be coarse, is what Gene here's tryin' to say," Larry explained. "Ain't no man around here gonna want a coarse woman."

"Well, now, that news certainly brightens my morning. Care to leave and make it perfect?"

His deputies appeared to be at a loss, and Matthew could certainly sympathize with their plight. Lacey Garder was definitely one for the books, and certainly not one to tangle with when it came to a battle of wits—especially not for three dim-witted barrelheads like Larry, Bill, and Gene.

The snow beneath him was starting to melt and seep through his denims, but he felt his men had been sufficiently distracted that it was now safe for him to stand. He pulled his hat on tighter, and rose to his feet. "Close your mouths, boys, before your tongues freeze to your teeth."

"Where the hell did you find this she-cat?" Larry demanded. "I've seen shorter claws on a mountain lion."

"And smaller feet on an elephant," Gene remarked,

staring at the overlarge shoes Miss Garder was wearing.

"He followed his gun," she remarked. She took hold of the sides of her trousers and hiked them back up around her hips. The strange way she'd tied her shirt through the belt loops was managing to keep the damn trousers on, but, judging by the shape of the sleek little body he'd just handled, Matthew figured the pants had to be several sizes too big.

Larry gave him an odd look. "His gun?"

Not in the mood to explain himself, Matthew ignored the question. "Any news on Lorraine Rawlins?" he asked.

"That's why we're here," Gene replied.

"Got a lead she might be holdin' up at an aunt's house in Geneva," Bill added.

Matthew nodded. "Ned and Henry feeling any more talkative after a cold night in jail?"

"Not a bit," Larry answered.

Bill smiled eagerly. "I say we string 'em up from a tree and see if that don't loosen their tongues a little."

"Oh, that's brilliant," Lacey Garder remarked. "Let's strangle them and see if that'll get them to talk."

Bill gave her a dark scowl. "I suppose you've got a better idea."

"As a matter of fact—"

"She's got no part in this," Matthew interrupted. "You boys get to work clearing off this porch while I get my horse. If we're lucky this lead in Geneva will pan out and we'll have that money back by this afternoon."

"Don't count on it," he heard Miss Garder remark as he walked past her for the barn.

He stopped and settled his stare on her red nose. "I suggest you get a coat on."

"I'm coming with you."

"We're not going to town. I'm sure the Martins will be happy to drive you there later to get some decent clothes."

"I don't intend to shop."

He cast a disparaging look over her baggy attire and couldn't help but wonder what lay beneath. "Suit yourself," he said and headed on his way.

"I intend to help you recover the stolen money."

Matthew froze in his tracks. He clearly heard the bewildered grumbles of his men a few yards away, but he was sure he had to have heard Miss Garder incorrectly. He turned once again to face her. "What was that?"

"I want to help."

"Go back in the house and have your cup of coffee, Miss Garder. Me and my men don't need your help."

She snorted derisively. "Is that why you had your gun planted in my face last night thinking *I* was Lorraine Rawlins?"

"But, boss," Gene Peers said, "she don't even have black hair."

"I'm aware of that," Matthew replied, his patience thinning.

"One would think, considering how important this money is to the town, that you'd welcome any help you could get in finding it."

He crossed his arms over his chest, wondering what game she was playing now. "And just how do you intend to help?"

She gave him a proud smirk. "I'll bet you a nice, warm new coat that I can get Ned and Henry to talk."

"Thanks, but those kinds of visits aren't allowed in my jail."

Her smile faded, but the determined glint in her

golden eyes only intensified. "Sex is not what I had in mind."

"The answer's still no."

"Afraid I might succeed and show you up?"

Fear didn't exactly cover it. It was more like doubt. Doubt that he'd be able to control himself if placed in the constant company of a wildly attractive woman that he was finding harder and harder to resist.

"Ya know, Marshal," Larry spoke up, "a man does tend to be susceptible to a purty gal. Maybe we should—"

"No," Matthew repeated firmly. He gave Lacey Garder an unflinching stare. "Absolutely not." Then he turned and headed off for the barn.

He'd been telling himself all morning that once he left the house, once he was out of her company, he'd be just fine. God, he'd almost kissed her. He still couldn't believe it. One minute he'd been angry as hell at her, and trying to keep from reaching for her neck, and the very next he'd been seized by an almost overwhelming desire to lay his hands on her in a entirely different manner. Thank God Hazel had walked in when she had.

"Mornin', Matthew," George Martin called as Matthew entered the barn. George was sitting across the way on a milking stool, doing his best with May the cow.

Matthew headed for his saddled horse. "Morning, George."

"You and Miss Garder get that porch taken care of all right?"

"I've got my deputies at work on it now."

George chuckled. "I always knew they were good for somethin'."

"Listen here, pal—just who the hell do you think you are?"

George looked up in surprise as Lacey Garder stormed into the barn, but somehow Matthew wasn't surprised at all. Of course she'd followed him; she hadn't had the last word yet.

"I happen to be the marshal," he retorted, tightening the cinch on his saddle, "the law around here, lady. I think's it's about time you came to terms with that, don't you?"

"And is that supposed to intimidate me?"

He turned to face her. "It should."

"Listen, sweet cakes, this tough guy image you're working on, here, it just doesn't impress me, okay? We both have a problem. You need to find that money, and I need to help you do it. I can get those two men to talk—"

"How? By flashing your pearly whites at them?"

"By getting them to think that I'm on their side. Place a man in the company of a woman who commiserates, and he'll open up like the cargo doors on a B-52."

"A *what*?"

"I can get them to talk," she insisted.

"I don't suppose it would do me any good to ask you why you're all of a sudden so interested in helping find this money?"

She pressed her lips together and looked down at her feet.

"I didn't think so. Look, it's an interesting idea, but in order for it to work you'd have to be left alone with the Rawlins brothers, and I'm not cruel enough to subject any woman to that. Even you. So do us all a favor and stay out of it." He turned to his horse and swung up into his saddle. "Thanks for the hospitality, George," he called.

"Don't mention it, Matthew," George replied. "See

ya Saturday night. Hazel and I are lookin' forward to having dinner with you and Mizz Simmons."

Amanda. Sweet, gentle Amanda.

Matthew glanced back down at the woman standing below him and found himself comparing the two women. Where one was gentle the other was brash. Where one was meek the other had nerve. Where one was resigned the other had fire—he could see it even now burning in her eyes. Here was the kind of woman who could take a man's best laid plans and grind them into dust beneath her heel. The smartest thing he could do was ride out of that barn and never give Miss Lacey Garder another thought.

He tugged his hat brim down low over his forehead, more to hide his thoughts than to block the daylight. "It's been interesting," he said to her.

"It ain't over yet, Columbo."

He shook his head at being called yet another name besides his own. "Yes, Miss Garder. I'm afraid it is."

He clicked to his horse and rode out of the barn. His men had finished clearing the porch, and they rode along behind him as he left the yard. He had six days to recover that money or he was out of a job.

The funny thing was, he wasn't thinking about his job or that stolen money as he and his deputies headed off down the road to Geneva. He was thinking about a copper-haired hellion with flashing golden eyes.

6

She wasn't giving up. And it was no longer just a matter of proving herself to her spiritual guide. No, now Lacey was determined to help find that money to show up that pompous windbag that Tranquility called a marshal if it was the very last thing she did!

He was afraid of her, that was obvious. Afraid that she was smarter than he was and would crack this case before he did. Well, that's exactly what she intended to do. She'd save the town, and his measly little job, and she'd do it all by herself.

What she needed was a plan.

She'd spent the morning cleaning up the feathers in her room. It was impossible to sweep them, so she'd had to pick most of them up with her bare hands. She never thought she'd see the day when she'd actually long for a Dustbuster.

And then Hazel had come into the room and announced that she and George were heading into town to their restaurant, and would Lacey like to spend the day in town with them. Considering that a trip into town fit neatly into the plan she was hatching, Lacey agreed. Now if she could only survive the ride there.

She ducked lower, beneath the thick quilt covering her, and barely suppressed a shiver. There was certainly nothing like speeding along through the freezing cold in a wooden convertible pulled by two gigantic draft horses to really get the old heart pumping. God, how she missed the warm California sun. She couldn't even feel her nose, and wondered if it was still attached to her face.

She tucked her hands up inside the sleeves of the large, wool-lined coat Hazel had lent her, and tried to keep her exposed face warm by pressing it into the coat's thick collar. Then she tried to focus her mind on something else, like the scenery rolling past her.

Cold though it might be, Washington in the wintertime was beautiful. She'd only seen scenes like the ones rolling past her on postcards, and never had she dreamed it would be this dramatic in full scope. The deciduous trees were bare of leaves, standing like sleeping sentinels awaiting spring, but the pines and the firs were still rich, deep green even though their boughs were covered in a sparkling layer of pure crystal-white.

The absolute silence was almost overwhelming, and until this moment Lacey had never realized how loud the twentieth century really was. Here there were no cars, no trains, no machinery of any kind to interrupt the perfect sounds of the horses crunching a path through the deep snow to the rhythmic jingle of bells around their necks.

"How ya doin' there, Lacey?" George asked.

Lacey looked up and managed to force her cold, dry lips into a smile. "F-fine," she said through the chatter of her teeth.

He and Hazel had seated her in between them to keep her as warm as possible. They'd also folded up the quilt and given her the entire thing to snuggle beneath. They were the nicest people she'd ever known, always thinking of others before themselves. Frankly, she couldn't quite understand it.

George smiled. "We're gonna to have to fatten you up, girl, or you're gonna freeze as solid as a icicle on a water pump."

"I think just gettin' her some clothes that fit might help," Hazel remarked. "George, you think you and Tyler can handle the lunch crowd all on your own?"

"Doubt many folks'll be comin' into town to eat in weather like this."

"Good. 'Cause Lacey and me are goin' shoppin'."

"Oh," Lacey said, shaking her head. "I'm afraid I don't have any money—"

Hazel held up her hand. "Not another word. What kinda folks would we be if we let you run around lookin' like that?"

Lacey glanced up at George, to gauge how he felt about his wife's plans, and he smiled down at her again. In all her life nobody had ever been this generous to her, and she was suddenly besieged with guilt. "I really can't accept—"

"Sure is a peaceful mornin', ain't it, George?"

"Sure is."

Lacey frowned at Hazel, realizing that the woman was not going to let her decline her generous offer. But she'd done nothing to deserve it.

"Here we are," Hazel said.

Lacey returned her attention to the road and noticed some ramshackle buildings coming up on her left. As they passed, she saw that the buildings were barely standing beneath the weight of the snow. "Where is *here*?" she asked.

"Tranquility," Hazel replied. "I know it's not much to look at now, but this town has big plans and high hopes."

And that's about all it had, Lacey thought, as George drove the sleigh down a narrow street between small, unadorned buildings with faded signs and cracked windows. Logging Tools, one sign said. Trapping and Hunting, said another. They drove past a large corral and building that proclaimed itself the Harness and Blacksmith Shop, and a large bearded man stepped out from a low tin roof to wave at them.

"Mornin', George. Hazel."

"Mornin', Ed," the Martins called back.

The man remained outside in the cold, staring blatantly at Lacey as they moved up the road. Then the buildings began to look a little newer—and a little more stable. There was a general store. And a tiny telegraph office. A Clothing Boutique boasted ready-made dresses and had a few hanging in its tall window. Next to that was a colorfully painted restaurant with a large sign that said Hazel's, and that's where George pulled up and brought the massive horses to a stop.

"This is our restaurant," Hazel proclaimed proudly. "We've got three employees and can feed fifty people at a time. Across the street there is Matthew's office."

Lacey turned to stare at the tiny building marked Marshal's Office and City Jail. The meat of her plan resided somewhere inside.

Laughter came from farther on down the road, drawing Lacey's attention. There were more buildings, these a little larger, and men were milling about in abundance.

"Farther on there is logger's row," Hazel whispered. "It's mostly saloons and a few other unmentionables."

Unmentionables most likely meaning prostitute joints—bordellos, Lacey believed they were called. She untangled herself from the quilt covering her as George reached up and helped his wife down to the street. Then the man turned toward Lacey and she stared hesitantly at his outstretched arms. To anyone else they would have represented shelter, security, but to Lacey they seemed like long, snaking weapons ready to grab her, hurt her.

George raised his brows in expectation. "You comin'?"

Lacey tried to steady her mounting panic. This man had given her food, shelter, kindness, clothing, how could she decline his offer to help her down without offending him?

"I'd hate for ya to fall," he said, seeming to read the apprehension in her expression.

"Oh, George, the girl's young and strong. She can get down on her own."

Finally George lowered his arms and smiled. "How 'bout if I just stand here real close in case ya slip?"

Lacey sighed in relief. "That would be very considerate of you." Fortunately she managed to touch down in the street without any problems at all. "Thank you," she said to George.

He chuckled. "I didn't do a thing."

But he had.

Suddenly the door to the boutique slammed open and a tornado with black hair and sparkling blue eyes came flying out onto the street. "Hazel!" the young woman cried. "Why didn't ya *tell* me there was a new girl in town!"

"Because Miss Garder only arrived just last night,

Nettie. Goodness, did you expect we'd come tromping to your place through the storm just to introduce the two of ya?"

Nettie laughed and turned her big blue eyes on Lacey. "Well, now. Aren't you a *beautiful* thing."

Lacey thought she managed to smile very nicely, considering she was fighting an urge to run. She'd come across enough of them in her life to know, instinctively, that this woman was a hugger.

She backed up a step, but didn't get away. Long, slender arms came reaching out to snake around her shoulders and pull her close. "It's so good to meet ya," the woman said in a lilting Irish accent. "We get so few new women around here."

Lacey bounded back like a bent tree branch once the woman finally let go of her, and then she sheltered herself by stepping slightly behind Hazel.

"This is Lacey Garder," Hazel said. "Lacey, meet Nettie O'Rourke. She's the sister of our reverend."

Oh, well that explained it, Lacey thought. She'd never met a man of God, or any of his immediate family, who weren't militant huggers.

"Pleased ta meet ya, Lacey," Nettie said. The woman was still smiling, and Lacey was trying to figure out how the hell she kept it up in such cold weather without her lips cracking. "It's always so excitin' when a new woman comes ta town."

"I won't be staying long," Lacey replied. She planned to run for the warm sun as soon as her "mission" was completed. She couldn't believe that these people actually chose to live in such a harsh climate.

"I'm headin' on into the restaurant," George announced, waving as he walked away. "You ladies have fun with your shoppin'."

"Shoppin'?" Nettie exclaimed. "Oh, please tell me

yer shoppin' fer clothes, Hazel, and not somethin' mundane like flour and oats."

"Lacey got caught in the storm last night and lost her luggage," Hazel explained.

The young woman's face scrunched in sympathy, and for a moment Lacey thought she was in for another hug. "Ohhh. Well, come on in and we'll get her all fixed up," Nettie said enthusiastically. She turned and preceded Lacey and Hazel into the shop.

"Happy, isn't she?" Lacey whispered to Hazel as they walked single file through the narrow door.

"Deliriously," Hazel grumbled. "But Nettie O'Rourke would cut off her right arm and give it to ya if you needed one."

Well, that would certainly prevent her from perpetrating spontaneous huggings, Lacey thought.

She was ushered to the back of the shop and shown into a small room where measurements were taken and the narrowness of her waist was exclaimed over. Then she was given two plain, button-up-the-front dresses to try on that would have made Cindy Crawford look dumpy. Lacey stood in front of the mirror scowling at herself. She'd always been kind of particular about the way she dressed, and she realized in that moment that she and nineteenth-century clothing were not going to get along.

Nettie and Hazel came back into the changing room, and smiled at what she was wearing. "That looks lovely on you, girl," Nettie said.

Lacey smiled politely. "I don't suppose you have any . . . jeans? Maybe some simple cotton shirts?"

Nettie frowned, and exchanged a perplexed look with Hazel. "Jeans?"

"Made from denim?" Lacey clarified.

"But Lacey," Hazel said with a laugh, "you're not

gonna need trousers. It's not like George and I are
gonna be workin' ya while you're stayin' with us."

"That color is wonderful on you," Nettie insisted.

Lacey looked down at the pale yellow dress. It had
long fitted sleeves, a narrow waist, and a high round
neckline. She tried to imagine herself dressing this
way for the rest of her life and couldn't. In her opinion she looked absolutely ridiculous.

"That is a very flatterin' color," Hazel agreed. "But
I get the impression from Lacey's expression that it's
not quite what she's used to."

"Yer from back east, aren't ya," Nettie said with a
knowing smile. "In that case I kin imagine that to you
my frocks are a bit on the plain Jane side. If you'd
like, I can order some fancier things for ya from the
Montgomery Ward catalog."

Fancier? Lacey could only imagine the horror that
might be mailed her way: bows and flounces, bustles
and ribbons. "No. You're right. This is a nice color."
These dresses would serve her well while she was in
town. But once she left she planned to go on a frantic
search for someone who could make her some normal
clothes.

"Good," Hazel said, smiling. "She'll take the yellow and the red sprigged muslin. She'll need some
wool stockings, a union suit, a petticoat, two pairs of
drawers, and some fleece-lined gloves—oh, and a
coat."

"She needs underthings too, eh?" Nettie replied.

"Everything she was wearing shrunk down to
nothin' in that storm. You should have seen her
corset and drawers."

Lacey smiled to herself at Hazel's explanation for
her demi-bra and panties. She must have caught sight
of them the night before when she'd ushered Lacey

into the bedroom and helped her out of her wet things.

"And she's gonna need a good pair of lined boots, Nettie," Hazel called as Nettie left the room.

"What size?" Nettie called back.

Hazel gave Lacey an inquiring look, and Lacey opened her mouth to tell the woman that she was buying her too much. That she was being too generous. But Hazel seemed to read Lacey's thoughts and gave her a censoring stare that said she would listen to no more arguments. Lacey sighed and relented. "Size five."

"A little bitty size five, Nettie," Hazel shouted back.

Twenty minutes later Lacey stepped outside dressed in insulating long underwear, which Hazel called a union suit, a thick petticoat, which Lacey called an annoyance, and the pale yellow dress. Hazel had bought her a beautiful brushed suede, fleece-lined coat that hung to her knees, and a soft pair of leather gloves lined with rabbit fur. For the first time since arriving in 1878, Lacey was warm.

A dark-haired man dressed all in black came walking up to them, smiling, as Hazel was putting their packages into the sleigh. "Good afternoon, Hazel," he said. "Nettie. And who is this?"

"This, brother dearest, is Miss Lacey Garder," Nettie replied. "She's stayin' with the Martins for a while. Lacey, this is my brother, Conal. He's our local man of God."

They looked like twins, both with rich black hair and sparkling blue eyes. Their smiles were even the same, Lacey realized, as Conal O'Rourke tipped his head in greeting. "It's a pleasure ta meet ya, Lacey."

"Lacey, ya just have to come by fer dinner," Nettie

stated excitedly. "We'd just love to have ya, wouldn't we, Conal?"

"Of course we would. And you'll have to join us for church this Sunday."

Lacey had never set foot in a church, and, after the events that had happened to her lately, she was afraid the roof might cave in on her if she tried. But they were all staring at her with such great expectation, she didn't see how she could refuse. "All right," she answered slowly.

"Wonderful." The reverend smiled. "Well, I'm off to Mrs. Kellogg's house."

"How is Judith doing?" Hazel asked. "That baby is due any day now, isn't it?"

"Doctor Colby tells me we could have a new resident by the end of the day."

"Wonderful!" Hazel exclaimed. "Well, you tell Judith that I'll have Tyler bring her over a platter for her's and James's supper tonight."

"I'm sure she'll be very grateful," he said. "Good afternoon, ladies." He dipped his head, and walked on down the street.

"Speakin' of babies, Nettie, how's that litter of new kittens comin' along at your house?"

"Oh, they're growin' like spring weeds. . . ."

Lacey turned her attention to the jailhouse across the street and let the two women's voices drift off to the back of her mind. Ned and Henry Rawlins were being held in there. And she had to figure out some way to get herself inside—

"Whoo-wee, what have we got here?"

Lacey turned to find a group of very large men converging upon her. "Three women hopin' for some quiet time alone, Paul Smith," Nettie said. "The bathhouse is at the end o' the street."

"How 'bout some quiet time alone with me?" he teased. He was a huge man, at least six and a half feet tall, with straggly blond hair and piercing blue eyes. He turned his bright smile on Lacey. "How 'bout your new little friend, here?"

A bath was exactly what this man and all his friends needed; Lacey was surprised she hadn't smelled them coming. They were covered in dirt from their heads to their toes, and had what looked like tree bark stuck in their hair and beards.

"Gentlemen," she greeted cautiously.

"Shoot, Paul, she called us gentlemen!" one of them shouted, elbowing the leader.

"That she did," he agreed, his grin broadening. "Where you from, pretty thing?"

"A galaxy far, far away," she answered.

"You boys best move on," Hazel warned.

The men ignored her. "What're you doin' tonight, beautiful?" Paul asked.

"Clipping my toenails," Lacey replied.

"Can I watch?"

Another man, dark-haired and bearded, elbowed his way past Paul. "Can I?"

And then another man came forward. This one took off his hat and began twisting it in front of him. "Would . . . would you do me the honor of allowing *me* to clip your toenails?"

Lacey threw Hazel and Nettie a disbelieving look, and both women shook their heads hopelessly. "What about you, Nettie?" someone called out from the crowd. "You need anything clipped?"

"I'll do ma clippin' on my own, thank you very much," Nettie replied.

"Holy B. Mary, you sure are a pretty little thing, ain't she, boys?" Paul said, still staring at Lacey. He reached toward her and she flinched back. "I ain't gonna hurt you," he crooned. "Lacey sure is a pretty name."

"You're gonna have a pretty big welt between your pretty big eyes if you try to touch me again, Hoss," she warned.

He laughed, his blue eyes sparkling. "She's got spirit in her. I think I'm in love."

"Whatcha got there, Paul?"

Hazel and Nettie let out a synchronized groan as another even larger group of men joined the crowd already gathered around them. "I say we bolt for it," Nettie whispered.

"And risk gettin' trampled? No thank you," Hazel remarked. "No, we best just sit tight until they've had their fill of lookin' at her for the time bein'."

The new men packed tightly around Lacey. "Have you gentlemen been rolling around in the mud?" she asked.

The crowd broke into laughter. "She likes to call us gentlemen, Reed," Paul told the new man, who then promptly broke into laughter himself.

"This isn't mud, ma'am," Reed explained. "This is pitch and saw grease, with a little dirt and tree pulp thrown in. We're lumberjacks."

Lacey nodded, finally understanding. "Well, listen, it's been real nice talking to you, but we were just on our way to Hazel's restaurant. So if you could just clear a path through here—"

"Now, now, not so fast," Paul interrupted. "I'd like to have dinner with you tonight, and I need to know where you're stayin' so I can pick ya up."

"*You* pick her up?" one of the others broke in. "What makes you the big winner?"

"Yeah!" the crowd erupted.

"I swear!" Hazel shouted. "You fellas are all like a pack of dogs in rut. Can't ya see she's not interested in talkin' to ya at the moment? And who could blame her. Look at yourselves. You look like you've been dragged through ten days of bad weather."

The men broke into loud murmurs and started looking around at each other. "If I clean up, will ya have supper with me?" someone called out.

"You went out with Nettie just last week!" another man countered.

"Like you ever stood a chance," was the reply.

"I don't know about you boys, but I'm headin' for the bathhouse!" somebody cried.

"Me too!"

"I'm with ya!"

"Step aside, I'm first!"

In the blink of an eye, twenty men were stampeding in the same direction, and getting absolutely nowhere. Then they began arguing over who would be getting the first baths, and that's when all hell broke loose.

Hazel pulled Nettie and Lacey close against the side of the sleigh as the fists began to fly.

"Looks like a ruckus startin' up across the street, boss."

Matthew looked up from the wanted poster he was writing at his desk to Larry who was standing by the window. "What's the problem?"

Larry squinted his nearsighted eyes. "Not sure. You don't think they've cornered Nettie again, do ya?"

Matthew stood up from his desk and walked to the

window. There was a ruckus all right. It looked like
every man in town was beating the hell out of every
other. He'd warned them about fighting over the
women, but apparently his threats hadn't sunk in.
After the day he'd had so far, this was the last thing
he needed.

"Come on." He grabbed his hat off the peg on the
wall, and threw the door open.

He strode across the street, with Larry two steps
behind, and stopped just short of the sleigh parked in
front of Nettie's boutique. He took his gun out of his
holster and fired it into the air. The fighting stopped
immediately, and Hazel Martin poked her head
around the sleigh at him. "Would you get these nin-
compoops out of here, Matthew!" she shouted.

The men were fighting over Hazel? A married
woman twice their age? They must be getting desperate. "The next man to throw a fist gets a night in jail!"
he called out.

"Be worth it if the young lady would agree to a
night out!" Paul Smith called from the midst.

Hazel Martin certainly wasn't considered young,
so Matthew assumed that poor Nettie O'Rourke was
somewhere at the center of the fray. "Let her out,
boys," he ordered.

"What's all the noise?" George Martin called from
the doorway of his restaurant.

"Just a little ruckus," Matthew replied. "Nothing to
worry about. Come on, boys, clear a path."

They began to part down the middle like the Red
Sea, and Nettie O'Rourke slowly made her way
down the passage toward him. Hazel Martin was
right behind her, but Matthew was unprepared for
the sight that greeted him next. It was Lacey Garder.
He should have known that a woman like Nettie,

someone who'd been living in town for over a year, couldn't suddenly cause this level of discord among the men. No, it had to be a fresh face, a bright new female possibility.

He muttered a curse violent enough to get a startled look from Nettie. Just when he'd finally managed to get Lacey Garder out of his head for a moment, here she was to torment him again.

She stopped in front of him and stared at the gun in his hand. "What is it with you and that thing?"

"Well, well, well. If it isn't our fearless marshal."

Matthew looked past Miss Garder to see Reginald Sterling standing on the boardwalk. The capper to a perfect morning.

"We didn't mean to cause problems, Brady," Paul Smith said. "We were just greetin' Tranquility's newest flower." He gave Miss Garder a lopsided smile that made Matthew grit his teeth.

"Lacey isn't interested," he warned.

"*Lacey* is it?" Reginald Sterling called. "Now why am I not surprised? I suppose you'll be paying court to this one too before we know it."

Matthew wasn't sure why he'd called Miss Garder by her given name. It had just sort of rolled very nicely off his tongue.

"But you're already courtin' the schoolteacher!" Reed Baxter called out.

"That he is," Reginald added with a cool smile. "Apparently one woman isn't enough for him."

The crowd broke into angry shouts, all directed at Matthew, and he lifted his gun again. But before he could fire it, Miss Garder stuck her fingers in her mouth and let out an ear-piercing whistle.

The crowd fell silent. "Are you people out of your minds!?" she shouted. "And I don't know who the hell *you* are," she added, pointing at Reginald Sterling, "but I suggest you back the hell off."

"Young lady," Reginald replied, affronted, "I am the mayor of this town, *and* the bank president."

"Well whoop-dee-do for you. For your information I am not being courted by the marshal—or anyone else in this town, so keep your two cents to yourself."

Reginald sniffed and lifted his high-falutin' English nose, which Matthew had an intense desire to shoot right off his narrow face. "Where I am from a decent woman would never address a gentleman so rudely."

"Well, welcome to my world."

Reginald's thin lips tightened. "Certainly, Mr. Brady, you can do a better job of maintaining order in this town. We hired you to keep the peace, not incite riots with your philandering. One would think you'd be out trying to capture the little heathen who has carted off my money."

"Don't you mean the town's money?" Matthew asked smoothly.

"Of course. But I treat it as lovingly as I would my own. Which is obviously more than we can say for you."

Matthew had never wanted a piece of a man so badly in his life. But one threatening move toward Sterling would mean the immediate loss of his job—which was probably why Sterling always seemed to go out of his way to provoke him.

However, Lacey Garder had no such restrictions. She crossed her arms over the front of the new coat she was wearing and glared at the man. "You're English, aren't you," she stated more than asked.

"And quite proud of it," Sterling sniffed.

"I've always heard that you Brits walk around like

you've got sticks crammed up your butts, but I never really believed it until now."

The entire street burst into laughter and Reginald Sterling's white face darkened to a deep pink.

"You need to loosen up, Reggie," she added. "Unclench that sphincter muscle before you do permanent damage to yourself."

"All right, fellas," George called from where he'd been watching in the restaurant doorway. His face was a little ruddy, meaning he'd been doing a little laughing himself. "Go on your way now. You can talk with Miss Garder some other time—and maybe one at a time would be your best bet."

"When she's not spending time with our esteemed marshal," Reginald had the nerve to remark.

"You're not encouragin' the marshal, are ya, Lacey?" Paul Smith asked in a pathetic whine of a voice.

There was a long pause as everyone perked their ears to catch her answer. She sighed, smiled, and said, "We're partners."

Matthew stared at her in shock. In fact, a tree could have fallen on his head at that moment and he wouldn't have felt a thing.

"Partners?" somebody shouted.

"What the holy hell are you talking about?" Matthew demanded.

"Oh, now," she said, smiling and giving him a playful nudge with her elbow, "don't be shy. I told you it's a brilliant plan."

"Did you," he remarked darkly.

"What plan?" Paul Smith demanded.

Matthew's sentiments exactly.

"The marshal has devised an ingenious plan to find the money that was stolen from the bank yesterday morning."

Reginald Sterling chuckled. "Really?"

"What's that got to do with you?" Reed Baxter demanded.

"I am going to help him."

Matthew slowly closed his eyes and prayed for patience.

"She is?" Larry whispered to him.

Reginald Sterling broke into laughter. "It sounds like our marshal is getting a little desperate."

"Let's hear the plan," someone called out.

"Yes," Matthew said, smiling tightly at her, "let's hear it."

"Oh, it is so brilliant," Miss Garder prefaced. "The marshal, here, is going to put me in jail with the Rawlins brothers."

"Oh God, shoot me now," Matthew groaned.

"His brilliant plan is to arrest you?" Sterling said. "Well, why didn't *I* think of that!"

The crowd broke into laughter again, and Matthew wanted to crawl back into bed and start the whole day over.

"He'll arrest her over my dead body," Hazel stated.

"Matthew Brady, how could you even be thinkin' such a thing?" Nettie O'Rourke demanded.

Matthew's store of patience evaporated in that moment. His deputies' lead on Lorraine Rawlins that morning had turned out to be false, he was still hitting a brick wall when it came to getting any information out of her brothers, and now he was having to deal once again with Miss Lacey Garder. Meanwhile that money was getting farther and farther away, and he was beginning to wonder why he didn't just climb up onto his horse and ride the hell back to California where he belonged.

Lacey Garder was frowning. "It's a perfect plan!"

she shouted above the din, and the men quieted immediately—not to listen to what she had to say, Matthew suspected, but because they were still interested in starting something up with her and didn't think it would be wise to be impolite. "He arrests me," she continued, "and I sit in a cell and complain to the Rawlins brothers about how miserable this town is. About how low-down, stinking, filthy, pathetic, and dastardly its marshal is," she said with a pointed look Matthew's way. "And slowly but surely they'll start to commiserate."

"What's . . . commiserate?" someone asked.

"We'll start swapping stories," she clarified. "I can practically guarantee you that I can get them to tell me where their sister is before you've even got half of that sap and mud scraped off you."

It was the craziest idea Matthew had ever heard in his life. Crazy enough to possibly work, if the Rawlins brothers didn't chew her up and spit her out before she had a chance to open her pretty little mouth.

"That is the most preposterous idea I have ever heard," Reginald stated. "And I absolutely forbid it to take place in my town."

Well, that certainly sold Matthew on the idea. "You want to give it a try?" he said to Miss Garder. "I'll give you one hour with them."

"Matthew!" Hazel exclaimed. "Lacey, are you sure about this?"

"Sounds to me like the idea's got merit," George stated.

"I said I *forbid* it!" Reginald called out. "This poor young woman has no idea what she'll be subjecting herself to."

"We're behind ya one hundred percent, Marshal!" Paul Smith shouted.

"Yeah. I think she can do it!" Reed Baxter agreed. "And I'll get a bath and meet her at the restaurant when she's finished," he added with a bright smile.

Matthew scowled at the lumberjack as Miss Garder lifted the hem of her skirt and marched past him through the snow toward his office. "Coming, Marshal?"

Matthew's intention was to follow right along behind her, but he stopped in place as his gaze landed on the shapely calves she was showing off above her ankle-high boots. She had the kind of legs that made a man start thinking about what he'd find a little higher up, and he was frozen in place for a moment.

Then he realized that the crowd had fallen silent behind him, and he looked back to see every male eye glued to what he'd been staring at so avidly himself. A twinge of irritation settled into his stomach. He didn't like the idea of them ogling her legs, he didn't like the idea of them accosting her on the street. And he downright despised the notion of any one of them cleaning up to vie for her attentions. All this for a woman he didn't even like.

He was obviously losing his mind.

7

Once in the jailhouse, Lacey took off her coat and gloves and hung them on a peg by the door. Then she turned to the marshal and held out her wrists. "Lock me up."

"I'd like to do a whole lot more than that to you," he stated angrily. "Just what the hell did you think you were doing out there?"

Lacey gave him an impatient stare. She wished to hell this man would come down off his high horse and give her a little credit so she could get this mission of hers over and done with. "What's the problem now, Marshal?"

"Maybe you better let me explain the situation, here, Miss Garder. You see, I've got two criminals locked up in a cell back there, and they aren't exactly friendly. In fact, I've got a pretty good idea they'll chew you up and spit you right out."

"They'd choke on me first," she shot back.

"That wouldn't surprise me either."

"You do have more than one cell back there, don't you?" Lacey asked.

"I wouldn't be agreeing to this if I didn't."

Suddenly Reginald Sterling burst into the office with one of the marshal's deputies fast on his heels. "This, sir, is outrageous!" the man proclaimed. "You cannot possibly allow this woman to risk life and limb for the sake of our fair town! As the mayor, I cannot permit it!"

Lacey rolled her eyes; the man was just one giant pain in the neck. "Back off, Reggie."

"Good lady," the man said, "those two men are depraved. They're uncultured, uncivilized . . . vulgar."

"Vulgar?" Lacey said breathlessly. "Oh my. You mean they might curse at me?"

"Oh, I'm sure they'll come up with something a little more colorful than that," the marshal commented.

"Give *me* the opportunity to speak with them," Reginald demanded. "I will make them see reason—"

"We've tried man to man," the marshal broke in, "it's gotten us nowhere fast."

"I'm not even going to be in the same cell with them," Lacey pointed out in exasperation. "I don't know what you guys are getting so worked up about."

"Them gettin' their hands on ya is the least of our worries, ma'am," the deputy stated. "A man don't have ta . . . have ta *touch* a woman ta . . . well, ta—"

"What Larry is tripping all over himself to say, Miss Garder," the marshal said, "is that a man can violate a woman in a number of ways. Not all of them include touching." To prove his point, he folded his arms across his chest and proceeded to stare hotly, flagrantly at her breasts.

Even though a fine line of heat sizzled down Lacey's spine, she prided herself on not batting an eyelash. By the time the marshal's eyes had finally lifted back to hers, however, a tight, restless knot had gathered in the pit of her stomach, leaving her feeling slightly weak in the knees. The very last thing she felt was violated.

"I'll be fine," she assured them.

"Lady," the deputy said, "you're plumb outta your mind."

"And the marshal is plumb out of his!" Reginald interjected. "I insist—"

"Shut up, Reggie," the marshal interjected. He reached out and took Lacey by the arm. Her breath caught in her chest at the physical contact, but she resisted pulling away. His grip, though tight, wasn't painful, and she concentrated on that instead of the usual burst of panic.

He must have noticed the subtle shift in her demeanor, however, because he hesitated in front of the cell-room door. "Changing your mind?" he asked.

"I'm capable of walking on my own."

"I thought you'd want this to look good."

He had a point, and Lacey nodded, giving him permission to drag her forward as he threw open the door. He pulled her into the cold, bare room that sported only one small barred window, and two scraggly looking men instantly came to attention in the right-side cell. "Got some company for you, boys," he announced.

"Well, all right, Marshal!" the smaller man shouted.

The other rattled their cell door. "Whoo-wee! Bring her on in here!"

"She'll be spending a little time back here with you boys in return for stealing hats from the general store." He led Lacey in to the other cell and sat down on a cot against the far wall. "You keep away from those bars," he whispered to her.

"Hats?" she whispered back. "You couldn't come up with something a little more sinister than hats?"

He gave her a twisted smirk. "You've got one hour," he said loud enough for the two men to hear.

"Ahhh, one hour?" the men groaned. "Is that all?"

"Have a heart, Marshal. Give the three of us some time to get acquainted."

The men certainly weren't hiding their enthusiasm for her presence—or their ogling stares—and Lacey began to think that maybe the plan she had might be just a little bit harder to pull off than she'd originally thought. After all, a very different breed of man populated the old West, and who was she to think that she could leash one in—or even two? She looked back to the marshal as he closed and locked her cell door. It wasn't too late. One word from her and he'd let her out. But one word from her and she'd never hear the end of it from him.

"You boys be nice now," he warned and left the cell room, banging the office door closed.

"Sweet as cream, Marshal."

"Pleasant as a flower."

Lacey leaned back against the mortar wall behind her and closed her eyes. She took a deep breath and imagined the best angle to take on the role she was about to play. And then, effortlessly, she settled herself into it.

She opened her eyes and looked across the small space of her cell into the one beyond. Two pairs of beady green eyes glittered back at her. The actress in her smiled as both men licked their lips and slipped their arms through the flat wrought-iron bars that divided the two cells. They saw her as their prey, but it would soon be the other way around.

"Well, now," the taller one said. "Whatever shall

we do to entertain ourselves for one whole hour, Ned?"

"I got me some ideas," the smaller man said. "Care ta join me, honey?"

The other let out a deep, gritty laugh. "Literally?"

"How do you think she'd like it, Ned? Laying on her back with her legs in the air, or bent forward with her pretty derriere stuck up for the world ta see?"

"I dunno, Henry. Let's ask her," Ned replied.

"How 'bout it, honey?" Henry reached down and began fumbling with the buttons on the front of his pants. "You wanna look inta my eyes as we rut, or would you rather bend forward and offer yourself to me like a proper little woman."

Lacey watched them both with an unconcerned expression, though she had a strong impulse to gag. She'd never seen two more ugly, disgusting men in her life. Mission or not, Marshal Matt was going to owe her big time for this.

She knew she'd have one chance to get them both under her thumb. One chance, or one entire hour of hell. Knowing the best defense is always a good offense, she did the very last thing either one of them expected. She stood, and began unbuttoning the front of her dress.

The men immediately stopped fumbling with the fronts of their pants and frowned at her through their thick, black beards. "What the hell's she doin'?" Ned whispered to his brother.

"Hell if I know," Henry said.

Lacey paused on her fifth button. "You don't like your women naked? Well, I can do it dressed. I'll stay warmer that way. Oh, and I prefer it on my knees. Always have."

They both gave her a look that said she'd clearly

lost her mind. Her dress front had to have fifty buttons going from neckline to waist, so it wasn't as if she'd exposed herself. No, the simple action of going along with them instead of curling into a terrified ball in the corner had apparently taken the wind right out of their sails—so to speak.

Ned and Henry were bullies. Plain and simple. And bullies operated under the premise of fear: no fear, no fun. All she really needed to do was keep her cool and refuse to react to whatever they chose to throw her way.

The taller man, Henry, narrowed his eyes. "What kinda woman are you?"

Lacey sighed and began rebuttoning her dress. "I guess it *will* be a boring hour after all."

"You're new in town, ain't ya?" Ned stated.

"And I'll be yesterday's news as soon as I get out of this cell," Lacey grumbled.

"You got somethin' against our fair city?" Henry asked.

"Other than it's the most pathetic place I've ever wandered through. Can you imagine that marshal arresting me for stealing one lousy hat? I've stolen horses, money, jewels, and here I am in jail over one lousy hat. Doesn't he have better things to do with his time?"

Henry snorted. "In *this* town?

"Shee-it, he wouldn't let an ant steal a crumb at a picnic, let alone let poor souls like us make a decent livin'," Ned added.

Lacey shook her head. "I don't know how you boys stand it." Ignoring the marshal's warning, she walked toward the center bars, but was careful to stay at least an arm's length away. "I'm Lacey Garder. And who might you two be?"

"Henry Rawlins," the taller man returned, "and this here's my little brother Ned."

"Nice to meet you, gentlemen. I wish it were over a strong drink and not through a sturdy pair of iron bars."

Both men grunted in agreement.

"Just what minor offense did you two commit to get yourselves thrown in here?"

"We let ourselves get talked inta somethin', is what we did," Ned replied.

Henry gave him a sharp, sudden jab with his elbow. "We robbed the city bank."

"I was gettin' to that part," Ned grumbled, rubbing his injured ribs.

They were talked into the robbery? Lacey thought with bewilderment, but she covered her avid interest with a broad smile. "I take it your plan went awry?"

"Awry, hell. We got away with five thousand dollars," Henry answered proudly.

Lacey let out a low whistle. "I'm impressed. But it looks to me like 'got away' isn't exactly the right phrase."

"We might not have got away," Ned told her, "but the money did." He exchanged a grin with his brother. "And we intend ta keep it."

"As well you should," Lacey said with feigned admiration. "You boys risked your lives to get it. I say it's yours, fair and square. But . . . "

"But what?" Henry demanded, scowling.

"But how are you going to protect it if you're stuck in jail?"

"We gave it to somebody for safekeeping," Ned informed her.

"Somebody you can trust, I hope."

"We can trust her," Henry asserted. "She wouldn't dare double-cross us."

"As opposed to *other* parties," Ned grumbled.

Henry threw him a dark look, and Ned glared right back at him. "He *ain't* double-crossed us," Henry stated in a harsh whisper.

"We been in jail for almost two days now, Henry," Ned retorted in a tight low voice. "I'd call *that* a double-cross. One word from us and he's in here right along with us."

"One word from us and we'll never get out of here!" Henry shot back. Then they both smiled hesitantly at Lacey, and she gave them her best smile back. There was definitely more going on with this robbery than the good marshal knew.

"Ya know, I ain't seen you around these parts before. Where did you say you was from?"

"California," she said.

"Oh, well that explains it," Henry replied, and Ned nodded in agreement. "A different breed a human bein' runs down south."

"Tough as nails, we hear," Ned piped up. "Like Bill Longley."

"And Clay Allison," his brother added.

"And Billy the Kid."

Ned had said that last name with such open admiration, that Lacey couldn't resist playing just one more card. "I'm his sister," she said, smiling proudly.

Ned's gaze widened, and he broke into a worshipful grin. "His *sister*?" he repeated.

But Henry wasn't so quick to believe. "I never knew the Kid had a sister," he said with narrowed green eyes.

"His half-sister, anyway," Lacey commented, shrugging. "We share a father."

"So that's where you got that reddish colored hair," Ned put in, still grinning stupidly.

"Billy the Kid doesn't ride in California," Henry said.

Lacey gave him an affronted glare. "I said I was his *sister*," she replied sharply, "not that we rode together. I make my own way in this world."

Her brisk retort seemed to mollify Henry well enough, but Lacey reminded herself to tread carefully. One wrong word could blow it all.

"So what are you doing all the way up here in Washington Territory?" Ned asked with a new light of admiration in his eyes.

"Heading for Canada," she answered, thinking quickly.

"For the gold?" he asked.

"Yeah, for the gold," she confirmed, jumping on the excuse. "I hear there's a damn fortune to be made."

"If pannin's your thing," Henry commented.

Lacey smiled slyly. "Who said anything about panning for it?"

Ned started to laugh, and after a moment, so did Henry. "Aw, hell, Henry, it's too bad she's headed north. This town could use a woman like her."

"She is a hoot, ain't she?"

"Now what would you boys do with a woman like me underfoot all the time?"

"First of all," Henry remarked, his eyes darkening, "under my feet ain't where you'd be mosta the time."

Ned snickered, and Lacey smiled at them both. "Stop teasing me, Henry." She leaned closer and whispered, "I've got a real bad thing for bearded men with sparkling green eyes."

Both men's pupils dilated, and they squeezed

their big bodies against the bars. "Maybe . . ." Ned began. He paused and swallowed thickly. "Maybe we could think up some way to keep her around, Henry."

"Maybe," Henry agreed. His eyes were riveted to where Lacey's breasts were pressing against the front of her dress.

"You know what. I'll bet she could help us out with our little problem."

"Ain't we already got inta enough trouble trustin' one stranger?" Henry reminded him.

"But she's—she's just a woman."

"I can damn well see that."

"She wouldn't double-cross us. Women are faithful by nature, ya know."

Now where the hell had he heard that? Lacey thought sardonically. The most faithless people she'd ever known were women.

"Ya don't say," Henry drawled, his hungry gaze still glued to the full rise and fall of Lacey's chest.

"You boys have a problem?" Lacey inquired.

The two men exchanged a look, and then nodded at each other. "It's our sister," Ned blurted.

"Shhhh!" Henry shot out.

Both men cast glances over their shoulders at the office door. And then Ned continued in a softer voice. "She's who we left in charge of the money, and, well—"

"She ain't exactly experienced in hidin' out," Henry added. "She's sorta new at robbin' banks."

"She ain't the only one—" Ned got another jab from his brother, but this time he wasn't putting up with it. "You do that one more time and I'm gonna steal myself summa your teeth," he threatened darkly.

"Then watch your damn tongue," Henry hissed at him. They glared at one another, and then turned and looked back at Lacey. Henry considered her for a long moment. "You wouldn't be interested in earnin' yourself a hundred dollars, would ya?"

"Depends on what you have in mind."

"Like we said," Ned interjected, "our sister's sorta new at the outlaw business, and well, we wasn't exactly plannin' on gettin' caught."

"We're afraid she's gonna screw up and get herself and our money arrested," Henry added.

"A smart woman like you," Ned said. "You could help her stay hid until we break out of this place and join her."

Despite Lacey's feeling of excitement that they were on the verge of telling her where their sister was, she shook her head calmly. Any great criminal worth her salt never jumped at the first offer. "Sorry, boys. Like I said, I'm on my way to Canada. There's a lot of money to be made up there for a woman with just the right smile—"

"Five hundred dollars," Henry cut in, and Ned gave him a startled look. "We'll just give her some of Lorraine's share," Henry explained.

Lacey wondered how Lorraine would feel to know that her brothers were trying to give her share of the loot to someone else. "That's very generous of you, boys, but, really, I can't accept. You see, the authorities in Seattle are rather eager to pick up my trail, and I think it would be best if I left the country for a little while."

"A thousand then," Ned blurted.

"And that's our final offer," Henry warned.

Lacey arched her brows and let a little bit of surprise show in her expression. "That's a lot of money."

"Not for two lucrative gentlemen like ourselves," Henry replied.

"Yeah. You do a good job helpin' out our sister, and maybe we'll keep you around for a while and give ya a few tips on how ta get rich quick."

Lacey broke out in a flirtatious smile. "Mr. Rawlins, are you asking me to join your gang?"

The two men turned to each other and broke into leering smiles. "What an interestin' idea," Henry said.

"She could be with us day . . . and night," Ned added.

Lacey had them right where she wanted them. Just one more twist . . . and they would be hers. "You boys ever taken a woman at the same time?" she whispered suggestively.

If they hadn't been draped over the bars, Lacey suspected they both would've fallen to the floor. "Say you'll join us," Ned rasped.

"We'd set this territory on fire," Henry added.

Lacey made a show of hesitating. "I'll have to meet your sister before deciding on anything permanent," she finally said. "I won't join a gang without first being sure that all of its members are competent outlaws. I don't need any slack-nerves guarding my back."

"Tell you what," Henry said. "You go take care of our little sister. Make sure she lays low in a safe place until we get there, and if it turns out you don't like her, she's out."

Well. So much for family loyalty.

Lacey wasn't aware of how close she'd gotten to the two men until Henry reached out and took hold of a lock of her hair. Her impulse was to lurch back, but she forced herself to remain very still and impassive.

Henry's eyes slid closed in a pained look of ecstasy as he rubbed her hair between his two gritty fingers. "A smart, purty little thing like you is much more important than our scrawny, pain in the ass little sister." He began rubbing the bulging front of his trousers back and forth against the cell bars. "Right, Ned?"

"Right, Henry."

Lacey carefully stepped back, and was relieved that Henry let go of her without a fight. "You know, you're asking me to risk an awful lot, boys. If I get caught, they'll hang me in Seattle."

"Wha'd you do there anyway?" Ned asked.

Lacey gave him a steady look. "I shot a man for double-crossing me. Where's your sister at?"

Both men smiled, apparently liking this crude, violent woman she'd invented, and Henry stole a furtive glance over his shoulder. "She's hiding out in Fairhaven," Ned said softly. "In one of the hotels down by the coal mines. She's registered under the name Henrietta Rodgers."

Henry took a wide, steel band off his little finger and pressed it into Lacey's hand. "You show her this and she'll know you came from us. We'll meet ya there."

"Planning on getting out for good behavior?" Lacey asked, slipping the ring onto her middle finger.

Henry smiled. "Don't you worry your pretty little head over us, sugar. You head on down to Fairhaven as soon as you get outta here . . . and when we meet up again we'll get better acquainted."

"All three of us at once," Ned added with a lusty chuckle.

Both men gave her a slow once-over with their eyes, and Lacey managed to keep smiling. She'd gotten all the information she needed to find the money. Now if she could only keep down her breakfast for the rest of the hour.

8

"Think she's gone insane yet?"

Matthew angled a glare at his deputy. He was staring at the clock, counting the minutes until he could barge back in there and drag Miss Lacey Garder out of that cell room. She was already insane. She had to be to have gone back there alone. And he had to be as thick as an oak tree to have let her.

Larry suddenly sat up straight in the chair beside the potbellied stove. "Was that a scream?"

"A horse outside," Matthew replied. Larry was about as jumpy as Matthew was frustrated.

"Well, I for one am going to hold you personally responsible if anything has happened to that poor young woman."

Matthew glared at Reginald Sterling. It seemed the man was so hot to get him out of the way he was even against any plan that might get the town back its money.

"Ain't it been an hour yet?" Larry whined.

"She's still got five minutes."

"And our generous marshal is determined to give her every single second of her torture."

"What the hell is wrong with that woman, anyway?" the deputy burst out. "No lady in her right mind would set foot back there with those two men, let alone demand to be left with 'em for one entire hour."

"Miss Garder seems to have her own personal set of rules," Matthew grumbled.

"Yeah, well, I'm glad she's not my responsibility or I'd be in my grave by now. Women are supposed to be sweet and retirin', like that little Simmons woman you're seein'. She don't make demands, she don't curse a man out, and she sure as hell don't visit outlaws in jail. You hitch yourself up with a woman like that, boss, and you'll live a long and prosperous life."

"Not if I can prevent it," Matthew heard Reginald mumble.

He narrowed his eyes on the man. "Just why are you bothering to hang around, Sterling, if you're so sure this plan isn't going to work?"

"Someone has to look out for the poor woman's best interests."

"How charitable of you," Matthew stated.

Finally the clock began to chime. All three of them watched it and waited for the final moments to tick off. One o'clock. Matthew scooted back his chair, and had his hand on the door to the cell room before the sound of the single *gong* had stopped reverberating through the small room.

"The woman will likely be out of her mind with terror when you bring her out here," Reginald called after him.

That statement slammed hard into Matthew's stomach as he strode into the back room and was surrounded by echoing, deep male laughter. He steeled himself for what he was about to see. He should never have let her do it. Despite her obstinance and goading, he should have stopped her from going through with this crazy scheme.

He turned his attention to the cell on the left, expecting to see Miss Garder huddled in a ball in the far corner, and he stopped cold. She was huddled all right. In a tight little group with the Rawlins brothers by the center bars, and they were all having a real good laugh over something.

Fury overrode all his senses, and he strode toward her cell door. He wasn't sure what was making him angrier, the fact that she'd apparently fit right in with the two scurrilous bastards, or that he'd actually spent the past hour worrying over her. "Time's up," he ordered gruffly.

The laughter stopped, and she raised her head and looked at him with her sexy tawny gaze. Her smile was wide and entrancing, her eyes were still sparkling from her laughter, and Matthew just about shot Henry and Ned Rawlins right then and there. She pushed her hand through the front of her copper hair and gave it a shake. "Hello, Marshal," she said. "Is my time up already?"

He yanked open her cell door. "Out."

"Ah, come on, Marshal," Henry Rawlins pleaded. He made an unsuccessful grab for the back of Miss Garder's yellow skirt as she turned away from him. "Just a little longer."

"I'll see you boys later," she called.

This must have been some sort of inside joke, because the two men broke into laughter again. "Yeah, see ya, Lacey," Ned called.

"See more of ya," Henry added with a chortling leer.

Matthew clenched his jaw as the woman brushed

past him and smiled her way out of the back room. He shut the cell-room door behind them both, and then barely kept himself from taking her by the shoulders and giving her a good shake. If more had gone on back there than just a clandestine gathering of information, then he damn well wanted to know about it.

Reginald minced toward her the moment she entered the office. "Well, she certainly looks all in one piece," he said, studying her carefully. "But who knows what kind of horror has been done to her mind. I'll take her to my office immediately and she and I will have a nice long chat—"

"Stand aside, Sterling," Matthew commanded. "She's not going anywhere until she tells me exactly what went on back there."

"Well, thank you for your concern, Marshal," she said sarcastically. "It was a little messy, but I survived just fine."

The sigh Larry heaved could have knocked over a sleeping cow.

"You three have yourselves a little party back there?" Matthew asked pointedly. That remark had sounded nothing short of childish, but he didn't give a damn. He wanted to know what had gone on between them to make them all so chummy, and he wanted to know now.

"They were a little tough to play at first, but things went well in the end."

"They did?" Reginald returned. "Frankly, Marshal, how can we even be sure that they didn't know Miss Garder's ploy and feed her a crop of lies?"

"They told me the truth. And now I've got all the information we need to recover the money."

Matthew should have been thrilled, elated by that

news, but her "we" took him by the scruff of the neck. "*We* need?" he echoed.

"That's right. I'll be joining you in the search."

"*What*?" Larry exclaimed.

Matthew gave her a stoic stare. "On a cold day in hell you will, lady."

She stepped closer to him, glaring stubbornly up into his face, and his nostrils filled with the sweet, spicy scent that always clung to her. "Like I said, Marshal, I've got all the information we need. The question is . . . how badly do you want it?"

"How badly do you want it," Nelson stated. "Those were her exact words, sir. How badly . . . do you want it. The dastardly misbegotten is now using her mission as a bargaining tool."

Stella rolled her eyes at Nelson's dramatics. "Was I or was I not given the opportunity to turn this young woman around? It's scarcely been one day, for goodness sake."

"Gentle lady," Nelson reminded her, "the heavens and earth were created in less time. Sir, I must now insist that Miss Garder be put back where she belongs—in jail, in the twentieth century."

"On what grounds?" Stella demanded. "That she's flirting with a man?"

"Flirting?" Nelson replied incredulously. "If that's her idea of flirting then I'd rather be hit by a Mack truck! Sir, she is toying viciously with this man's life. He is only trying to do his job, and lead a quiet, respectable life as his dying father wished him to do— noble ambitions, I'd say. And this Garder woman is knowingly—I repeat, *knowingly*—standing in his way."

"Mr. Brady is being entirely too stubborn where Miss Garder is concerned," Stella insisted. "I think it's entirely reasonable that she maintain her demands be met before she shares her information with him."

"Oh, poppycock," Nelson blustered. "That woman wouldn't know reasonable if it sprouted horns and bleated in her face."

"You two are beginning to give me a headache," Maximillian finally spoke up. "Has Miss Garder done anything untoward that has adversely affected the lives of anyone she has come into contact with?"

"No," Stella stated.

"But she's on the very verge of it as we speak, sir. She has information that will lead Mr. Brady directly to his goal, and she is willfully withholding it from him."

Maximillian settled his steady gaze on Stella. "Is there a problem brewing, Stella?"

"The only thing my client is guilty of at the moment is playing with the man's mind. It's classic behavior between a woman and a man, and not surprising between these two considering their connection."

Maximillian's brows arched in interest. "Have there been signs of spiritual recognition?"

Stella hesitated. She'd been so hoping that Lacey Garder would take one look at Matthew Brady, recognize him as her soul mate, and fall head over heels in love—and that Matthew Brady would do the same. In fact, she'd been counting on that occurrence to help her turn her client around. But so far she'd seen no signs of that happening, even after Miss Garder and Mr. Brady had spent an entire night together under the same roof.

"Not that I'm aware of, no," she answered truthfully. "But, as I said, it has only been one day."

"Well, I haven't been informed of any recognitions," Nelson stated. "In fact, Mr. Brady's guide has asked me to make it very clear to you, sir, that he is beginning to grow concerned about his client's continued exposure to Miss Garder. So far she's proved to be nothing but a nuisance."

"And you'd know a lot about nuisances, wouldn't you, Nelson," Stella grumbled.

Maximillian frowned at her, and Stella realized how much this case was really getting to her. She wanted so desperately for Miss Garder to succeed.

"Nelson," Maximillian said. "Stella is correct. Unless something truly dire happens, her client shall be given ample opportunity to complete her mission."

"But sir—"

"And minor flirtations between a man and a woman are not what I would consider dire, Nelson. Do you understand?"

"Yes, sir."

"Furthermore, you will remind Mr. Brady's guide of his oath to prevent his personal opinions from unduly influencing his client."

"Yes, sir."

"I don't expect to see you in my office again, Nelson, unless the world has exploded and Miss Garder's hands were on the plunger."

"Yes, sir." With that, Nelson turned and left the room.

Stella thanked her superior and turned to leave herself, but Maximillian stopped her. "A word, Stella," he said. "You know, it is entirely possible that Mr. Brady and Miss Garder's paths together have been irreparably damaged by her altered evolution in the twentieth century. You must be prepared for the possibility that they may never recognize each other."

Stella nodded. But the idea of Lacey Garder living the rest of her life without her one true love was just too sad for her to contemplate. And too tragic for her to accept.

Lacey slammed out of the jailhouse and onto the deserted street. The day had warmed up a little since her ride into town that morning. The calf-deep snow was beginning to melt, turning into a gray slush that hid mud holes and patches of horse manure. She managed to avoid both of these as she trudged toward Hazel's restaurant, knowing the Martins would want to be informed immediately of her progress with the Rawlins brothers.

"Maybe I don't believe you got a single bit of information out of them!" the marshal shouted at her from his office doorway. "Maybe that's why you're not telling me a goddamned thing!"

"And maybe you're an idiot!" she shouted back without turning from her path. What she'd learned from Ned and Henry could keep until the marshal had learned some manners. She was sick of him constantly being suspicious of her—and before she'd even given him a reason to be! "If you want to know what Ned and Henry told me, then you can damn well come over to the restaurant and apologize for being such a pigheaded bastard!"

"Oh, now I'm supposed to apologize?"

She heard him marching across the street after her. He cursed, and she knew he hadn't been as lucky as she about avoiding those hidden mud holes and dung piles. She turned and faced him head on. "Come to your senses so soon?" she asked sarcastically.

He hooked his thumbs in his gun belt and replied evenly, "Tell me what they said."

"Apologize. And then agree to let me go after the money with you."

He threw his hands up in the air. "What the hell is the matter with you? This isn't a game, Miss Garder! This town's future is at stake!"

"And to think you're letting two little things like an apology and a tiny compromise stand in the way of saving it." She turned and continued toward the restaurant.

"Don't you walk away from me, goddamn it!" he shouted. She heard him sloshing through the wet snow after her.

"Touch me," she warned, walking onward, "and you'll pull back a bloody stump."

Suddenly she caught a glimpse of her spiritual guide standing by the restaurant door. The woman was frowning, as if Lacey had done something terribly wrong. Before Lacey could open her mouth and inquire about the problem, the wet snow beneath her feet turned into solid ice. Her eyes flew open wide as she lost her footing. She let out a startled shriek, and the angel smiled and vanished as quickly as she'd appeared.

Lacey instinctively made a grab for the nearest stable object, which just happened to be the marshal. Unfortunately his situation wasn't any better, and he had to make a grab for her at the same time. "What the . . ." he muttered.

"Don't move," she commanded. She crouched to balance herself, but her left foot betrayed her and slipped sideways. She did an odd little dance in front of him while he held onto the sleeves of her leather coat. Somehow she managed to remain standing.

"I thought we weren't supposed to move," he remarked.

She glared up into his dark green eyes. "Back up," she ordered.

"If I fall I take you with me."

"Then let go of me," she said tightly.

He shrugged and did as she asked. Her feet instantly began a slow slide away from each other, and she tried to leverage herself by gripping the front of his jacket. "You're just going to stand there and let me fall, aren't you?" she demanded.

"I was considering it." But then he took her by her elbows and hoisted her back into a standing position.

Lacey's indignation got the better of her survival instinct and she gave him a little shove. He arched backward, and his left foot slipped out from under him. The two of them did a shimmy, a slow slide, and then gravity finally won out and they landed, hard, in the road.

"You lumbering ox!" she shouted at him. "Why did you have to grab hold of me! Like I could hold up a two-ton elephant like your sorry ass! What are you trying to do, kill me! And haven't I told you about a thousand times not to touch—" A glob of slushy snow came flying through the air and hit Lacey in the chest.

"Would it be possible for you to shut up?" the marshal demanded. "Christ, if I'd known you would be my punishment for leading a questionable life I would have entered the goddamned clergy!"

Lacey gritted her teeth and struggled to her knees. She scooped up a handful of snow, packed it into a tight, hard ball, and then turned to the marshal. "So much for hindsight!"

"Don't you dare—"

Her snowball hit him smack-dab in the center of

his forehead, where it shattered and poured down the sides of his face and neck. He brushed the ice away, and smiled coldly at her. Then he crouched down and began to pack another missile of his own.

Lacey tried to scramble away, but the ice made that nearly impossible. Finally he straightened, grinned maliciously at her, and hefted up the grand-daddy of all snowballs. It was as big around as his head, and, seeing a concussion in the making, Lacey managed to get to her feet and began backing toward the restaurant. Of course she forgot all about that mysterious icy patch, and her feet went flying out from under her the moment she stepped onto it. She landed hard on her back.

The marshal loomed over her, his gigantic snow-ball clutched tightly in his hands. His hair was wet and dripping down into his eyes, his forehead was red where she'd hit him with her iceball and his breath was coming hard and fast. He looked like Conan the Barbarian with a giant boulder, and she covered her face with her hands.

"Matthew Brady!"

Lacey let out a relieved sigh. It was Hazel, come to save her. She sat up as the woman strode toward them from the doorway of the restaurant looking fit to kill.

"What in tarnation do you think you're doin'?" Hazel demanded.

"Getting even," the marshal returned between grit-ted teeth.

"Not in front of my restaurant you're not. And not with my houseguest." She slipped her hands beneath Lacey's arms, and hauled her to her feet as if picking up a rag doll. "I swear, you two act like a couple of children when you get together. Come on inside where it's warm, Lacey, honey."

The marshal tossed his snow boulder aside. "I'm not finished talking to you yet, Miss Garder," he growled.

Lacey ignored him. Hazel looked flustered. "What is it?" Lacey asked her, concern overriding her anger.

"Oh . . ." Hazel waved a dismissing hand. "Things are a bit hectic inside today. Despite what we hoped, the restaurant's plumb packed full to capacity this afternoon, and one of our waiters is down sick with the flu. George and I just don't seem to have enough hands," she finished with a laugh.

Considering all George and Hazel had done for her, Lacey didn't even hesitate with her response. "Then toss me an apron, and consider yourself two hands stronger."

Hazel gave her a startled look. "Oh, no, Lacey. You're our guest. Me and George would never ask you to—"

"You're not asking. I'm offering." She began walking toward the restaurant with Hazel at her side.

"Miss Garder—" the marshal began.

"Later, law-dude."

"Damn it! This discussion is *not* over!"

"You know where to find me. Oh,"—she turned in the doorway and faced his hot glare—"and don't forget to bring your apology." She flashed him a quick smile, turned, and followed Hazel into the crowded restaurant.

9

The moment the restaurant door closed behind Lacey twenty pairs of interested male eyes swung her way and she realized why the Martins had such a crowd. The lumberjacks had bathed, and then decided to hang around in hopes of catching sight of her again.

"So how did it go?" Hazel asked.

Knowing she was alluding to Lacey's time with the Rawlins brothers, Lacey gave her a victorious smile. "Great. I know exactly where the money is." She flashed Henry Rawlins's ring. "And how to get it."

"Ya hear that boys?" Paul Smith called from a nearby table. "Lacey's done it! She's found our money!"

A loud shout went up from the crowd, and the men began to rise from their seats. "Hold it!" Hazel shouted. "The first man to stand is the first man to leave. If you wanna eat in my restaurant, you'll keep your hineys in your chairs and leave Miss Garder to herself."

"But I'd so much rather keep my chair to myself

and leave my hiney to Miss Garder!" someone shouted, which made the room burst into laughter.

Hazel gave Lacey a sympathetic look. "You think you're gonna be able to handle this hungry crowd?"

It was what they were hungry *for* that had Lacey so worried. "Hey. No problem."

"After spending the past hour with the Rawlins brothers, if you're not up to this George and I'll understand."

"No, no." Lacey tried to smile brightly, but figured the action probably looked more like a grimace. "It'll be a piece of cake."

Three hours later Lacey was rethinking that statement, and her impulsive generosity in offering to help.

"Where's that piece of cake, Lacey?"

"Hey, Lacey, I ordered of platter of fried chicken fifteen minutes ago."

"How long does it take to fetch a mug a coffee, Lacey?"

"Lacey, can I get a little service over here, please?"

She paused in the middle aisle of the restaurant and blew a loose strand of hair back from her eyes. It was nearly five o'clock. The lunch crowd had blended into the dinner crowd without even giving her a chance to catch her breath. She'd taken close to sixty orders, received more than twenty marriage proposals, and had been pinched on the butt so many times she was going to be black and blue for a week.

"Hey, Lacey, come on over here and meet my pal, Johnny!" a man in the back called.

Word had apparently gotten out around the lumberjack camp that a new lady was in town, and that she was going to help find the stolen bank money. As a result, the stream of curious men filing into the restaurant appeared to be endless. She was the center of attention amidst a horde of gigantic men who acted as if they hadn't seen a real live woman in months.

"Hell, Lacey, as a waitress you've got about as much get up and go as a two-legged horse!"

"She sure is a hell of a lot more in'erestin' to look at, though!"

Lacey felt the by now familiar sensation of someone pinching her bottom, and spun around to face her abuser. There were three lumberjacks sitting at the table behind her, all three within pinching distance, and all three now looking as innocent as lambs. "Looks like you found her start-up button!" somebody shouted, sending the room into laughter again.

Lacey pointed her finger at the offending group of men. "I'm going to warn you one time, gentlemen. *Hands off the waitress.*"

"Or what?" one of them dared to ask. "Come here, li'l gal."

Before she could move a step back, the big smelly man reached out and pulled her onto his lap. The crowd cheered their approval and panic took Lacey tightly by the throat. She struggled with the man, but his strength far surpassed her own, and she fought down a gag when he attempted to press his mouth to hers.

But then another arm was snaking around her waist and lifting her off the man's lap. She let out a shout and kicked backward, and was dropped to her feet on the floor. She turned, prepared to fight this new threat, and came face to face with Matthew Brady.

Her breath coming hard and fast, she stared up into his face and noted his grim expression. The clapping and cheering in the restaurant had stopped. "There a problem here?" he asked.

The big man who'd pulled her onto his lap looked instantly contrite. "Sorry, Marshal."

Lacey saw red. "Oh, yes, do forgive him, Marshal, for pinching *your* butt and then attempting to shove his tongue down *your* throat!"

"See that you leave the lady alone," the marshal said. The man nodded, and promptly went back to talking with his two friends without even giving Lacey so much as a conciliatory glance. She leaned on the table toward him. "You ever touch me again and I'll be serving your ears to you on a plate," she hissed.

Meanwhile the marshal walked to a small table near the front window, took off his coat and hat, and sat down. Lacey glared at him moodily, hoping he wasn't there to pick up where they'd left off earlier. She was just too damned tired to deal with anything or anybody right now.

She strode toward him with a sigh. "What do you want?"

"Coffee. And little cooperation."

"Cup of coffee coming right up," she replied, and turned for the kitchen.

"Just how long do you intend to go on like this, Miss Garder?"

She turned back to him. "Like what?"

"Do you have any idea how important that money is to this town?"

"I know how important it is to you and your job."

His features tightened. "Is that why you're holding out on me? Because this directly involves my job?"

"Strange as it may seem," she replied dryly, "that's why I'm trying to *help*."

He arched a skeptical brow. "*You* are trying to help *me* save my job?"

"I'm a kooky sorta gal, aren't I?"

"And just what, exactly, do you expect in return?"

Lacey sighed and folded her arms. "Let's start with a little consideration. You've been on me since the moment I hit town. You've been suspicious, narrow-minded, and offensive—and I haven't even had the chance to do anything wrong yet. Out of the goodness of my heart I've offered to help you find that money, and you've been nothing but rude and ungracious. And when I finally do convince you to let me help by having a go at the Rawlins brothers, you insult me by insisting that something other than talking went on during the enchanting hour I spent with them."

He stared hard at her, his eyes searching hers. "Did something else happen?"

"What could have happened?" she demanded. "We had a set of iron bars between us, for God's sake."

"How about a meeting of the minds?"

"Listen, Marshal," she said tightly, leaning close to him. "I may run with a suspicious sort of crowd at times, but I wouldn't be caught dead in company like theirs. And for you to even suggest it makes me want to take a long hot soak in a tub full of lye. Understand?"

His stare held hers for a moment longer, and then dropped down to her mouth. The action took her off guard and she quickly straightened. She'd recently eaten a muffin, and, thinking she had food stuck to her lips, she brushed at them with her fingertips. "I'll get your coffee."

She turned to leave, but he caught hold of her hand and yanked her back around so fast it snapped her neck. "What the hell is this?" he demanded darkly.

Lacey jerked her hand from his, and glanced down at the steel band on her finger. "It's called a ring."

"I know what the damn thing is. I also happened to know whose it is. What I want to know is why the hell *you're* wearing it."

His olive-green eyes were flashing lightning, and Lacey knew what he was thinking. That she'd lied to him. That she and the Rawlins brothers had come to a meeting of the minds—and then some. "Well, you see," she said, "Henry and I are engaged. We haven't told our families yet, so if you could just keep it to yourself—"

"What the hell did you have to do to get it?" he said viciously.

"Why, lift my skirt and fanny up to the bars—*what else!*" She turned and marched across the room, ignoring the standard taunts and proclamations of love from the other men, and barged into the kitchen.

"How's everything goin' out there?" George asked her. He was frying pan steaks at the stove while Hazel peeled potatoes over the garbage bin.

"Fine," she retorted. "Just fine." She reached for the tin coffeepot on the counter.

"You might want to heat that up," Hazel suggested.

"Oh, this'll do just fine."

She took the entire pot and headed back out into the dining area where she ignored the cups that were raised her way and headed straight to the marshal. "Apologize," she stated.

"I only apologize when I've committed a wrong, lady. Now I suggest you start talking before I toss you in jail for withholding vital information from me that might help my investigation."

"Oh, is that what you call it? An investigation? I'd

say it looks more like a three-ring circus. You being the biggest clown, of course."

"Don't make me ask you again, Miss Garder."

"What? For your coffee? Gee, I'm sorry, Marshal. Here you are." With that, she turned the pot over, dumping the lukewarm contents into his lap.

He was on his feet in seconds, probably thinking she'd ruined his chances of ever procreating, and the entire dining room burst into hoots of laughter. "Will there be anything else?" she asked him sweetly.

His hands formed into claws, and she wisely took a step back from him. "Miss Garder . . ." he sputtered.

"Looks like you could use a change of clothes there, Sparky."

"First thing tomorrow," he growled, "I want you . . . in my office. *First thing tomorrow*."

"Wanting can be such a frustrating thing, can't it?"

"You be there, or so help me I'll ride out to the Martins' and drag you back by your hair," he seethed. "And be prepared to talk. Because you're not leaving until I've heard every single damn word that was said between you and Ned and Henry Rawlins."

And with one, final, hostile glare, Marshal Matthew Brady turned and . . . sort of *hobbled* from the restaurant.

Amanda Simmons's house was as quaint and as pretty as the schoolteacher herself. Dressed in a clean pair of pants, Matthew paused at the white picket gate and stared at the neat little moonlit walk lined with snow-draped shrubbery. He hadn't found the time to talk to Amanda at all that day, or at least hadn't found the energy to make the effort, but he knew he couldn't let the evening end without apologizing to her for not showing up to take her to dinner the night before.

He pushed open the gate, scraping aside a thin layer of shoveled snow, and headed toward her front stoop. His heart just wasn't in this visit, and he chalked it up to two tiring days of trying to save his job while doing his best to keep the unpredictable Miss Lacey Garder in line. He hadn't had a moment's peace since she'd come to town.

Three neatly shoveled steps later he was knocking on Amanda's front door. And then she was standing there, with the moonlight reflecting off her warm smile. Dressed in a high-collared blue flowered dress and wearing her blond hair in a bun at the back of her neck, she was the epitome of respectable. Everything a decent man was ever supposed to need.

He took off his hat. "I've come to say I'm sorry about last night."

"Oh, don't apologize, Matthew," she said gently. "God Himself wouldn't have ventured out in that storm. Come in. Have you eaten?"

Instantly Matthew's thoughts returned to Hazel's restaurant and inevitably Lacey Garder. No, he hadn't eaten. But he had had an entire pot of coffee. He followed her into the parlor, after being sure to wipe his feet on the reed mat outside the door. She took his coat and hat and hung them on the coat tree in the entryway.

"You look tired," she said. "Please, come in and sit down."

Matthew followed her into the front room and sat down on the comfortable sofa. He *was* tired. He'd slept very little the night before, and figured he wouldn't do much better that night. He swore that if that woman wasn't in his office by the time he arrived in the morning—

"Matthew?"

He blinked, and refocused on Amanda.

"I asked if you'd like some cookies. I just made them."

He managed a smile. "Sounds good."

She rose from the rocker she was sitting in and headed for the kitchen. With an almost scientific curiosity Matthew watched the subtle sway of her skirt until she disappeared through the swinging door at the back of the room. He found himself doing that often, watching Amanda when she wasn't aware of it, trying to figure out why he didn't feel even a smidgen of attraction toward her. She was pretty enough, shapely enough, certainly intelligent enough. But although they'd been courting for over three months now, he'd never so much as had a single desire to touch her, to clandestinely brush his arm against one of her breasts, or even to kiss her. He'd always considered himself a pretty passionate man, and, frankly, his lack of reaction to her perplexed him.

She returned a moment later carrying a small plate of cookies, which she handed him, and then, once again, sat down in the rocker. "They're cinnamon."

But Matthew already knew that. His nostrils had flared the moment she'd handed him the plate, and he now finally knew what the scent was that always clung to Lacey Garder. The sweet, spicy smell of cinnamon instantly conjured up an image of copper hair and golden eyes, and he threw the plate onto the couch beside him in his haste to banish the infuriating woman from his thoughts.

"You don't like them?" Amanda said, frowning.

Realizing what he'd just done, Matthew smiled and

reached down to rearrange the scattered cookies back onto the plate. "I'm . . . uh . . . they give me hives."

"Oh good heavens, I'm sorry, Matthew." She rushed forward to pick up the plate and set it on the sideboard a few feet away. But that didn't lessen the aroma that had already filled the room. It positively exuded Lacey Garder. "Can I get you something else?" she asked. "A cup of coffee perhaps?"

Matthew closed his eyes and prayed for patience. "No, thank you."

"Are you sure you're all right, Matthew?"

She looked so distressed that Matthew suddenly regretted coming to her house. He should have known that she wouldn't be angry at him for not being able to make it to dinner the night before. Amanda could never be that petty. He should have waited until morning, when he'd been more in charge of his own thoughts and emotions, before coming to apologize.

"You know, I am really tired." He stood up from the sofa. "I just wanted to stop by and apologize. I'd better get home and at least try to get a good night's sleep."

"Try? Are you having trouble sleeping?"

"Uhh— It's the wolves," he offered with a smile. "I haven't gotten used to the howling yet."

She frowned. "Yes, that can be very disturbing."

The fact that wolves rarely howled in the middle of winter either didn't occur to her, or she was just too polite to mention it. Knowing Amanda, Matthew suspected the latter.

She led him to the front door and offered him his coat. "Perhaps we can get together for dinner at the reverend's on Sunday night?"

He draped the coat over his arm. "Oh, the Martins

have invited us over for dinner tomorrow night. I told them we'd come."

"Well, that sounds nice."

The fact that he'd already accepted without even bothering to check with her first didn't seem to bother Amanda in the slightest. But that really didn't surprise him. Amanda was kind, honest, unassuming, completely uncomplicated and totally gracious—a *saint*, for crying out loud. But if she was so perfect then why the hell couldn't he feel passionate about her? Why was it a woman like Lacey Garder could make his heart pound with just a glance, and this sweet, gentle lady didn't even have the power to create the tiniest bit of longing within him?

Maybe he just wasn't trying hard enough. Maybe one simple kiss was all it would take to light a fire between them.

"Come here," he said softly.

Slowly, he reached for her. She looked bewildered, hesitant, but still allowed him to take her in his arms. Her eyes were wide as he bent his head and had a brief, tender taste of her lips. She was graceful, pleasant to embrace, but didn't fit quite right in his arms.

One kiss was all he took before releasing her. And, to the best of his estimation, it appeared as though their kiss hadn't had much of an effect on her either.

"I'll see you at five," he said, reaching for his hat.

"Yes. Good night, Matthew."

He headed down the snowy walk toward the street with a rock the size of Texas in his stomach. The woman he planned to marry left him cold as an Arctic fish. But the woman he wanted out of his life as fast as he could chase her ignited a fire in him like nothing he'd ever felt before. And he wasn't sure how much longer he could control the flames.

10

Lacey curled up on the Martins' sofa that night and kept warm by the fire while she considered her next move. She'd decided that the possibility of Matthew Brady allowing her to go along on the hunt for Lorraine Rawlins was about as probable as the space shuttle Atlantis landing in the Martins' front yard. But if she relented, gave him the information he needed and then stayed behind, how could she trust that he and his men wouldn't scare Lorraine away before they ever got within ten feet of her or the money?

There were only five days left for Lacey to accomplish her mission, which didn't leave a whole lot of room for mistakes. Her freedom was at stake. How could she possibly trust that to the whim of the marshal and his deputies?

With all this in mind, her only choice seemed simple. She would damn well go to Fairhaven and get that money back herself.

All she had to do was find out where Fairhaven was. "Hazel's all settled in for the night," George said, coming into the room. "Told me to say thank you for helpin' us out today."

"She was falling asleep on my shoulder on the way home."

"Ah, we're gettin' too old to handle crowds like that one." He eased down into the leather chair. "The more this town grows, the more employees we're gonna need."

Lacey knew that the oversize, never-ending crowd had been mostly her fault, and she thought it kind of George not to mention that fact. "I'll help out as long as I'm in town," she replied. It was the least she could do after all the Martins had done for her.

"'Preciate the offer, Lacey."

"Then I did all right today?"

"Well . . ." He rubbed the back of his neck.

Lacey smiled ruefully. Her first day on the job had fallen a little short of sterling. She'd spilled more coffee, dropped more plates, and messed up more orders than the three stooges on a bad day.

"The important thing is," George continued, "you did your best."

"I guess we've both discovered that I'm not exactly the greatest waitress in the world."

He smiled. "I'd say you were meant for somethin' other than restaurantin'."

"Guess so," Lacey mumbled. Like stealing wallets and robbing jewelry stores.

"I'll give ya this, Lacey, you've certainly shown a knack for standing up against adversity. Although I don't suppose Matthew would appreciate being described as that. Heard you did a real good job with the Rawlins brothers this afternoon. Everybody's talking about it. Whole town appreciates it."

"Not the *whole* town."

"Ah, Matthew'll come around. He's a real sharp fella. Gets that from his daddy. Gets his stubbornness from his daddy too."

"I don't suppose his daddy tended to change his mind easily."

George laughed. "Hank? Not rightly. He'd sooner gnaw off his own foot."

"Great," Lacey grumbled, "I guess I'll just stick with my plan then."

"What was that?"

"Oh, nothing. Just talking to myself. So you and Hazel must have made a killing in the cash department today."

He gave her an odd look.

"You must have taken in a lot of money," she clarified.

"Oh. Yeah. Couldn't a done it without you, though."

"It was the least I could do considering all you two have done for me. I mean you're feeding me, sheltering me, *clothing* me. I never intended to be such a problem—"

"A problem?!" he exclaimed. "Hazel was just tellin' me how much she wishes you'd stay around for a long time to come."

"She was?"

"Absolutely. She thinks you're the greatest thing since canned vegetables. We both do."

A warmth spread through Lacey, filling her heart, and she felt a powerful moment of connection, as if she'd finally found her first allies in the world. "That was very sweet of her to say," she replied through a slightly tightened throat. "I think very highly of her as well. Both of you."

"But you don't have to feel beholden to us for bein' a friend to ya, Lacey. That's what friends are for, to be there when the goin' gets rough. Like you were there for us today. But you know the next time you help us out in the restaurant we're gonna have ta get you an iron bustle," he added. "Hazel told me tonight what was goin' on out there before Matthew arrived, and your fanny must look like the bad side of a twice dropped apple."

She was a little sore now that he mentioned it. "I survived. And I'm surprised you'd let me come back after I ran off so many of your customers."

"Apparently some of 'em needed runnin' off. Besides, they'll be back. The nearest restaurant is just outside of Fairhaven, and I doubt they'd be willing to ride twenty miles in the snow to get there."

At the mention of Fairhaven Lacey straightened on the couch. "Fairhaven is only twenty miles from here?"

"That's right. You got business there?"

"I . . . an aunt, actually."

George brightened. "Really? Well, I know just about everybody who lives in Whatcom County. What's your aunt's name?"

Lacey gave him a hesitant smile. Never having had an aunt, she had to think quickly. "Uhhh . . . Aunt . . . Jemimah." The words "aunt" and "Jemimah" just sort of went together naturally.

"Jemimah . . ." George repeated, frowning thoughtfully. "What's the surname?"

"Umm . . . Jones?"

"Know a Carl Jones. He any relation?"

"Not that I know of."

"Well, I can't exactly say I've heard of your aunt. She a married woman?"

"No," Lacey said, simply because she didn't want to have to come up with an uncle's name as well.

"What does she do to get by?"

"She . . . Uh . . . She makes pancakes."

"Pancakes . . ." George said to himself, still wracking his brain.

"I hear they're the best around."

"Well, you'll have to ask her if she'll share the recipe with us."

Lacey nodded. "I'll ask her tomorrow . . . when I go for a visit."

George's brows arched in surprised. "You're goin' to visit her tomorrow?"

"Is that all right?"

"Well, sure. But isn't it a little cold for you to go traipsing down to the bay?"

"But you said it's only twenty miles."

"*Only* twenty miles?"

At his incredulous stare, Lacey suddenly remembered where she was. It wasn't as if there was a truck parked in the barn by the cow. "I don't suppose it's an easy walk?" she asked meekly.

George broke into laughter. "I'll saddle up Big Red for ya first thing in the mornin'. Who've you got goin' with ya?"

"With me?"

George broke into a disapproving frown. "You aren't plannin' on goin' alone, are ya?"

Lacey could tell, by his censoring tone, that if she admitted she planned to ride to Fairhaven by herself he'd change his mind about lending her the horse. "No," she scoffed. "Of course not. Marshal Brady's going with me. He said something about checking into some leads about Lorraine Rawlins, and I figured that would be a perfect opportunity to see my aunt."

George nodded, believing every word she was telling him, while Lacey's stomach slowly tied itself into knots. She hated lying to this decent, trusting man.

"Well, it's good to see you two are finally tryin' to get along."

"We're doing our best."

"Matthew's a good man."

"If you say so," she replied.

"He's just a bit headstrong, and a tad stingy with his affections." George gave her a pointed look. "You two have a lot in common."

Lacey's smile was replaced by wide-eyed affront. "I am not stingy. Cautious maybe, but not stingy. And I am not half as stubborn as he is—he can't even give me credit when it is plainly obvious that I am right."

George smiled, and stood from the chair. "No need to get your back up. Just makin' an observation. You got a temper like him, too," he added with a smirk. "I'm headin' off to bed."

"I do not," Lacey grumbled.

"See ya in the mornin', Lacey."

"Good night," she answered moodily. Then she listened to the comforting sound of his footsteps as he walked through the entryway, entered his bedroom, and shut the door.

She leaned her chin on the thick arm of the sofa and stared into the fire once again. "I'm nothing like Matthew Brady," she grumbled. The man was hot-headed and suspicious, stubborn and unreasonable—she was nothing at all like him.

"Sounds to me as if you are protesting too much, Miss Garder."

Lacey straightened, and looked over to the leather chair to find her spiritual guide making herself at home. "And where have you been?"

"Here and there. How was your first full day in the nineteenth century?"

"You ask that as if you don't know the answer."

"Perhaps I don't."

"Well, let me see. I was assaulted by a mob of lumberjacks, ogled by a pair of smelly outlaws, pinched until my butt turned black and blue, and repeatedly insulted by the man I am supposed to be helping. Oh yes." She narrowed her eyes. "I went ice dancing. And I have a sneaking suspicion that you had something to do with that."

"Why haven't you told Mr. Brady where he can find Lorraine Rawlins?" the woman asked, ignoring Lacey's insinuation.

"Don't even try avoiding the subject, lady. I saw you just before that snow turned to solid ice. You were the one who told me that everything you do has a purpose, and I want to know what purpose that served."

"Are you attracted to him, Miss Garder?"

To Lacey's ultimate chagrin, her entire face heated. "What difference does that make."

"It makes a great deal of difference. Have you felt any desire for him?"

"Sure. Desire for him to get the hell out of my life," she retorted.

The woman sighed. "I created that situation so that you and Mr. Brady would stop fighting long enough to respond to one another."

Lacey slowly leaned forward. "Respond how?"

"Don't you see it in his eyes?" the woman asked.

"I see anger in his eyes. I see animosity, dislike—"

"Then you're not looking deeply enough."

"Maybe it would help if I knew what I was looking *for*."

"When you find it, you will know."

Lacey fell back onto the sofa. "Maybe I don't want to know."

"You haven't changed your mind about staying, have you?"

"Not if I'd still do a nosedive into a nine-by-twelve cell."

"Then I ask you again, why haven't you told Mr. Brady where to find Lorraine Rawlins?"

"Because I've decided to go to Fairhaven and get the money back myself."

The woman turned downright pale. "That is not a wise decision."

"Why?"

"You need each other. Neither of you can do this alone."

"Look, I've lived my whole life doing things on my own, lady, and I've managed just fine." The woman gave her a dubious look. "All right, just fine until recently. But if I tell him what I know, he'll go without me. And I can't take the chance of him and his three caballeros scaring Lorraine off."

"Perhaps you should ask—"

"I already have. The man practically laughed in my face when I told him I wanted to ride with him. Trust me. He's no more interested in my help than I am in offering it to him. You said my priority was seeing that money returned to Tranquility, and that's precisely what I intend to do."

"If you're determined, then there's nothing else I can say."

"No. There isn't. I'm going to Fairhaven tomorrow alone, and I'm going to get that money if I have to drag Lorraine Rawlins back by her nose hairs to do it."

"If that's what you've decided. I am only here to guide you, Miss Garder. I cannot force you into decisions you don't care to make—no matter how foolish your own may be."

"Good." Although Lacey was beginning to feel a little uncomfortable by the woman's lack of enthusiasm for her plan. "I'll be fine," she said, hoping the angel would agree with her.

But the woman didn't. She simply pursed her lips and disappeared.

Matthew was standing, stark naked, at the end of a long aisle as a woman in a sleek white dress and veil walked toward him.

Everyone he'd ever known was there, gathered in a meadow beneath a bright blue sky. And they were all as fully clothed as the bride, making him feel more than a little disconcerted about his nudity.

She reached for his hand, and he hesitated at first, not sure who he would be giving it to. But finally he took a deep breath and grasped her cool fingers, helping her to step up beside him.

They both turned and faced George Martin, who then proceeded to marry them before God and all mankind.

Matthew thought it strange that George Martin, a simple restaurant owner, was presiding over his wedding, but his bride seemed all right with the idea, so he ignored the small oddity. She said her vows in a gentle, sweet voice, swearing to love him till the day she died, and he slipped a golden wedding band on her finger.

Then came the time for him to lift her veil and seal
their future with a kiss. He was afraid to do it. Afraid
of who he might find beneath. But the crowd became
restless, and finally he performed the traditional deed,
and raised the veil.

It was Amanda Simmons who smiled back at him.
He heaved a very relieved sigh, and smiled back at
her. But then suddenly, before his eyes, she turned
into his late mother. Then she turned into his obese
Aunt Elinor, and finally his childhood dog. Instead of
kissing her, he tossed the veil back over her face,
spun her around, and sent her back up the aisle to
wherever she'd come from.

Entrancing laughter filled the air, and he turned to
find Lacey Garder standing where George Martin
had been. Like Matthew, she was wearing nothing—
except the smile on her face. His body reacted
instantly, powerfully to her sleek beauty, and he was
forced to stand there in front of all his gaping friends
as his body went as hard as an ax handle. "Don't you
see?" Lacey said to him. "Don't you understand? It's
me, Matthew. I'm finally here. And you can't run
from me any more than you can run from yourself."

Matthew woke up with a start and sat bolt
upright in his bed. His upper body was a sheen of
sweat, and he was breathing hard as he struggled to
orient himself.

He set his elbows on his bent knees, and pushed
his fingers through his damp hair. "Christ," he said,
dropping his forehead into his hands. "I can't even
get away from her in my sleep."

He glanced toward his window, and noticed the
dark sky beginning to brighten. Dawn was breaking.
Time for all respectable folks to be climbing out of
their respectable beds.

He fell back to his pillow and stared at the shadowed ceiling. Today was the day he'd get to the bottom of where Lorraine Rawlins was hiding. Today he would finally conquer the indomitable spirit within Lacey Garder.

But then, there were no guarantees that she'd show up in his office that morning as he'd commanded.

Damn, the woman was so infuriating. She called his every bluff, nagged his every waking thought—even when he was with Amanda—and now she was actually giving him nightmares.

He tossed back his blankets and got out of bed. The cold air raised gooseflesh over his naked body. He walked to the window to stare out at the trees that made up the one hundred acres that was now his home. The home his father had built with his own two hands.

And he wasn't giving it—or his job—up without a fight.

In a sudden burst of determination, he grabbed his denims from the wooden chair by the window and pulled them on. Time waited for no man. And he wasn't about to wait for any woman. He was dressed, cleaned up, and out the door in minutes.

The sun was growing bolder just beyond the tops of the fir trees as he rode out of his yard. By the look of the clear blue sky, Tranquility was in for one beautiful day.

He urged his horse onward. Toward the Martin ranch.

When he arrived ten minutes later he spotted George coming out of the barn. "Morning, George," he called.

The man stopped cold, stared oddly at him for a moment, and then strode in his direction. "What in the livin' hell are you doin' here, Matthew?"

"I've got an appointment with Miss Garder this morning—"

"Yeah," the man said sharply, "and you best get movin', 'cause I don't like the idea of her sittin' out there all by herself."

Now it was Matthew's turn to look confused. "Sitting out where?"

"Out at Three Forks. Frankly, I'm a bit miffed that you couldn't take it upon yourself to just meet up with her here, 'specially since you're here now anyway."

"Three Forks Road?"

"Don't tell me you forgot that you were supposed to meet her there this mornin' so's the two of ya could ride out to Fairhaven together."

Fairhaven? What the hell was she up to now? Matthew thought suspiciously. "How long ago did she leave?" he asked. Three Forks Road was five, maybe six, minutes away. It was the main route that led down through the city of Geneva and toward the communities surrounding Bellingham Bay.

"'Bout a half hour ago," George replied curtly. He was obviously irritated with Matthew for what he saw as a distinct lack of responsibility. "You best get movin'," the man added. "She's real anxious to see her Aunt Jemimah and I don't want her headin' off alone."

"Right," Matthew replied. *Her Aunt Jemimah?* "We wouldn't want her getting into any trouble, would we."

He turned his horse around and headed for the road, settling his eyes on the mountainous horizon. He knew damn well he wasn't going to find Miss Lacey Garder waiting for him or anybody else at Three Forks Road. Aunt Jemimah his ass. She'd gone after that money. As sure as the sky was blue.

11

Getting George to give her directions to Fairhaven had been—as Hazel would say—easy as pie. Certainly easier than navigating the snow-covered and sometimes icy road Lacey was now traveling. She'd simply expressed an interest in the distance she and the marshal would be traveling, and in any obstacles they might encounter, and George had told her, without any qualms, that they'd be taking Three Forks Road between Geneva Lake and Lake Whatcom, and down into the bay communities. Nothing to it, she'd thought to herself.

Now, thirty minutes later, she was realizing there was a whole lot more to it.

Though breathtakingly beautiful, everything around her looked exactly the same. The same snow-heavy trees, the same snow-covered rocks, the same bends in the road, the same silence in the air. And with every successive plod of the horse beneath her, the risk of her getting lost out here in the middle of nowhere increased to almost overwhelming proportions.

"All you've got to do is stick to the road, Lacey," she told herself. "Easy as pie."

At least she was warm, even though the sun was still hanging low in the morning sky, and an occasional frigid breeze pressed against her exposed face. She was dressed in the two union suits Hazel had bought for her, the two pairs of bloomers, *and* the yellow muslin dress. She was bundled up in her fleece-lined coat with the wide collar hiked up past her chin. She had on her lined gloves, and she was wearing her boots over two pairs of itchy wool socks that she'd found in the bottom drawer of the dresser in her room. She'd even taken a towel out of Hazel's linen closet and was wearing that as a scarf over her head to protect her ears. She felt like an overstuffed turkey jammed into a miniature oven, but, damn it, she was warm.

She would make it to Fairhaven, and she would recover that money—even if she had to *steal* it back, and then she would ride back to Tranquility and toss it in Matthew Brady's face. Mission accomplished. Then she'd finally have to start facing the task of figuring out what, exactly, she intended to do with the rest of her life in the midst of the wild, wild West.

But first she had to find Lorraine Rawlins. She had Henry's ring tucked down inside her purse, which was tucked down inside one of her saddlebags. She planned to start with the choice hotels in Fairhaven and work her way down, bandying the name of Henrietta Rodgers around as if she were searching for a long-lost friend. Lorraine was bound to be curious rather than suspicious of a woman asking about her, and Lacey figured she'd have her prey before the day was out.

The horse beneath her pivoted its ears at a bird

fluttering through one of the trees and Lacey reached forward and patted his neck. He was a handsome animal, red in color with a dark stripe running down the length of his back. "You and I are doing just fine on our own, aren't we," she said to him. She couldn't wait to see Matthew Brady's face when she handed him all that money.

And then Big Red stopped cold in his tracks, and Lacey glanced up and realized why. They'd come to a fork in the road, and the horse didn't know which way to go. Of course, neither did she. She supposed if there hadn't been so much slushy snow on the ground she might have known the main road just by the wheel ruts in the dirt, but all she saw before her now were two distinct paths going at two distinctly different angles to her original direction.

"Now what?" she muttered.

She stood in the stirrups and stared down one path and then the other, trying to make out anything further on that might distinguish either one of them as the road to take. Nothing stood out, and she sat back down in disgust.

Big Red shuffled beneath her, probably sensing his rider's disquiet.

"A lot of help you are," she said to him. "Aren't you local boys supposed to know the way to the big city?"

He snorted and tugged at the bit in his mouth.

"Then I don't suppose you know of a place where we can stop and ask for directions?"

The horse merely blinked in the sunlight.

"Too hard on the pride, huh? Isn't that just like a man. Well . . ." She studied her two choices one more time. "I choose the left. It looks a little smoother, and widens out quite a bit past those trees. "To the left, faithful steed," she announced, and touched her heels to the animal's flanks.

A few minutes later Lacey rode into a clearing with nothing but snow surrounding her and nothing but trees and mountains in the distance. In fact, since arriving in the nineteenth century she'd never seen such a large clearing. Normally the thick-trunked trees grew so close together she had to turn sideways to walk between them.

Then she heard something and reined in Big Red. A loud pop. A sound she probably wouldn't have paid any attention to if the silence around her hadn't been so oppressive. The horse beneath her became animated, prancing sideways, snorting and tossing its head as it tried to take control of the bit in its mouth. But Lacey kept a firm grip on the reins and managed to settle him down.

Then she frowned at the scene around her, both peaceful and foreboding, and knew she must have taken the wrong road. She tugged on the reins, but didn't have to exert much pressure in order to turn Big Red around; he was all for the idea. And then Lacey finally realized why.

There was another loud *pop!* Followed by a sharp, spine-tingling *crack!* And then a racing sound, as if a million marbles had been dropped onto a linoleum floor. The ground beneath Big Red's hind legs gave way.

The animal bellowed and lunged forward, sending Lacey bouncing over the back of the saddle as its hindquarters dropped like a falling elevator. She lost the reins, and scrambled to hold onto the cantle, but the horse's frantic struggles to save itself sent her tumbling backward. Plunging her into icy darkness.

*   *   *

He almost had her.

Matthew had been following Lacey Garder's tracks for almost thirty minutes now. A few more and he'd catch up to her. What he intended to do with her once he got his hands on her still wasn't decided, but one thing was for sure: She was going to be giving him a damn good explanation for why that money was so important to her that she'd risk riding through the cold wilderness alone to get it.

He came to the fork in the road that led to a small lake named Geneva on the left and would take him past Lake Whatcom and to the tri-cities of Fairhaven, Sehome, and Whatcom to the right. He reined in his horse, and stared down at the tracks in the snow. A frown settled over his features as he looked off toward the smaller lake. "Now why the hell did she ride that way?" he mumbled to himself.

And then he heard a scream. A loud, panic-stricken scream that raced up his spine and took him tightly around the chest. He dug his heels into his horse's flanks and took off toward the lake. Snowy trees sped past him, along with rocks and tangles of dormant salmonberry bushes. The frigid wind tore at his face, and watered his eyes, and he prayed his horse wouldn't slip on the treacherous path.

When he finally broke into the lake's clearing, the first thing he saw was Big Red charging toward him across the snow-covered ice. Matthew looked a little harder, a little further, and saw a bright head of coppery hair sticking up from a hole about twenty yards out.

"Damn it, woman!" he swore furiously. He swung down from his horse, and grabbed his rope from his saddle. "What the *hell* did you think you were doing!"

He tied one end of the rope to his pommel, and then marched out over the ice until he was about ten feet from her. He could see that she was struggling to hold onto the edge, fighting to keep her head above water where the temperature alone would kill her in less than a few minutes.

"Get me out of here!" she cried. "Get me out of here!"

He stretched out flat, and then scooted the rest of the way on his belly.

Her lips were blue. That was the first thing he noticed when he gave one last push with his feet and came face to face with her. That and her teeth were chattering like castanets. The air pockets beneath her clothes had puffed her up like a giant blowfish. But the water had saturated her clothing, tripling her weight and preventing her from crawling out on her own.

She grabbed hold of the collar of his coat. "What t-took you s-so long?" she whispered, clenching her jaw against the cold.

He pulled off his gloves with his teeth and crammed them into his back pocket. "Maybe you should have waited for me at Three Forks like we'd obviously planned."

"L-leave it to a man t-to k-keep a g-girl waiting."

He leaned closer and reached into the water to wrap his rope around her back. His hand went numb the instant it came into contact with the icy water, but Matthew barely noticed as the side of his face brushed against hers and he caught the spicy cinnamon scent of her. Her cheek was so close to his mouth, he could have pressed his warm lips against it with barely a thought.

She was shivering loudly, and he quickly finished

his task, and pulled back from her. Her breaths were beginning to come in quick, shallow gasps, and he knew that getting her out of the water wasn't going to be his biggest problem. Warming her up before hypothermia set in was going to be the tricky part. But he couldn't think about that now.

He tied two good knots, securing the rope around her chest. "Get ready."

She held on tightly to his collar. "W-where are you g-going?" she demanded, her voice raspy and keyed high with panic.

"To pull you out.

"Y-you w-wouldn't leave a g-girl, would ya?"

It was a question tinged with sarcasm, but Matthew could see the fear in her golden eyes. She was afraid he was going to turn around and leave her there. "I'm going to pull you out," he said firmly. But she still wasn't letting him go. Knowing they had little time, he took hold of her gloved hand and pried it from his coat, placing it instead on the rope around her chest. "Hold on," he told her, and began scooting backward.

A few yards back, he climbed to his feet and hurried to his horse. "Come on, boy." He used his shoulders to crowd the animal, impelling it backward. "Come on, boy, back up."

He heard the ice crack, and looked back to see it giving way where Lacey was being dragged forward, providing a perfect ramp for her to be pulled out. He continued to crowd his horse until she was lying on a thicker span of ice. Then he strode toward her, took her by the back of her coat, and dragged her the rest of the way to the bank.

She was shivering so loudly the sound was a hum in his ears. He dropped down beside her and took hold of her chin to look into her eyes. She was dazed, unfocused, and mumbling incoherently. Her complexion had a bluish tinge to it, and she was chilled to the touch. The lake hadn't claimed her, but the cold still might. If he didn't warm her up quick, she would die from exposure.

He cut the rope from around her, and then made short work of stripping off her wet coat and gloves. The towel around her head had managed to stay above the water, and he used it to dry off her hands and feet after he'd taken off her sodden boots. Then he dressed her in his coat and gloves, quickly packed up her wet things, and then picked her up and put her in his saddle. He swung up behind her on his horse, and with his arms wrapped around her shivering body, he set out for the nearest shelter.

Geneva was the closest town, but it was still five miles to the west and uphill all the way. So, knowing of a closer, easier-to-reach place, he galloped his horse back up the road in the direction he'd come until he saw the carvings in the tree that marked the spot he was looking for. At that point he left the road, and followed a narrow, well-marked path that led straight to the mouth of a large cave.

Big Red wasn't far behind, following faithfully as Matthew rode right inside the cave and dismounted. Miss Garder collapsed into his arms, and he gently set her down on the soft, dirt ground and turned to retrieve his bedroll. Then he crouched down beside her.

"Miss Garder? Lacey, can you hear me?" Her violent shivers were echoing loudly through the cave, and he took hold of her chin and looked into her unfocused eyes. "You have to get out of these wet clothes. Do you hear me? You're going to freeze to death if you don't get them off."

"Wet c-clothes," she repeated, nodding.

She at least agreed to his assessment. Now the question was, how did he go about getting her undressed? "Can you stand?" He frowned, wondering if she could even hear him above the sound of her own shivering. And she was shaking so violently he doubted she'd be able to sit, let alone rise to her feet to get out of her clothes.

And then her eyes focused on his. "W-where are we?" she asked.

"A cave.

"A *c-cave*? C-could you start a f-fire or something? I'm r-really c-cold."

"A fire won't do you any good if you're soaked to the bone. You have to get your wet clothes off."

He reached for the coat he'd let her borrow, but she crossed her arms to prevent him from taking it. "I'll f-freeze without it!" she cried angrily.

"You'll freeze with it, goddamn it. Now, we're wasting time." He reached out and yanked his gloves off her small hands and she let out a faint sound of protest. He ignored it, and the other weak signs of resistance she offered as he forcefully uncrossed her arms and finally got his coat off her. Her shivering increased.

"Y-you're going to k-kill me," she rasped.

She was going to kill herself if she didn't give him a little cooperation. He reached for the buttons on the front of her dress, but only managed to undo four of them before she realized what he was doing and slapped his hands away. "G-get away from me!"

"Listen, lady, you can fight me till the sun turns as blue as your lips, but these clothes are coming off!"

"G-go to hell!"

They were wasting precious time, and Matthew

knew he wasn't going to get her undressed without a fight. So he pulled his long knife out of the scabbard inside his boot.

She let out a gasp when he brought it toward her throat. He ignored her look of horror and took hold of the neckline of her dress. "This is for your own good," he said. And then he sliced the garment down the center.

That's when Matthew's challenge changed from simply getting her undressed, to cutting her clothes off without slicing her skin to ribbons. Considering what she'd just been through, he was surprised that she had any fight left in her, but then he reminded himself that he wasn't exactly dealing with an ordinary woman here.

"Hold still, goddamn it!" he ordered, finally pinning her to the floor with his arm over her chest. "I'm only trying to help you!"

"Don't touch me!" she kept shouting, squirming frantically. "Don't *touch* me!"

He cut off her dress, cut off *two* pairs of bloomers, and finally cut through her union suit, only to find that she had another one on underneath. "Christ almighty, woman, how much have you got *on*?"

Her strength had waned considerably by this time, and he had no trouble at all slipping the edge of his knife between her last article of clothing and the delicate, pale skin at the base of her throat. In order to protect her skin from the double-edged knife, he made a small incision in the wet cotton material, and then took hold of the edges with his fingers.

Up until that point Matthew had been too busy fighting Lacey to really think about what he was doing. But now she was calm, close to unconsciousness he suspected, and the instant his warm fingers came into contact with her soft, silky skin, he was reminded of just exactly what he was about to do.

He was about to strip her naked.

He hesitated for the first time since finding her in the lake. She was lying beneath him, still shivering like a leaf, freezing, and half-conscious, and his mind was beginning to race with all kinds of lascivious thoughts. Sure she was aggravating as hell, infuriating to the core, but he was only human, for God's sake. He was a man, and she was a woman—and he wasn't made of stone.

So here he was, about to get a good look at what his mind had only imagined up to this point, and he was terrified by the prospect. So far he'd been able to control this strange desire he'd felt for her since the moment he'd set eyes on her. But what would happen when all her charms were spread out before him like a Sunday morning buffet? What if he just couldn't resist having a little taste?

But his fears were pointless. He sure as hell couldn't just let her freeze to death, and freeze she would if he didn't get these wet clothes off her—*all* of these wet clothes.

And then what? he finally allowed himself to wonder. His bedroll and whatever meager fire he could manage to build out of the few scraps of wood lying about the cave floor weren't going to warm her up quickly or thoroughly enough.

Matthew closed his eyes and let out a low groan. Shared body heat was the only answer. Which meant her clothes wouldn't be the only ones coming off.

He was doomed for sure.

She let out a soft moan, and he put his knife away and bent back over her. He could see the outline of her perfect body through her tight, wet union suit:

the length of her sleek legs, the curve of her hips, the lush fullness of her breasts. With slow precision, he took the cut edges of her neckline between his fingers and began tearing the sodden material away from her.

The deep, creamy valley of her cleavage was revealed to him, and he clenched his jaw at the burst of arousal that jolted him. His fingers brushed against the sides of her silky breasts, but he forced himself to continue without pushing aside the severed material and lingering over them fully bared. Her stomach was soft and flat, and he felt the tickle of the soft hair between her legs as he tore the garment all the way down to the crotch. It was all he could do to not groan as springy copper curls came into view.

He picked up his knife and cut two more slashes in the garment along the inside of each leg. Then he set to work tearing it down her smooth thighs, past the sexy curve of her knees, to her ankles.

Pausing to take a deep breath, he moved back up to her chest, and pushed aside the red material. He let out a long, slow breath of air as he stared at her full, large breasts, and her tight pink nipples.

"Don't . . . don't touch me," she whispered in her delirium.

God help him, he wanted to do a hell of a lot more than touch.

He slipped his arm beneath her shoulders, feeling every inch of her cold skin, and pulled the sleeves of her wet union suit off her. She shivered and curled against his chest, instinctively pressing her face against the warmth of his neck. He ran his hand down the length of her delicate back, and felt desire pulse through him. His lips tingled to kiss hers, his hands itched to caress her breasts, he ached to roll her over and give her the kind of body heat his own was crying out for. But he resisted, though he'd never felt such torture in his life.

He removed the rest of her union suit, and scooped her up into his arms to set her down on his bedroll. Then he moved away from her, being sure to cover her with the blankets. She curled into a tight ball and moaned at the absence of his heat. She needed his body against hers.

He began unbuttoning his shirt, swearing all the while that he would keep his hands and his lust to himself. This was not a woman to be toyed with, unconscious or not, and he owed his loyalty to Amanda, the woman he intended to marry. Some day.

He shucked his clothes and the cold air in the cave made the breath catch in his chest. It did nothing to lessen his arousal, however, and he was glad Lacey was so incoherent, otherwise the sight of him coming toward her like a ship at full mast might have started an all-out war between them. But he had no intention of making love to her. And he kept telling himself that over and over again as he joined her sleek, chilled body beneath the blankets of his bedroll.

He didn't even have to pull her toward him. The moment he lay down beside her she turned eagerly toward his heat and curved herself against him, tucking every cold appendage she had into every warm crevasse he possessed. He felt as if his entire body were being doused in ice. But his desire for her raged on.

She buried her face in his neck, wormed her cold hands beneath each of his armpits, sighed, and then fell fast asleep.

Matthew closed his eyes, trying to remain detached

even though he could feel every inch of her soft body pressing against his own. Her legs were entwined with his, her silky abdomen was rising and falling against his hardness, her breasts were burning twin holes into his chest, and her warm, sweet breath was tickling the side of his neck. He was out of his mind to subject himself to this willingly. Completely out of his mind.

He moved his hand without thinking, and discovered the satiny smooth skin of her thigh. And he didn't stop there. He couldn't stop there. He skimmed his fingers over the arch of her hip, and around to the small of her back. Then he slowly, carefully, pressed her against him, and swallowed hard at the sensation of her soft stomach cradling his erection. Before he knew it he was cupping his large hands over her delectable little bottom and grazing his lips along the top of her shoulder.

"Ah, Lacey, what you do to me," he whispered hoarsely.

He gently ground his hips against hers, and touched his tongue to the arch of her neck. She shifted, unconsciously moving her hips against his, and he sucked in a sharp breath. Her head lolled back and settled in the crook of his elbow, and he stared down into her beautiful, fragile face. He mentally traced the fine, high arch of her golden eyebrows, the straight, delicate line of her nose, and the full, lush lines of her pouting lips.

She sighed in her sleep, and he gave in to impulse. He bent forward and brushed his lips over hers. A thousand tiny sparks shot through his body at the contact, and he pulled back in surprise. His breathing had picked up, his heart was pounding, and he felt an unmistakable craving taking hold of him. This was desire, white and hot. And like a starving man getting his first taste of food, he wanted more.

He moved in for another, more lingering kiss. And that's when she suddenly opened her eyes.

12

Lacey had never been so cold in her life. Her skin felt raw, as if someone had taken a piece of sandpaper to it.

And yet . . . there was warmth, pressing close, battering at the frigid wall surrounding her, pulling her up from the darkness. And it wasn't an *intangible* warmth either, her groggy mind told her. It had substance, power, and it was draping itself over her like . . . like a strong man's arms.

She opened her eyes and looked straight into the olive-green depths of Matthew Brady's intense stare. She blinked, not sure whether she was dreaming, and when he didn't vanish she tried to grasp what his presence there beside her meant.

She slowly began to realize that the weight over her legs and pressing against her upper body wasn't just the coarse heavy blankets covering her. It was him, strong and powerful, muscular and warm. *He* was her source of heat.

Her eyes flew wide and she attempted to shove away from him by arching her body backward. He sucked in a sharp breath, and the strong arms around her tightened. "Hold still," he said through his teeth.

"On a c-cold day in hell!" she snapped, fighting a bone-jarring shiver. She tried to unwedge her legs from between his, but he clamped down his knees and wouldn't let her free. "What the *h-hell* do you th-think you're doing!"

"Trying to keep you alive," he growled.

She finally managed to free one of her legs, and dug her foot into the blanket beneath her to shove her lower body away from his. But, with a muttered curse, he took hold of her bottom and hauled her back against the strong, warm length of him.

That's when Lacey froze, her eyes widening into his. There were no barriers between his palm and her skin, and his touch seared both her body and her mind. She was stark-raving, no-bones-about-it *naked*.

Her first impulse was to scream and go for his eyes, but her hands were trapped between their two bodies. He must have read the alarm in her expression, because he shook his head at her and warned, "Don't panic."

Don't panic? She'd awakened to find herself lying next to him in a cave, with him touching every square, naked inch of her body, and he had the nerve to tell her not to panic?

"I'm just trying to warm you up," he added, as if that explained everything.

"W-Warm me up f-for *what*?" she demanded, though not sure she wanted to hear his answer.

"You fell in the lake, remember?"

"And you th-thought you'd g-get me warm by t-taking off my clothes?"

She moved her face back from his, but couldn't

quite get far enough away to suit herself. She could still see the tiny crease between his eyebrows, and the flecks of gray in his green eyes. He was suddenly no longer a distant, irritable annoyance. He was a warm, attractive, flesh and blood man—with his hand on her ass.

"This isn't any easier for me than it is for you—"

"Oh, I s-somehow doubt that—would you get your d-damn gun out of my stomach!" she snapped, shifting her hips.

His jaw clenched. *"Stop wiggling."*

"I'll s-stop wiggling when you s-stop breathing, p-pal. And if you d-don't get the h-hell up and out of here th-that'll be sooner than you think!"

He closed his eyes, his nostrils flaring. "If you don't stop squirming around you're gonna find yourself flat on your back with more problems than you care to deal with."

"Your th-threats don't scare me, M-Marshal."

"That's not a threat." He opened his eyes and she saw a heat in them that she'd never seen before. One that made her decidedly nervous. "That's a fact."

Ignoring his tone, and his warning, Lacey rounded her back and slipped her hand down to shove his intrusive gun aside. The fact that she'd encountered muscular male flesh all the way down didn't really register until she brushed against a hard, silky object that felt nothing at all like a gun—inside a holster or otherwise.

The marshal let out a violent curse, and Lacey yanked her hand back as if she'd touched a hot plate. "Oh my God," she whispered, finally realizing that she wasn't the only one naked beneath the blankets. *"Oh my God!"* she shouted, and renewed her struggles to get free.

But he only held on to her tighter. "I am not going to hurt you—*stop wiggling, goddamn it!*"

Realizing now that his earlier threat of her finding herself flat on her back had been very real, Lacey went perfectly still. She and the marshal were both breathing hard, both watching each other intently, but she suspected that his actions had little to do with panic, and everything to do with that kickstand between his muscular thighs.

Remain calm, Lacey, she told herself. Above all else, remain calm.

She took a deep breath and asked, "Where are your clothes?" in the same tone she would have used to ask where he kept the peanut butter.

"Body heat, Miss Garder. It was the only way to warm you up."

"So you're trying to tell me that this is all for my benefit?"

"Well, it certainly isn't for mine," he replied, anger and, she suspected, sexual frustration grating through his voice.

"I suppose underwear wasn't a consideration?"

"Clothing is meant to keep body heat in. Hardly a benefit when attempting to share," he added with a wry twist of his lips.

She realized she was staring at his mouth—anywhere but into his dark, penetrating eyes—and quickly refocused on his chin. "Well, I'm . . . I'm feeling much warmer now." And she wasn't just saying that. Her shivering had all but stopped, and she was beginning to feel a definite heat coiling within her stomach.

She sucked in a startled breath as he glided his hand across her lower back and sent a different kind of chill skittering through her body. "You still feel cold to me."

Now there's a compliment every girl waits a lifetime to hear, she thought ruefully. "Nothing a nice
little fire wouldn't solve," she suggested sweetly.

"Your lips are still blue. When they're not blue, I'll
see what kind of firewood I can scrape up."

"I'm sure I'll be fine now."

"We'll wait."

Lacey clenched her teeth. She was trying to be
diplomatic, but, as usual, he was determined to be
pigheaded. Despite his assurances to the contrary, she
suspected he liked where he was, and doubted he'd
be budging any time soon.

She couldn't believe she'd woken up in the arms of
a naked man and not had the slightest clue. Until,
that is, she touched his—

She closed her eyes. Her hand was still burning
from the contact. And her body was growing more
and more aware of his by the second. She could now
feel the hard planes of his chest pressing against her
breasts, the soft hair on his legs tickling her knees,
the fierceness of his desire pressing insistently into
her stomach. She'd aroused him, whether from her
movements or just her nakedness alone, and the
slightest, falsest move could land her in one hell of a
lot of trouble. He was bigger, stronger, and if he got it
into his head to have her, she wasn't going to be able
to stop him.

She stole a glance up into his eyes and found him
staring intently at her. She swallowed against the dry-
ness in her throat. "What are you thinking?" she
asked.

"That this is the strangest situation I've ever found
myself in."

"I can relate."

He shifted slightly, and her nipples grazed his muscular chest. A tiny, unexpected thrill shot through her and the crests instantly tightened into two hard pebbles. She was stunned by her body's reaction to him, and horrified to see a knowing look come up in his eyes.

"Now what are you thinking?" she dared to ask.

"That you're warming up a lot faster than I expected."

His fingers were starting to make little tantalizing circles on her back. "Are—are my lips pink yet?" she asked, and hoped he hadn't noticed the tremor in her voice.

His gaze drifted down her nose, and settled on her mouth. To her great chagrin, her stomach did a little flip-flop in response. "They're usually more like a tawny rose."

Had she heard him right? All the fights they'd had, all the arguments, all the confrontations, and he'd somewhere along the line taken the time to notice the color of her lips? "A tawny rose?"

"A tawny rose."

His gaze lingered over her mouth, making her feel very uncomfortable, and she bit her bottom lip self-consciously. His eyes narrowed on the action, and she realized that with every subtle move she made she seemed to turn him on even more. The man was definitely hard up for a woman, and here she was lying naked in his arms like a sacrificial lamb.

"Hey. We hate each other, remember?"

His eyes rose back to hers. She smiled reassuringly at him. But then he began to slide his big hand down the curve of her bottom, making her eyes grow wider and wider, until he'd hooked his fingers along the inner cleft between her thighs.

Lacey let out the breath she was holding, and

found she had to make a conscious effort not to groan. A damp, cloying heat was gathering between her thighs.

"Yeah," he said softly. "We hate each other all to pieces."

Lacey was in trouble. A definite ache of the erotic kind was slowly beginning to build within her, and if she didn't do something quickly to distract the man so effortlessly seducing her, she was going to be a willing partner in an afternoon of sexual escapades.

"So . . . how's . . . how's that little girlfriend of yours? Amanda, isn't it?"

He pulled back a little, telling her she'd hit her mark. "She's fine."

His stock answer. Was the woman ever anything other than fine? "I bet she's never fallen into a frozen lake."

"She's bright enough never to put herself into that kind of situation."

Great. She tries to make conversation, conversation intended to help them both out of this jam they'd found themselves in, and he tosses out some cutting remark. But, thinking they could both use a good, knock-down, drag-out argument, Lacey took the bait. "Are you implying that I'm stupid?"

"Are you implying that you've never been called that before?"

Now that was downright mean, and Lacey would have hit him if she'd had just a little more elbow room. She had to settle for a flinty glare. "I think I've more than proven that I can outwit you any day of the week, Marshal."

"If you had outwitted me today you'd be sleeping at the bottom of the lake."

"And what makes you think I wouldn't have been able to pull myself out alone?"

"The five hundred pounds of clothes you were wearing at the time."

She clenched her jaw, hating that he was right, hating that she had been a fool to ride off into the unknown alone. Even the angel lady had tried to warn her. But she'd been too stubborn to listen.

"How long are you planning on keeping me here like this?" she demanded.

"I already answered that question."

"Are they at least *starting* to turn pink?"

His eyes flicked down to her lips once again. "I could try speeding up the process."

"How?"

"The perfect moment. Your willingness." His gaze lifted and captured hers. "My mouth."

Lacey felt her face heat.

"In fact," he added softly, "if I really thought about it, I could probably come up with a few ideas on how to turn your whole body a nice healthy shade of pink."

She swallowed hard at the erotic image that statement conjured up in her mind, and quickly shook her head. "I'll— I'll warm up the natural way, thank you."

"There's nothing more natural than a man and a woman, Lacey, tangled beneath some blankets."

He leaned closer, and bent down to kiss her, but she quickly turned her head. "No," she said breathlessly. "I can't . . . "

He placed a hot, lingering kiss on the top of her shoulder. "Sure you can."

"But I've— I've never . . . "

He began nuzzling her ear, and she wanted to scream and sigh all in the same breath. He was exciting.

He was terrifying. She wanted his touch, but she didn't. She'd never been quite so confused.

"You've never what?"

"Never . . . never . . . "

He slid his hand down her leg and brought her knee up to rest on his bare hip. His whole body was beginning to move against hers in one giant lover's caress, and her entire being was coming alive.

But she couldn't afford to lose control.

"I've never been with a man."

She'd finally gotten the words out, and he suddenly went very, very still. Then he pulled back to search her face. "You're lying," he finally said.

The surety with which he said that made anger well up inside her. Why would she lie about being the oldest living virgin on the planet? The one woman too cold for mankind to touch? The original ice princess?

"Well, you sure the hell don't act like it," he added angrily.

"And how the hell am I supposed to act?" she demanded.

"First of all, a virgin doesn't curse."

"Well, they do now, Sparky. Hell, hell, *hell!*"

"Why would you wait until now to tell me this?" he demanded.

"I wasn't aware that I was supposed to wave a sign!" she shouted back. "What the hell business is it of yours, anyway!"

"I'd say it's definitely my business now," he stated darkly.

"Hey, I didn't invite you to crawl between these blankets with me. As a matter of fact, as far as I'm concerned you can reholster your tiny little gun, and crawl the hell back out!"

He gritted his teeth. "You know, just once I'd like

to hear one simple word of gratitude slip out from between those sweet lips of yours instead of bitterness and complaints."

"Don't hold your breath!"

"Oh, I wouldn't waste my time!"

"You'd be too busy wasting everybody else's!"

"Now there's the pot calling the kettle black!"

"At least I'm trying to help this town!"

"Yeah, help it right off the map!"

A throat cleared a few feet away. "Uhh . . . pardon me . . . Marshal?"

They both shot glances to the cave entrance. Larry Dover was standing there, looking chagrined. And he was quickly joined by Tranquility's other two deputies.

"Well," Lacey stated. "If it isn't the Brady Bunch."

"What the hell are you three doing here?" the marshal demanded.

"We, uh . . ." Larry began, but he had to pause to control a grin that seemed to have a mind of its own.

"Sure ain't no question what you two are doin'," Gene remarked, making Bill burst into laughter.

Lacey looked down at herself and suddenly remembered where she was—how she was. More importantly, she realized how all this must look to three feeble minds like Larry, Bill, and Gene. News of her and the marshal's exploits would infiltrate the town within the day, and it would definitely reach the ears of the Martins. She'd never be able to look the couple in the eye again.

With an anguished groan, she threw the blankets over her head, and prayed the earth would swallow her whole.

*　　*　　*

Matthew now knew what a true paradox was. Heaven and hell. That's what it had been lying naked with Lacey Garder. His desire for her was fierce, as plain to her as it was to him, and every lithe little movement of her luscious little body had brought him closer and closer to throwing caution to the wind and seducing her into giving him what he wanted.

And then she'd sprung her little surprise on him.

The woman was a virgin. *A goddamned virgin!* He never would have guessed it. Lacey Garder was the furthest thing from his image of chaste that a woman could get. Virgins were shy and soft-spoken, not stubborn and mouthy, the bane of a man's very existence.

And thank God he'd come to his senses; bedding a virgin was supposed to be a dangerous practice. *First in their bed, always in your head.* And that was a cage he didn't want to enter if Miss Lacey Garder was holding the key.

No, nothing permanent had happened between them. Now if he could only convince his deputies of that.

He propped himself up on his elbow and stared at their grins. Convincing these three not to jump to the wrong conclusions was going to be like convincing a monk not to pray.

"Whatcha doin', boss?" Larry asked.

"Looks like he's cornerin' bad guys, Larry," Bill replied.

"Can't wait till I'm a marshal," Gene said with a waggle of his brows.

"*Get rid of the three stooges!*" Lacey shouted from beneath the blanket.

Bill scowled at Gene. "I forgot how much we didn't like her."

"We got some news this mornin', boss," Larry said. "We knew you'd wanna hear it right away, so we followed your tracks. . . . By the looks of the hole in the ice out at Geneva Lake, we figured somebody must have fallen in."

"Miss Garder fell in. I was forced to share body heat with her to keep her warm."

"Did he say forced?" Bill remarked.

"Yeah," Gene said, still grinning. "Forced."

"Nothing happened," Matthew stated. "*Nothing.*"

"Uh-huh."

"*Nothing!*" Lacey shouted from beneath the blanket. "And if any one of you tells otherwise, I'll be wearing your testicles as earrings!"

The three deputies paled, and for once Matthew appreciated Lacey's no-nonsense way of putting things. The last thing he needed was this moment getting repeated to Amanda in full living color.

"What's the news?" he demanded.

"Huh?" Larry grunted, obviously still recovering from the image of having his balls made into jewelry.

"The news you were so hot to bring me?"

"Oh. Got a telegram from Fairhaven this mornin'. A desk clerk at the Royal checked a woman in yesterday fittin' Lorraine's description."

Fairhaven? Matthew thought, angling a sharp look at the lump beside him. "You boys wait outside while I get the lady some dry clothes."

"Sure we can't help?" Gene asked suggestively.

"Like he needs your help," Larry remarked, and shoved the other two outside ahead of him.

Matthew sat up, letting the blankets fall down his bare chest. "Don't suppose it's just a coincidence that you were headed to Fairhaven and that's where Lorraine Rawlins has been spotted."

There was a moment of silence, and then Lacy said, "Don't suppose it is."

He pulled the blankets back from her head, and she stared up at him with large golden eyes. "You're after that money for yourself, aren't you?" he demanded.

She didn't answer, she was too busy gaping at him, affronted. But if there was one thing Matthew had learned about Miss Lacey Garder in the past three days, it was that she was a consummate actress.

He cursed, tossed aside the blankets covering him, and rose to his feet. She instantly looked away and focused her eyes on the cave wall. "Are you going to answer me, or not?" he demanded as he reached for his pants and began pulling them on.

"I've already told you why I'm after it."

"Oh yes, you're trying to help me save my job. How noble of you, Miss Garder. Unfortunately I'm well aware of your background."

She gave him a startled look. "That's impossible."

"It's written all over you, lady. In your walk, your talk, your actions. You're a thief. From your forehead right down to your dainty little toes. Why should I believe for one second that you don't want that five thousand for yourself?"

"Taking money from this town would be like stealing candy from a baby," she replied tightly. "I do have some standards."

"Is that suppose to be funny?" he asked incredulously. "I call you a thief, a criminal, and you don't even flinch? What the hell kind of woman are you!"

Her chin came up defensively. It was at least nice to see that she wasn't entirely made of ice. "A resourceful one," she said simply.

"Yeah? A stupid one's more like it. I can't believe

you'd risk your neck riding off alone after that money. You must want it pretty badly."

"I do. But for the town, not myself."

"Then why the hell didn't you tell me yesterday that Lorraine was in Fairhaven?" he shouted.

"Because you wouldn't have taken me with you!" she yelled back.

"Damn right I wouldn't have."

"The money can only be recovered if we're together!"

He gave her an incredulous look, thinking whatever sanity she had was slipping for sure.

"I didn't believe it either at first. But after what happened to me today—"

"What happened to you today was born of pure stupidity, lady. Any halfwit knows not to ride out onto a frozen lake—let alone by themselves."

"Well, I didn't know that," she answered tightly. "Just as you didn't know how to get the information from the Rawlins brothers that Lorraine was in Fairhaven. Don't you see? It makes sense that we work together!"

"Well, now that I know Lorraine is in Fairhaven," he returned smoothly, "your part in all this seems pretty irrelevant, doesn't it?"

Her golden eyes flashed. "You go there without me and you'll be wasting your time! And mine!"

And hers? He narrowed his eyes, wishing he knew all the answers to what made her tick. "Just what the hell is your stake in all this?"

She looked away. "I can't tell you that."

"Fine. Then don't expect me to trust you enough to take you with me to Fairhaven."

He strode toward his horse and retrieved his extra set of clothes from the saddlebags. "Put these on," he said, tossing them at her, "and meet me outside. Me and my men'll see you back to the Martins'."

"How hard would it be to just let me trail along behind you to Fairhaven?" she demanded.

He paused in leading his horse outside and shot back, "How hard would it be for you to give me a straight answer for once?"

"My life and who I am have no bearing on the search for Lorraine Rawlins."

"Really?" He grunted. "You could have fooled me."

He turned and left, furious that she was so stubborn, and that he was so totally intrigued by the mystery surrounding her. She was poison to him, and to the life he had planned for himself. He couldn't let her get under his skin like this. It was time he cut his losses and stayed the hell away from her.

But as he walked toward his men the sun caught in the trees just right and flashed a brilliant copper light into his eyes. The memory of Lacey, naked, and all sleek and silky flashed through his mind and dropped his stomach to his knees. And he knew that the image, the feel of her naked in his arms, would be forever branded in his memory.

13

It took thirty painfully cold minutes for Lacey and her escorts to reach the Martins' house. Then, without a single word, the marshal retrieved his coat and gloves from her, and he and his deputies rode off toward Fairhaven, leaving Lacey on the porch to quietly simmer.

The only thing that kept her from chasing after them was the cold. She was still recovering from her dunk in the lake, and doubted she would be able to stay in the saddle another minute, let alone the two hours it would take to reach the bay city. So she could only stand there feeling frustrated as they rode off without her.

The front door of the house flew open and Hazel burst out onto the porch. "Oh, my dear!" she shouted. "Ya look like a drowned possum!"

Well, that was certainly something Lacey needed to hear about now. "I fell through the ice on the lake," she grumbled.

The woman's blue eyes rounded. Then she marched forward and wrapped her heavy arm around

Lacey's shoulders. "Get on to the barn, Big Red," she ordered. The horse obeyed with a faint whinny. And Hazel led Lacey across the porch and into the warm house.

Two hours later Lacey was freshly bathed, and wearing the red dress Hazel had bought for her the day before. Warm once again, she curled up in the big leather chair by the fire and sipped hot coffee while Hazel sat on the couch and darned socks. She'd not asked a single question about what had happened to Lacey, hadn't prodded, poked, or insinuated. She had simply been determined to get her guest warm, comfortable, and feeling right at home once again.

The woman was a matriarchal wonder, and Lacey figured that if she'd had someone like Hazel Martin in her life all along things might have turned out very differently for her. "Your children are very lucky," she said without thinking.

Hazel's head popped up. "What was that, Lacey, honey?"

"I said, your children are lucky to have you and George for parents."

"Oh, George and I were never blessed."

Lacey scowled. "You mean you don't have any children?"

"Not a one."

"You're kidding." Lacey had assumed the two of them had a horde of children, and that they'd all grown up and left the nest.

The woman smiled sadly. "George and I always hoped, but a little miracle never did come our way."

Lacey felt a hot flash of injustice. If any two people were meant to be parents it was George and Hazel Martin. What a shame for them. What a shame for the children they might have had. And then people like her mother were popping babies out left and right.

"It used to really bother us," Hazel said. "But George and I left all our tears behind when we left Chicago."

"Chicago?" Lacey repeated. It seemed as if she'd heard that city mentioned recently.

"Chicago, Illinois. That's where George and I are from. We came out to Washington Territory in '76, to get a taste of the good life. Fresh mountain air, wide open fields, forests with trees as thick as boulders. Men were being recruited from all over the country to come out and fell trees for the mills. We figured somebody was gonna have to feed all those big strappin' lumberjacks, so why not us? We sold our house and our restaurant, and headed out west."

"Are you telling me that you left everything behind in Illinois to start over again here, with nothing?"

"Here's a pretty wonderful place, Lacey," Hazel reminded her. "And nothin' isn't so hard. An adventurous spirit is a definite must, but it does the heart good to build somethin' from nothin'. You're a strong, adventurous woman. I'm sure you know exactly what I mean."

Adventurous, Lacey knew plenty about. But to give up a stable, successful life and everything you owned for a complete unknown? Especially out here in the middle of nowhere? Lacey couldn't even fathom that idea.

"You sure you're not hungry?" Hazel asked for probably the third time in the last ten minutes.

Lunch had come and gone, but Lacey doubted she'd be able to keep down anything but hot coffee. "I'm fine. Really."

"Well, you must be tired. How 'bout if I promise to

stop yammering your ear off, and you close your eyes and try to get some sleep?"

With a final warm smile, Hazel went back to her darning, and Lacey sighed and turned back to stare at the fire. It had been one hell of a morning, and she was incredibly tired. But every time she closed her eyes, Matthew Brady's handsome face insinuated itself back into her mind and any hopes of sleep went south for the winter. She couldn't believe he'd made a pass at her. She couldn't believe that she'd admitted to him that she had never been with a man! This whole situation between them was so bewildering.

"Now what's that scowl for?" Hazel asked. "All of a sudden ya look like you've got the whole world on your shoulders."

"It's nothing," Lacey hastily replied.

Hazel laughed and rested the sock she was darning in her lap. "Nothing doesn't cut a crease the size of the Grand Canyon down the center of your forehead, honey, so let's have all of it before that dark cloud over your head hits you with a bolt of lightning."

"The-marshal-tried-to-kiss-me," Lacey said so fast it all sounded like one word.

Hazel blinked in surprise. "He did?"

"I know, it's laughable. Don't ask me why he did it. I think this cold weather affects the brain—"

"Oh, I know *why* he did it," Hazel cut in. "I'm just amazed it didn't take him a little longer to get around to it. That Matthew's a stubborn little cuss."

Now it was Lacey's turn to blink in surprise. "Well, I could certainly stand to hear a theory or two on his odd behavior. I mean, is he desperate for a woman or what?"

"Desperate? Matthew? And what's so odd about a man being attracted to a woman?"

"We're not talking about any woman, Hazel. We're talking about me."

"Which, in my opinion, makes it even less baffling."

"Are you saying he's attracted to me, not just the idea of being with a woman—any woman?"

"The same way you're attracted to him."

Lacey frowned. "And just what makes you think I'm attracted to him?"

"Because you're interested in his attraction to you."

"Maybe I just feel that if I can understand his reasons for doing what he did, I can avoid the situation in the future."

"That sounds very sensible, Lacey. But sensible won't getcha squat in the game of love."

Without meaning to, Lacey burst out laughing. "Love has absolutely nothing to do with this, Hazel."

"Maybe not yet, anyway," the woman remarked, sobering Lacey instantly.

"Not ever," Lacey said.

Not only was she unreceptive to the emotion, she was incapable of expressing it. She admitted that Matthew Brady was handsome, intelligent, and powerfully sexy. He may have been able to thaw out her body, but nobody was capable of cracking the ice surrounding her heart.

"I knew from the first moment I saw you two together that there was something between you," Hazel stated.

"Yeah, his gun," Lacey remarked dryly.

"He insisted on you telling him all about yourself. He was interested."

"He was interrogating me, Hazel. It's a common habit among lawmen, believe me."

"Interrogating you for what? He knew the moment

he clapped eyes on you that you weren't Lorraine Rawlins. The Rawlins family is known for their black hair and green eyes. No, Matthew was too curious about you to let you get away, so he kept his gun trained on ya until you'd satisfied his curiosity."

"You think you've got this all figured out, don't you? Well, I hate to burst your bubble, but I didn't tell him a damn thing about myself, then or later."

"Good idea. A man loves a mysterious woman."

"I am not being mysterious. I just don't happen to think it's any of his business where I'm from or why I'm here."

"He saved ya from the lake," Hazel said, as if that proved everything.

"That proves he's got human qualities at least," Lacey grumbled.

"You musta been mighty cold after that. How ever did you get warmed up?"

By the way that question was asked, Lacey had a sense that Hazel already knew the answer. But Lacey replied anyway, refusing to let it seem as if what Hazel was suggesting made any sense. "Shared body heat."

To Hazel's credit she didn't break into a irreverent smile like Larry, Bill, and Gene had, although Lacey could see one dancing in her sparkling blue eyes. "Then he saved your life. Again."

"When? When other than that has he saved my life?"

"I recall you bein' ablaze at one point."

"Oh, this is ridiculous. You haven't given me one solid reason to think that Matthew Brady wanted anything more from me than a few hot kisses and a lusty roll in the dirt."

"He admires your strength."

"My what?"

"Your strength. Your get-up-and-go. That's a rare thing to find in a woman so young. You get his heart pumpin', girl. You keep his mind workin'."

"I infuriate him is what I do."

"At times. But men aren't like women. They can't really tell the difference between one emotion and the next. That heart of theirs starts pumpin', that blood of theirs starts rushin', and *bam*! they're in love."

"So now you're trying to tell me that Matthew is in love with me?"

"It's just a matter of time."

Lacey shook her head and laughed. But when Hazel casually went back to darning socks, she realized that the woman was totally serious and sank back into the leather chair in astonishment. The very idea that Matthew Brady felt anything other than contempt for her was ludicrous. She'd baited him, berated him, and battered him every chance she got. He hated her. He had to.

She closed her eyes and his face came to her instantly, every line and nuance. She heard his voice in her mind, the soft, seductive tone he'd used on her in the cave, and felt a little tingle. He was a strong, powerful man. One that challenged her every move. One that she enjoyed challenging back.

But what would happen if they began to feel something other than flirtatious competitiveness toward each other? How, then, would she protect herself from him and the vulnerability that inevitably came with caring?

The very idea sent panic racing through her, and she knew that, no matter what, she could never let any tender feelings grow between them.

His anger she could deal with. But his love was too frightening for her to even consider.

Matthew had never been so frustrated in his life. He'd spent the entire day in Fairhaven and come up with absolutely nothing. And to top it all off, he was beginning to believe that bringing Lacey Garder along might have made all the difference in the world. Lorraine was obviously on the lookout for men asking around about her, but she probably wouldn't have paid any attention at all to a woman—especially one as crafty as Lacey Garder.

He rode into his barn just before sundown, cold and worn out, a dinner party the very last thing he needed. But he'd promised the Martins that he and Amanda would join them that night for dinner. He'd also told Amanda he'd pick her up at five, and, after missing their date two nights before, he wasn't going to pull another no-show. He washed up, changed into some clean clothes, and headed for town.

It was the setting sun, glowing crimson and orange through the cloud cover, that suddenly reminded him of Lacey. A coppery glow settled over the mountainous horizon. She hadn't been far from his mind all day. Lacey Garder was nothing but trouble, a catastrophe waiting to happen. The funny thing was, that very quality was what seemed to be drawing him toward her.

Once in town, he headed toward the livery and rented a buggy for the night. Then he guided the two horses three blocks to Amanda's house. He ambled up the walk not thinking about his future wife, or Lorraine Rawlins. No, he was still thinking about Lacey Garder.

She'd felt amazing in his arms. A perfect fit. He'd wanted to make love to her more than he'd ever wanted anything else in his life. But then she'd sprung her virginity on him like a rabbit snare, and he'd been temporarily knocked off balance. Up until that point he'd felt fairly confident that he'd be able to coax her into giving herself to him. But the only time a man needed to get tangled up with a virgin was when she was lying in their marriage bed. And marrying an unpredictable woman like Lacey Garder was completely out of the question.

Ah, but in his bed she'd be a wonder. He knew it as sure as daylight. She had a body that was made for loving, a spirit that would be wild and hot once ignited with passion. And the idea of how close he had come to being inside her made him ache from head to toe.

He was thinking of that very thing as he knocked on Amanda's door. When she opened it and smiled at him, a barrelful of guilt fell down upon his shoulders, and he immediately cleared his throat—but he wasn't so successful with his mind. "Evening, Amanda. Ready to go?"

"Good evening, Matthew," she replied politely.

Amanda was always polite, and Matthew suddenly found himself wishing she'd show a little backbone every now and then. Once they were married he was going to have to see to it that she argued with him at least once a day. A man needed that kind of balance in his life to keep a level head.

He helped her on with her long wool coat. She buttoned it, and they both stepped out onto the porch into the twilight as he closed the door behind them. "Nice evening," he said distractedly.

She frowned up at the dark, threatening sky. "Yes. Nice."

He looked up himself, only just remembering that the sky was so full of clouds not a single star shone through. Then he frowned at Amanda. Forget his lapse, why the hell had she agreed with him? He toyed with acting out Shakespeare and telling her the moon was the sun, just to see what she'd do. But, frankly, he was afraid of the possible outcome. He couldn't imagine her contradicting him.

He led her to the buggy, helped her up to the leather seat, and covered her legs with the warm lap quilt. Then he climbed up and settled in beside her for the fifteen minute ride to the Martins'.

"Did you have an interesting day, Matthew?"

This was asked a few minutes later over the crunch of the horses' hooves through the snow, and the jingle of bells on their harnesses. Matthew kept his eyes on the dark road that the lanterns on the sides of the buggy barely illuminated, and did his best not to react too strongly to the unintentionally loaded question.

Despite his warnings to his deputies, he knew that, by morning, what had happened between himself and Lacey in the cave would be all over town. He figured his best bet was to tell Amanda about it now and defuse the situation while he was still in control of it.

"I had to rescue a woman from Geneva Lake."

Amanda gave him a startled look. "Good heavens. Who?"

"Lacey Garder."

"The Martins' houseguest?"

Matthew nodded. "She went riding and fell through the ice."

"She went riding out on the lake?"

"The woman's a little nutty."

"Well, is she all right?"

"She, uh, she was pretty shaken up and shivering

pretty badly from the cold. I took her to the Indian cave. It was closer than Geneva City."

"That was very smart thinking."

Matthew rolled his eyes. At the moment her compliments were the last thing his guilty conscience needed. "I managed to warm her up before she froze to death."

"There was enough dry wood around the cave for a fire?"

The moment of truth. He couldn't lie to her—that's not to say he wouldn't have tried if the chances of her hearing the whole story the next day weren't so great. "There wasn't time for a fire. We shared body heat."

Amanda was silent for a moment, and Matthew used the time to think up a number of explanations that would hopefully stop her from ending their relationship right then and there.

"It seems that I am constantly being reminded of what a generous person you are, Matthew," she finally said.

Matthew quickly mulled over her words, and the tone in which she'd said them. For the life of him, he couldn't detect anything but sincerity in her voice. So he glanced over, and found her smiling at him.

"Miss Garder was very lucky that you came along," she added.

Matthew stared at her, feeling nothing short of baffled. He'd lain naked with another woman and she didn't seem to give a damn. He hated to admit it, but that stung his pride just a bit. "You do know what sharing body heat entails, don't you?"

She touched his arm. "I understand the sacrifice, Matthew. It must have been very difficult for you and the young lady."

Hell, difficult hadn't even figured into it. Taking the

naked Miss Lacey Garder into his arms had been one of the easiest things Matthew had ever done. The difficult part had been tamping down his flaming desire for the woman. And here Amanda was commending him for his nobility. His conscience couldn't stand it.

"It's not what you think—"

"She's all right, isn't she?" Amanda asked, frowning with concern.

God, he hoped so. To be honest, Matthew hadn't really considered whether or not she might still be in some sort of danger. Colds, flu, pneumonia, none of them were uncommon after experiencing what Lacey had that morning. And he'd just dumped her on the Martins' doorstep without even pausing to see that she made it inside all right. He suddenly felt a little sick himself, and gave the horses a light slap with the reins to get them moving faster.

"Is something wrong?"

"The wind's picking up," he lied. "We should hurry along."

Amanda frowned, and looked around them into the darkening night. She was obviously noticing that there wasn't the slightest breath of a wind. But once again she didn't contradict him.

Lacey Garder would have called him on his lie— even that small harmless one—and then she would have demanded that he tell her what was really bothering him. She would have badgered and provoked him until he'd given in and blurted out the whole truth, that he'd enjoyed lying naked with another woman.

And then she would have given him a lambasting like nothing he'd ever heard before. She would demand nothing less than his total faithfulness and complete respect.

Amanda. Lacey. Two different women with two different characters. One offered everything she had on a silver platter, no questions asked, and the other made you work for every tiny scrap of herself she was forced to give you. The problem was, Matthew had always loved a good challenge, appreciated hard work, and felt his best when he was rising to an occasion. So it stood to reason that he would be attracted to Lacey, and that Amanda would leave him cold.

This just wasn't going to work at all. And, from his point of view, there seemed to be only one answer. He needed to incite Amanda into standing up for herself.

"How was your Saturday?" he asked, settling back into the leather seat.

"I spent the day reading. There's a lovely new book out by Ibsen—"

"Christ, Amanda. You read too much. I'm surprised your eyes aren't crossed."

Silence answered him.

Finally he glanced over to find her looking wounded. "I enjoy reading," she offered softly.

"Don't you get enough of it teaching school?"

Her mouth opened and closed. She seemed to be at a total loss, and Matthew realized that the tactic he was employing was getting him nowhere. He was only hurting her feelings, which made her pull further away from him.

He turned away from her in frustration, and settled his eyes back on the road. It was obvious that he couldn't change her. And why would he want to, for God's sake? She was a sweet, unassuming woman. She'd be the perfect wife and the perfect mother to his children. No, the problem wasn't Amanda, it was Lacey Garder. Things had been just fine until she'd sashayed into town and turned his world upside down and sideways.

Damn it, he wouldn't think about her anymore. He'd attend this dinner and completely ignore her. He'd give his undivided attention to Amanda, and, in the morning, when he wasn't so damned tired, he'd be thinking a lot more clearly.

At least he hoped he would be. He had only five days left to find that money. And it seemed he'd been left with only one final option: to ask Miss Garder to accompany him and his deputies to Fairhaven.

And then, once the town had its money back and his job was once again secure, she would leave. She would take her tawny eyes, her flashing smiles, and her unending challenges, and she would go back to wherever it was she'd come from. And then he could get back to building his quiet, respectable life.

14

Lacey woke to the sound of voices in the entryway. She wasn't sure how long she'd slept, but it was now dark outside, and she had a kink in her neck from her awkward position in the chair.

She recognized the timbre of Matthew Brady's deep, smooth voice immediately, and quickly smoothed her hair. She folded down the top edge of the blanket in her lap, and then straightened the front of her red dress as the voices drew nearer. And with her eyes glued on the fire to her right, she pretended as if she hadn't heard anyone arrive.

"Lacey, honey? You awake?"

Lacey turned at the sound of Hazel's voice, being sure to keep a completely casual expression on her face. But when her eyes settled on the young woman standing next to Matthew Brady, it was impossible to keep her astonishment hidden. Amanda Simmons was beautiful. She was tall and graceful, blond-haired, blue-eyed, and with the perfect features and rosy complexion of a European model.

Matthew Brady was dating Barbie!

"Amanda Simmons," Hazel said, "meet Lacey Garder. Lacey's been stayin' with us since the storm."

Lacey remained perfectly still as sky-blue eyes met hers. She hadn't had any dealings with possessive women before, and figured she'd let the girlfriend make the first move.

And then a warm smile slowly began to form on a set of lips so perfectly pink they were nearly impossible. "It's a pleasure to finally meet you, Lacey. I've heard so much about you from Hazel and Nettie."

But apparently not from her main squeeze here, who, after that morning, had the most to impart about her, hands down.

The teacher came forward with her hand outstretched, and Lacey found herself rising from her chair to accept the gesture. Amanda Simmons's hands were just as perfect as the rest of her. She towered over Lacey by at least five inches, making Lacey feel very small and insignificant—and very stupid that she'd entertained for one second the notion that Matthew Brady might be attracted to her. Not when he had *this* waiting for him.

"I understand you're helping Matthew recover the money for the town," the woman continued. "That's very selfless of you. Not many women have the courage to spend an hour alone with the Rawlins brothers. In a cell or otherwise."

Lacey found herself searching desperately for just a tiny ounce of spite in the schoolteacher's tone, just a smidgen of female rancor that would justify a full frontal attack on her part. But there wasn't a trace. Amanda Simmons was obviously just as perfect on the inside as she was on the outside.

So Lacey turned her anger and frustration on the man at Amanda's side.

"So, Marshal. How does Lorraine Rawlins like her new home?"

He'd seemed a little on the guarded side since walking into the room, and Lacey had a feeling she knew why. "What new home is that?" he asked.

"Her cell. In your jail. Was she happy to be reunited with her brothers? I hope they weren't too hard on her for being captured. But then who could possibly elude such a competent lawman as yourself?"

A muscle at the back of his jaw twitched, and Lacey had her answer. His trip to Fairhaven had been a total bust. She hoped he and his bungling men hadn't scared Lorraine Rawlins away for good.

"Unfortunately Matthew and his men were unsuccessful," Amanda Simmons said. "But they'll prevail eventually."

And now Lacey could add supportive to the woman's long list of pedigree qualities.

"I'll fetch the coffee," Hazel said. "Oh, Amanda, honey, could you come along and bring the cups?"

"Certainly, Hazel. You know, I've been meaning to compliment you on your restaurant's apple pie . . . "

Amanda's soft voice trailed off as she followed Hazel from the room, and Lacey's gaze snapped instantly to the man left alone with her. "I told you to take me with you, didn't I."

"Don't start."

"If you'd taken me with you, you'd have that damn money back and I'd be free to—" She caught herself just in time, and let her sentence hang ambiguously in the air.

"Free to what?" he demanded. "Just once I'd love to get a straight answer from you on that."

Lacey circled the chair and stood beside the

hearth. "She's very pretty." Very perfect, she added to herself.

"Who? Amanda?"

"Well, I'm certainly not talking about that shirt you're wearing. Who dresses you? Howdy Doody?"

He looked down at his blue plaid shirt, and then back up at her again. "I take it Mr. Doody doesn't adhere to your particular taste in clothing."

"How did you ever talk her into going out with you?"

"Amanda happens to have manners, and would never cancel a date with a man simply because of the shirt he's wearing."

"I'm not talking about just tonight. I mean the whole relationship thing. She seems just a tad immaculate for you, don't you think?"

He came forward and leaned his arm on the back of the leather chair. "What man wouldn't want a respectable woman?"

That remark hurt more than it should have, especially since she was supposed to be indifferent toward him. But it had struck hard and true—straight in her heart.

"Realistic men for starters," she snapped back. "Men with enough brains to know that the perfect woman doesn't exist, and that the truth will show its ugly head eventually. Usually after the woman's got them tied to a hefty mortgage and two cars."

"Two what?"

"Never mind. You just go ahead and marry her. The two of you deserve each other." She couldn't believe how worked up she was getting over this. What did she care who the man married? What did it matter to her if Amanda Simmons was Snow White or the evil queen?

"Here we are," Hazel announced, coming back into the room.

Amanda Simmons was following along behind her, carrying a tray of coffee mugs and gliding across the floor as if floating on a cloud. She smiled warmly at Lacey as she set the tray on the coffee table, and try as she might Lacey couldn't bring herself to hate the woman. To the best of her knowledge perfect didn't exist, but Amanda Simmons was pretty damn close. Lacey paled in comparison.

They all sat and drank coffee, Lacey in the chair, and Hazel, Matthew, and Amanda Simmons on the couch. Lacey listened rather than taking part in the conversation, and with each passing moment her self-confidence wavered just a little more. Every time the woman touched Matthew, his arm, his hand, his shoulder, Lacey's throat tightened a bit, until she doubted she'd be able to swallow any of the roast Hazel was cooking for dinner. She considered pleading a headache and heading to her room for the night, but the idea of leaving the two of them alone for a single moment grated raw on her nerves.

She had to be out of her mind. What other reason could there be for her to feel this way? She felt panicked and dizzy, clammy, almost numb. But her mind was racing so fast she could barely keep up with the conversation going on across from her. And she had the distinct urge to jump to her feet and scream at the top of her lungs.

"Lacey? . . . Lacey, honey, are you all right?"

Lacey's attention snapped back into focus, and she realized that Hazel was talking to her.

"Amanda was wonderin' where you're from," Hazel continued.

Lacey glanced at the marshal, at his intense olive-green eyes. She knew he expected her to refuse to answer the question, to embarrass herself in front of his little date, but she wasn't about to give him the satisfaction.

"California," she replied, and the marshal's expression instantly hardened.

"Really," Amanda said breathlessly. "Matthew is from California."

"Really?" Lacey remarked, giving him a tight smile. "I'm sure he'll read plenty into that little coincidence."

"He's from San Francisco," Hazel supplied.

Lacey nodded and sipped her coffee. "Nice town."

"Then you've been there?" Matthew demanded more than asked.

"A time or two."

"A time or two in the past few years?" he persisted.

"I suppose so."

"Then that explains it," he stated.

"Explains what?" Amanda asked.

"Where I've met her before."

"You two have met before?" Hazel asked, looking astonished.

Lacey shrugged. "Don't look at me." He was obviously still trying to find an answer to the sense of recognition he felt toward her. The same one she felt toward him.

"It didn't involve a gun and a pair of handcuffs, did it?" he inquired.

"Matthew," Amanda said, laughing softly at what she apparently thought was a joke.

But Lacey knew he wasn't kidding. He was thinking he knew her because she'd been arrested in San Francisco. And if she hadn't been living in the twentieth century at the time, his theory might have had merit.

"A lot of the women you know get arrested, do they?" she commented.

"You probably met her at one of those flashy galas they're always holding in the big cities," Amanda said. "I can see it now, the two of you dressed in all your finery, dancing to a waltz in the middle of a marble floor."

Matthew nodded slowly over the rim of his coffee cup, but Lacey could tell by the look in his eyes that he didn't believe that theory for a moment.

And then George came home, and everyone moved into the entryway to greet him.

Lacey was very conscious of the fact that Matthew had his hand in the small of Amanda Simmons's back as the two of them stood chatting with George, and she forced herself to step up next to Hazel to block her own view.

They all moved into the kitchen where Hazel had the table set with a blue linen tablecloth and crystal stemware. Dinner was served, and the table settled into a series of quiet, amicable discussions. Amicable, that is, until Lacey got sick of watching Matthew fawn all over his girlfriend. She was sitting directly across from them, and felt she was doing reasonably well—until Matthew began to gaze at the woman like a love-sick puppy. That's when what little patience Lacey had with the situation snapped completely.

"Just exactly how did you two meet?" she asked, in a less than congenial tone. The entire table quieted and looked her way. "I mean," she added, laughing a little, "you're not exactly a matched set."

Matthew narrowed his eyes on her as Amanda

dabbed her perfect petite mouth with her napkin. "This is a small town," Amanda answered, smiling.

"So you settled for what you could get."

Amanda went downright pale, and Matthew's stare hardened. "That's not what she meant," he broke in. "In a town this small, it's impossible not to eventually meet everyone."

"Ohh," Lacey said, nodding. "But I can imagine the choice you must have had, Amanda. Him, or one of those god-awful lumberjacks. Personally, I would have chosen—"

"I don't think we care to hear what your choice would have been, Miss Garder," he stated.

"Matthew, don't be rude," Amanda whispered to him.

"Oh, but he is rude. And that's my point. The two of you go together about as well as a white dress and a mud hole—you, Matthew, being the mud hole, of course," she added with a sweet smile.

Hazel cleared her throat. "Lacey, honey—"

"Hazel was telling me just the other day how sweet and gentle you are, Amanda. And, from my point of view, *he's* about as pleasant as a sharp poke in the eye."

"That's enough," the marshal stated.

But Lacey wasn't finished. She was so full of bitterness that she felt she might explode if she didn't get it all out. "There has to be some other single man in town who's better suited to your disposition. Hey, how about Reggie? He's seems rather . . . immaculate," she said, giving Matthew a pointed look.

Matthew slammed his hands down on the table, making the dinnerware jump, and causing Amanda to let out a little squeak as he surged up from the table. *"That's enough!"* he shouted.

Mindless of the other people at the table, Lacey

held his volatile stare and rose up from her own chair. "What happened in the cave?" she demanded, though her throat tightened around every word. "Tell me what the hell you wanted from me."

"I was trying to save your life!" he bellowed.

"Don't make me spell it out, Marshal, because you know I will!"

His eyes narrowed and his nostrils flared. "The moment," he replied darkly. "I wanted . . . the moment."

Then it had been just as she'd suspected. He'd wanted nothing more than a quick tumble in the dirt with her. Without even thinking she picked up her roll and threw it at his face. "You *pig*!" she shouted. "You filthy, stinking—I wouldn't give you a *moment* if you demanded it with your dying breath!"

"You'd be the last thing on my mind during my dying breath!"

"Unless I was the one killing you—which isn't too far from reality right now!"

"I wouldn't put it past you to stick a knife between a man's shoulder blades!"

"I'd go straight for the heart, baby," she seethed. *"Straight for the heart."*

Hazel rose from her chair. "That is enough out of *both* of you," she stated angrily. "I've never seen such a horrible display around a dinner table. Just look at Amanda. She's about to fall out of her chair, for heaven's sake."

Amanda Simmons was about as pale as a white-haired rabbit, and looked twice as likely to bolt at any moment. "Matthew," she said softly, "I'm suddenly not feeling very well. I'd . . . I'd like to be taken home."

The marshal threw an accusing glare at Lacey, and she lifted her chin, refusing to accept his blame—she was already applying enough of it to herself. She'd stepped over the line. She'd obviously upset Amanda. Hell, she felt like she'd just drop-kicked a puppy.

Matthew helped Amanda up from her chair. He thanked the Martins and then apologized for his behavior. Then he and his Barbie doll headed for the door.

Lacey stood frozen at the table as the Martins showed the couple out. Her whole body felt hot and tingly, and she wanted to run, far and fast, but she was rooted to the plank floor beneath her feet.

And then George and Hazel came back into the room.

Lacey took one look at the disappointment on their faces and burst into tears.

The conversation on the ride back to Amanda's house was stilted to say the least. Amanda was quiet and withdrawn, leaving Matthew to wonder about her state of mind. Was she angry at Lacey? Or was she angry at him?

Finally he couldn't take the silence any longer. As they pulled up to her house, he set the reins over his knee and turned to her. "I'd appreciate it if you'd talk to me, Amanda."

She glanced over at him, but only for a moment. "I'm sorry, Matthew. I guess I'm a bit . . . over-whelmed by what I just witnessed."

"Yes, well, Lacey Garder tends to have that effect on people."

"I've never seen you quite so angry."

Matthew let out a heavy sigh. "The woman's a menace. She provokes me every chance she gets. And then she doesn't stop until the blade is driven home."

"But I've never known you to be so easily provoked."

"She knows exactly where my sore spots are and how to work them to her advantage. I'm sorry I lost my temper."

"Do you do that often with Miss Garder?"

"Unfortunately."

"There . . . There certainly seems to be a lot of emotion between the two of you."

"And none of it good, believe me."

"Maybe you're not looking hard enough."

He gave her a startled glance. "I beg your pardon?"

"I said maybe you're not looking hard enough, Matthew. For how you really feel, I mean. I've read that there's very little emotional difference between love and hate."

"What are you saying?" he asked incredulously.

"Matthew, I believe there's a spark between you and Miss Garder."

"A spark of what?"

"That's what you need to find out. By ignoring it, you could be letting something precious slip through your fingers."

Matthew couldn't believe what he was hearing. Was she actually telling him to pursue another woman? He took her hands in his. "I thought what we had was precious."

She smiled gently at him. "What we have is convenience. Just as Lacey said."

Just as Lacey said? She'd actually listened to the ramblings of that woman? "Lacey is a lunatic," he stated. "And I refuse to let her ruin what we have."

"And what do we have? Besides companionship, I mean? You were there as well as I for that kiss we shared last night. What I felt were the emotions of a warm gesture between friends. Can you honestly say you felt anything more?"

He couldn't. And that's what was eating him up so much inside. But maybe, with just a little more effort, he and Amanda could find the spark between them. "We just need more time."

"No. We're both wasting time, time we should be spending in finding our true loves. I don't love you, Matthew. Not like that."

Her words should have cut him to the quick. But they didn't. Because he didn't love her either. In his rush to find himself a respectable woman for his new respectable life, he hadn't even thought about love.

"Please don't be angry with me," she said, squeezing his hand.

"I'm not angry with you. I'm gonna strangle *her*," he added fiercely.

Amanda laughed softly. "Someday I hope to affect a man as passionately as she's affected you."

He shook his head, laughing ruefully. "You have no idea what you're saying."

"Oh, Matthew," she said, a warmth of sympathy in her eyes. "These past few days have been so hard on you."

"They've certainly been interesting."

"Take a lesson from something I read to the children yesterday. Don't fight the current of the river. It'll only tire you out and drown you eventually."

Great. Now all he had to do was figure out which way the current was headed.

"From what I understand, Lacey won't be in town long. Take advantage of the time you have together to look deeper into your feelings. Otherwise you may regret it for the rest of your life."

"Then you're sending me on my way?" He laughed. "I've got to admit, I've never had a woman do this to me before."

"Then maybe it was about time?" she said, smiling warmly. "Will you see me into the house?"

He climbed down and helped her up the snow-covered walk to her front door, where she turned and gave him a kiss on the cheek. "We'll still be friends, won't we?" she asked.

"That's always been the best part of our relationship."

"Then I'll see you at church tomorrow?"

"Without me sitting beside you you're sure to have Reginald as a hymn partner."

She smiled. "I'll survive. And so will you. Good night, Matthew."

She turned and went into her house. Leaving him to stare at her front door and wonder what the hell had just happened. Lacey, that's what had just happened. Lacey Garder and her scheming, interfering, high-handed ways.

He cursed beneath his breath and headed back to the buggy. He drove it back to the livery, and retrieved his horse. Then he started to ride—anywhere but back to his house. The house that represented his father's dreams and his dreams for a stable, respectable life. He felt like the world had just been yanked out from under him. And Lacey Garder had hold of it with both hands.

She'd ruined everything. And Amanda wanted him to explore his feelings for her? Well, it didn't take a genius to know he was infuriated by her, undone by her, unnerved by her. Even when he'd been in the company of the woman he thought he'd marry, she'd insinuated herself into his thoughts. Her and her damned sexy body.

The memory of their time together that morning returned to him in full force. He closed his eyes and let the sensations fill him, hoping to twist them, to turn them into something ugly that he could despise. But the memory of her silky skin gliding against his body invariably made him go hot and hard. He could still feel the sensation of her curves filling his hands, and smell the spicy scent that clung to her. He imagined the sensation of his fingers sliding down her thigh and lifting it just enough to probe her hot, damp secrets.

The spiraling sensation in the pit of his belly made him gasp, and his horse stopped and sidestepped beneath him. He looked up and found himself in the Martins' front yard. And sitting not ten feet away, bundled up in blankets on the porch swing, was the object of his anger and his desire.

It was time to stop fighting the current and plunge head first into the water.

"What do you want?" she demanded.

For once, he knew the answer to that question. Without saying a word, he swung down from his horse and strode up the porch steps.

"Don't you touch me," she warned, her voice rising a notch.

He reached for her and pulled her from the swing, letting her blankets fall. She let out a startled gasp, her eyes flying wide with alarm, and he took her tightly around the waist before she could strike out at him.

He stared down into her tawny eyes, feeling the softness of her body against his, and remembered the heady sensation of her bare skin in his hands. His attention lowered and fastened on her full lips.

"What do you want?" she demanded again, breathlessly.

"You. I want you."

He pressed her back against the outside wall of the house, and covered her mouth with his.

15

After breaking down like a five-year-old in front of Hazel and George, Lacey had been consoled—as if she'd deserved consoling—and told to go sit out on the front porch swing and take in some fresh air.

As if a thousand nights of fresh mountain air could make her forget what a fool she'd just made of herself over a man she didn't even like.

She'd taken the Martins' advice, though, grabbed a quilt, and headed for the porch swing.

She'd spent the past twenty minutes trying to understand her actions and trying to reach her spiritual guide. Maybe there was some way she could earn a second chance. But she'd had no luck, in the form of insight or angels, and she'd found herself struggling with tears again when she'd suddenly looked up and found Matthew Brady riding into the yard.

George had lit the lanterns on the porch for her before turning in for the night, and they'd illuminated the marshal's intense expression as he climbed the porch steps and headed toward her. She'd allowed him to yank her up from the porch swing, believing that she deserved his anger for what she'd done, but the last thing on earth she'd expected was for him to kiss her.

Lacey didn't know what to do with her hands—or her lips, for that matter. She was a little too stunned at first to react. She was being held prisoner between the wall and the pressure of his hard body. He had one arm wrapped tightly around her waist, and one hand tangled securely in her hair, obviously intending to keep her in place until he was good and ready to let her go. And, for the moment, Lacey was perfectly happy to remain right where she was.

The man was doing the most amazing things to her senses. Every slide of his lips, every tug with his teeth, every tantalizing brush of his tongue against her mouth, made a whole new set of nerve endings fire in her body.

He groaned deep in his throat as she started to respond to him. "Open your mouth," he whispered against her lips. He cupped her jaw in his hand and nipped her lower lip. "Let me all the way in, Lacey."

Yes, let him all the way in, something within her whispered. *Past the pain, and the sorrow, the bitterness and the hurt. Let him melt the ice surrounding your heart.*

But that ice was there for a reason, as a protective barrier against misery and loneliness, and Lacey had a strong instinct to guard it with every ounce of her will.

But then Matthew was kissing her again, pleading with insistent stabs of his tongue for her to part her lips and give him deeper access to her mouth. And with every ounce of potent male power at his disposal he was urging her to let go, to give in to him.

Suddenly it wasn't hard at all for her to let her inhibitions slip away. She simply slid her hands up his chest, curved her fingers around his neck, and opened her mouth beneath his.

He let out a groan, moved closer, and a jolt of sexual electricity shot through her like a bolt of lightning as her breasts were smashed against his chest. She felt herself being lifted, glided sensually upward along the length of his hard body as he straightened with her in his arms. Then he moved backward, and she found herself straddling his hips as he sat down on the porch swing.

She held onto his corded neck and kissed him back as he slipped his hands up her bare legs and shoved her skirt high enough to allow her to fit her thighs over his. She took a chance and touched his tongue with hers, and he pulled in a sharp breath and yanked her closer.

"Give me more of that," he insisted against her mouth. She complied, sliding her tongue into his mouth as he'd been doing to her, and their kissing took on a whole new urgency.

He eased his hands up under her skirt to her hips, and she felt his fingers tug on the narrow piece of elastic that made up the waistband of her French-cut underwear. "What's this?" he asked, his voice hoarse with desire.

"Panties," she replied breathlessly.

"Panties," he repeated, as if memorizing the word. He broke the elastic on both sides with one strong tug and then moved his hands down to cup the curves of her bare bottom.

His lips left her mouth for the line of her jaw. She bit her lip and felt her stomach leap as he licked her ear and sent her senses reeling.

When he began to work loose the top few buttons
on the front of her dress, she was too far gone to care.

"This is insane," she finally whispered as he kissed
the base of her throat.

"Completely crazed," he agreed. His kisses continued to travel lower, pushing aside the red cotton
material as each tiny button was freed.

She gasped as his fingers, inadvertently or otherwise, brushed against her sensitive nipples, and then
tipped back her head and laughed deeply when he
cupped her breasts through her dress and placed a
lingering, hot kiss in the cleavage he'd unveiled.

"It's nice to know you're enjoying this as much as I
am," he said in a sexy rough voice.

"It wouldn't be polite of me to make you wallow in
pleasure all by yourself."

Now he was undoing her buttons with his teeth,
and she suddenly had an almost insatiable craving to
feel his hot, wet mouth on her nipples, tasting them
as hungrily as he'd done her mouth.

"Get on with it, Brady," she demanded restlessly.
She arched toward him. "It isn't nice to keep a lady
waiting."

He suddenly pulled back from her, and she stared
into his eyes. The raw passion she saw there made her
swallow hard, and question just exactly what she was
getting herself into. "One moment," he whispered.

It took Lacey exactly one moment to realize what he
was saying. And for the briefest, tiniest second the realization stung. But then she understood the logic behind
it. A moment was all they would need. They were two
obviously incompatible people with lives to get on
with, and one brief encounter between them should be
all it would take to squelch once and for all this irrational desire that kept flaring up between them.

"One moment," she agreed.

One side of his mouth turned up in a roguish smile, and he yanked her toward him. She actually felt a flash of fear for a moment, until he eased his mouth back over hers and once again proceeded to take her breath away. The next thing she knew he was slipping his hand up her bare thigh, heading for that dampest and hottest of places, and she was mentally kissing her virginity good-bye.

"I think it's about time you were headed home now, Matthew."

Lacey instantly pulled back from Matthew's hungry lips, and looked over her shoulder. George Martin, bless his understanding soul, hadn't come outside. He was talking through the screen, standing at an angle where he couldn't see the sensual scene being played out on his porch.

Lacey turned back to the man in front of her— around her, beneath her—and their eyes met. And in the span of just a few seconds it was communicated that this would not be the end between them. They had business to finish, and neither would rest until it was done.

His gaze seemed to linger on her mouth, and for a moment Lacey thought he might begin kissing her again, throw George's statement laced with warning to the wind. But then he stood, slowly, letting her slide down the length of his hard body until she was back on her feet.

"See ya inside, Lacey," George said. And she heard the wooden door close tight.

Matthew was buttoning up the front of her dress, but he was lingering over the task. "You'll be having dinner at my place tomorrow night," he told her, finally finishing with her dress.

She wasn't about to argue. The sooner and the quicker this fire was put out between them, the better off they'd both be. "I'll bring dessert."

He gave her a dark, steady look. "You'll be dessert."

And with that, he crossed the porch, climbed up onto his horse, and rode off into the night.

It wasn't until after Lacey had gone inside and assured George that she was perfectly all right, affirmed that Matthew Brady had not been taking advantage of her, that she was finally able to escape into her bedroom to calm her rioting nerves. And that's when she realized that her panties were missing.

"Sir, we have a serious problem."

"What is it now, Nelson?"

"The woman has lost her panties."

"I beg your pardon?"

Stella laughed and clapped her hands. "He's stolen her underwear, sir. Isn't it wonderful!"

"In the vast bank of human rhetoric," Nelson commented dryly, "*wonderful* is not exactly the word that leaps to mind."

"Do you think it wise to be leaping into something so shallow?" Stella remarked.

Maximillian cleared his throat noisily as Nelson angled Stella a disgruntled glower. Finally Nelson jutted his square, dimpled chin in the air and continued. "Amanda Simmons's guide is in a complete state of pandemonium."

Stella sighed and gave Maximillian an impatient look. "Amanda Simmons was never meant to live her life with Matthew Brady. Her guide was well aware of that fact."

"But your client has reduced her to a puddle. A withering mass of self-recrimination. The poor woman is a mess, to say the least."

"Which you never seem to do," Stella grumbled.

Maximillian was scowling, and Stella was beginning to lose patience with both of them. She was certainly doing the best she could—and her client happened to be coming along very nicely.

"Stella? Do you care to explain this situation?"

"They've finally discovered each other—"

"They've discovered each other's physical attractiveness," Nelson cut in. "A basic human proclivity. Nothing more."

"She's allowed him to reach her like no one else—"

"I'd say she's allowed him to do a whole lot more than that," Nelson remarked.

Stella gritted her teeth and turned to the disputer. "If you interrupt me one more time I'm going to give you another dimple right between your eyes."

Nelson sobered. "You see there, sir? The dreadful woman is even rubbing off on your best guide. I insist that you remove her from the nineteenth century immediately and toss her back in prison where she belongs."

"And what would that solve?" Stella demanded. "Mr. Brady would lose his job, Miss Simmons would still be a withering mess, and I'd still think you were a pompous windbag."

Nelson's eyes bugged. He opened his mouth to speak, but this time Stella held up her hand and stopped him. "Not another word until I have said my piece," she stated. "Sir, Miss Garder's soul has been enriched by leaps and bounds in the past few days.

She has discovered compassion, faithfulness, loyalty, and, I'm suspecting, love. She's on the very verge of fulfilling her mission, and becoming all that she was meant to be. It would be a great injustice for you to remove her simply because she's hurt somebody's feelings."

"She will not be removed," Maximillian answered, making Nelson cut loose with an impatient sigh. "However, what has been done by your client, must be undone."

"It can't be undone, sir," Nelson spoke up. "Miss Simmons is feeling unlovable. Her history with men has been hapless to say the least, and now, because of Miss Garder's tirade, the poor woman has decided that she isn't worthy of any man."

"That woman needs to grow some backbone," Stella remarked.

"That woman would have been just fine had your client not come bulldozing in and driven her into the ground," Nelson stated. "She's blaming herself for Miss Garder's upset."

"Then perhaps if Miss Garder apologized," Maximillian replied. "If she accepted responsibility for her anger, and released Miss Simmons from fault."

Nelson broke into laughter, and Stella pursed her lips in irritation. "Sir," Nelson said, "Miss Garder wouldn't know an apology if it climbed up her leg and bit her on the—"

"Your point is made," Maximillian interrupted darkly. "Stella. What have you to say about this?"

"I think an apology can be arranged."

"Oh no," Nelson interjected. "Not arranged. Sir, remorse is a fact of life, something everyone must learn in order to face accountability and grow spiritually. If Miss Garder is to apologize, she must do so because she feels compelled to, not because her guardian has instructed her to do so. Miss Garder must apologize of her own free will." He broke into a tight, smug smile. "From the depths of her own sweet heart."

Stella glowered at the man as Maximillian leaned back in his chair and considered Nelson's words. "Stella, you've said yourself that Miss Garder has grown a great deal since her arrival in the nineteenth century. Eventually everyone's morality is put to the test. This seems to be the perfect opportunity to evaluate Miss Garder's."

"She will succeed, sir," Stella stated confidently. More confidently than she felt.

"I hope so, Stella," Maximillian warned. "I would hate to see this woman become a blot upon your record that would force me to reevaluate your promotion."

"I understand," Stella confirmed. And she crossed her fingers and hoped with all the stars in the heavens that Lacey Garder would not let her down.

16

She'd never set foot in a church in her life.

Lacey kept a watchful eye on the thick-beamed ceiling as she followed George and Hazel inside the one-room building. It was fairly evident, by the world map and the chalkboard hanging on the wall behind the pulpit, that it doubled as a schoolhouse.

The place was packed with lumberjacks.

Hazel quickly explained that the saloon and brothel were closed on Sundays, giving the local men no other social activity except church. Thankfully the men sat at the back of the room, slumped low in their seats like children who'd been forced to attend against their will. But they perked right up when Lacey walked by. They whistled and called her name, waggling their fingers if they happened to catch her eye. Lacey did her best to ignore them.

"Lacey!" Nettie O'Rourke hurried toward them from the center aisle, her blue eyes sparkling like diamonds. "Thank the stars yer all right. I heard what happened to ya yesterday." She frowned with concern. "How're ya feelin'?"

Lacey gave the woman a painful smile, hoping she wasn't in for another hug. She liked Nettie, she really did, but the young woman was definitely a personal-space violator. "I'm still a little numb here and there, but otherwise—"

And then Nettie took her firmly by the shoulders. "I want ya to know . . . that I don't believe a word of it."

"A word of what?" Lacey asked, stepping back from Nettie's firm grip.

"What're you jabberin' on about now, Nettie?" Hazel put in.

Nettie glanced around to be sure no one else was listening. "Rumor has it," she whispered in her soft Irish lilt, "that Lacey and Marshal Matt did the hokey pa-dokey in a cave yesterday."

Hazel scowled. "The hokey pa-*what*?"

"The hokey pa-dokey," Nettie whispered insistently. "The wild and woolie. The two of them communicated in the *conjugal* sense."

Lacey closed her eyes as a thick hot feeling of embarrassment surged through her. She was going to skin those deputies alive.

Hazel gasped, and threw her arm around Lacey's shoulders, yanking her to her side in a mother-hen gesture. "This girl was at death's door yesterday mornin'," she said loudly. "And Matthew risked life and limb to pull her out of that lake. If I hear a single word said to slander either one of 'em, I'll be servin' prune pie to the whole town come mornin'."

"And they'll be tastin' the unfriendly end of my shotgun," George added.

Lacey smiled gratefully at them both. She appreciated their support. Even if she didn't deserve it.

"Go get 'em, Martins," Nettie said exuberantly.

"Now, Lacey, yer sure yer all right? An ice dip like that's bound ta take a while ta recover from."

"I'm fine, Nettie. Really."

"Tell ya what. I'll bring over some of my sainted grandpappy's tonic this afternoon. That'll settle yer nerves."

"And make your hair fall out," Hazel mumbled.

Nettie gave Hazel an affronted look. "I beg yer pardon. My grandpappy used only the finest of ingredients in his tonic."

"Like snake venom and bull spit?" George put in.

"It'll make her hair fall out," Hazel repeated.

"Not to mention what it does to your bowels," George grumbled.

George had apparently been a victim of Nettie's sainted grandpappy's tonic once before.

"I heard that stuff was outlawed in four states," Hazel said.

"This isn't a state," Nettie quickly pointed out.

"She's got a point there," George agreed.

"Besides the one on the top of her head," Hazel retorted. "You can't feed that unholy mixture to our Lacey. The last thing she needs is to be knocked on her—"

George cleared his throat.

Hazel paused and glanced around at where she was. "Onto her back," she finished.

"Well, maybe she *should* stay shut in until these rumors are put to rest."

"What rumors?"

They all turned to find Matthew standing behind them. And if Lacey had been hoping that she'd purged him from her system the night before during their wild make-out session, then she was sadly mistaken. Her heart gave a little skip at the sight of him.

He was dressed in blue jeans and a white shirt, and had a black string tie tied around his collar. She'd never seen him look so handsome, or so intense. She would have smiled, said hello, but her mouth had gone dryer than a bag full of sand.

"The ones flyin' around about you and Lacey," Nettie returned.

"Outlandish rumors," Hazel added.

George cleared his throat. "While you hens are fillin' in the rooster, I'm gonna go hunt us up some seats before we wind up standing in the back with the sawdust gang."

"Rumors about us, huh?" Matthew said again.

He gave Lacey a vaguely inquiring look, and she nodded minutely. His jaw clenched, and he did a quick glance around the room, probably in search of his three deputies. But *she* had first crack at them when they were found.

"Seems word has gotten out about yer brave rescue of the fair damsel, here," Nettie explained, "and speculation has begun to arise as to what went on between the two of ya in that cave."

Matthew crossed his arms over his chest, looking fit to kill. And then his features suddenly relaxed. "Miss Garder, have you been starting rumors up about us again?"

She blinked, not sure how to respond. "I . . . Well, I guess I was bored," she went along, frowning at him.

"I hope dinner tonight will rectify that."

Lacey felt a hot blush tinge her ears. Only *she* knew the true meaning behind his words. He planned to make love to her that night. And the very idea had the power to just about send her out of her skin.

"You are still coming, aren't you?" he asked intently. As if she could refuse.

"Of course."

Nettie was staring oddly at the two of them. "You're havin' supper together?"

"And what is wrong with that?" Hazel demanded. "Two adult folks eatin' the same meal at the same table?"

"We've got some things to discuss," Lacey explained, knowing those rumors were beginning to seem more like fact to Nettie than fiction. "About . . . about . . . "

"Miss Garder is going to be riding with me and my men to Fairhaven tomorrow to help catch Lorraine Rawlins."

Now it was Lacey's turn to looked surprised. "I am? I—I mean, I *am*."

"Well, isn't that nice of you," Hazel commented.

"Yes," Nettie agreed. "Very nice of you."

Neither one of them believed a word. Nettie was alternating glances back and forth between Lacey and the marshal with a different light of understanding in her eyes. And Hazel was beginning to smile. "I'll bake a pie for her to bring for dessert," Hazel said.

"She won't need it." The marshal broke into a crooked smile, and Lacey wanted to reach over and punch him in the stomach. She was too embarrassed to look at anything but the floor.

"You can't have dinner without a good dessert," Hazel protested.

The marshal smiled. "Dessert'll be on me."

Lacey let out a gasp without even knowing it, and all three of them looked her way. "I . . . I can't wait," she said with a hesitant smile.

"And how does *she* feel about it?" Nettie asked, looking past their shoulders.

Lacey turned to see Amanda Simmons standing in

a burst of golden sunlight in the doorway. She looked like an angel standing there in her prim and proper coat and hat, and Lacey gritted her teeth as Matthew immediately turned and walked toward her. Lacey wanted to rip every perfect little hair out of Amanda Simmons's perfect little head.

Organ music started up, sending a hushed quiet through the small building, and Nettie hurried toward the front pew.

"Come along, Lacey, honey." Hazel led the way to where George had sat down. "You know, you'll have to talk with him about that."

"Talk with who about what?" Lacey asked tersely.

"Talk with Matthew about walkin' away from you to go talk with other women."

"He can do whatever he likes."

Hazel gave her a quizzical glance as they sat down on the pew. "That philosophy'll get ya exactly nowhere. Right, George?"

"What's that?"

"Letting a man do whatever he wants."

"Oh. That's right, Lacey," George concurred. "Ya gotta keep a tight rein on 'em." He leaned back and gave her a wink behind his wife's back.

Lacey smiled at him. These two people had come to mean so much to her. She absolutely had to keep them from finding out what she and Matthew intended to do that evening after dinner. Two decent people like this would never understand her need to purge someone from her system.

She took off her coat, folded it into her lap, and settled in on the pew, still a basket of nerves. And then Matthew Brady settled in right beside her.

Lacey refused to look at him as he draped his own jacket over the empty spot on the pew next to him.

She focused instead on the tall, handsome man who stepped up to the pulpit to begin his sermon. "Good mornin', ladies and gentlemen," the reverend said in his Irish lilt.

"Good morning, Reverend O'Rourke," the crowd replied in unison.

"Let us bow our heads for a moment in prayer."

Lacey followed suit and bowed her head, but instead of closing her eyes, she angled them toward Matthew Brady. His jeans were pulled taut over his thighs, showing off his thick muscles. She wondered what his legs would look like bare. Were they as sculpted as his upper body?

He shifted slightly, and Lacey slammed her eyes shut. Then she got a light elbow in the ribs, and she elbowed him back, harder. "The prayer's over," the marshal whispered to her.

She lifted her head to see that everyone had straightened and was now listening to the reverend with their eyes open. She had to stop letting Matthew affect her like this.

"Amanda sends her regards," he whispered.

How nice, Lacey thought spitefully. She stuck her chin in the air and pretended to focus intently on what Reverend O'Rourke was saying.

". . . I'm reminded of the story of Job . . . "

"You really should apologize to her for last night."

Not in a million years, Lacy thought rancorously.

"You've never been to one of these before, have you? . . . You're not supposed to pay attention. . . . You're supposed to fall asleep."

"Would you be quiet?" she whispered forcefully, causing Hazel to glance her way for a moment.

"The attire for this evening is casual," he went on softly. "Just a coat'll be fine."

Lacey tried to move closer to Hazel so that he'd be unable to continue whispering to her, but her skirt was caught beneath him. "You're sitting on my dress," she whispered, keeping her eyes on the pulpit. The last thing she needed was for the reverend to catch her talking and ask her to share her conversation with the class.

"Sorry," he said. And then he scooted closer, further onto her skirt, until their knees were touching. "Don't wear stockings," he leaned sideways to say. "Hate the things with a passion."

She would not respond. She would not respond.

"And none of these, either."

She glanced down at what he was holding, and just about choked when she saw her tattered silk panties lying in his open palm. She tried to snatch them away, but he was too quick and closed his fist back over them.

"Put them away," she hissed.

Hazel glanced over at her again, and Lacey gave her a hesitant smile. But as soon as Hazel had returned her attention to the reverend, Lacey reached over and gave the marshal a good pinch on the leg.

"Ow," he whispered, chuckling softly. "Save it for later, sweetheart."

Oh, she had plenty saved for later. First she was going to smack his smug face for embarrassing her in front of Hazel and Nettie with that dessert remark. Then she was going to give him a good kick for what he was putting her through now. And then she planned to kiss him until she was either completely satisfied or blissfully unconscious.

The sermon lasted for what seemed like a lifetime. And Matthew didn't keep his mouth shut for more than a minute at a time. He continued to whisper suggestive things to her, and nudge her with his knee when he thought she wasn't paying attention. But she was paying attention, she was taking in every word. And by the time the reverend had stepped down from his pulpit she knew well and good what lust was: she had a fire burning inside her to rival hell itself.

She couldn't wait to get outside in the chilly morning air, and didn't wait for either of the Martins or Matthew Brady to follow when the service ended. Bright sunlight hit her face, and she squinted into the glare and buttoned the front of her coat against the cold.

And then she heard a soft, gentle voice call out her name. Lacey turned, saw Amanda Simmons on the church steps, and seriously considered walking on as if she hadn't heard the woman. But, considering what she planned to do with the woman's man later that night, she couldn't quite bring herself to do that. She stood nervously as Amanda Simmons approached with her hands tucked inside a rabbit-fur muff.

"Thank you for stopping," the woman said.

"Why wouldn't I?" Lacey replied.

Amanda smiled. "Because I get the distinct impression that you don't like me very much."

That's putting it mildly, Lacey thought dryly. "You wanted to speak to me about something?" Could it be that little miss perfect had heard the hokey pa-dokey rumors and was vaguely shocked? Well, Lacey would gladly set her straight about the truth of her boyfriend's faithfulness.

"I wanted to wish you the very best with Matthew."

Lacey blinked. The very best? With *Matthew*? "Excuse me?"

"He and I had a long talk after he took me home last night and I think I may have finally made him see the light about you."

"About me?"

"About the two of you."

Lacey was only getting more and more baffled and confused. "About the two of us?"

Amanda frowned, puckering the perfect angle of her golden eyebrows. "He told me before the service that he saw you again last night. Didn't he talk with you about any of this?"

He'd hardly had the opportunity to say a word. "It didn't come up, no."

"Well, that blasted man—he probably didn't even tell you that he and I have decided to end our . . . understanding and remain friends."

All kinds of things went racing through Lacey's head at that moment. The fact that Matthew was available. The fact that he was no longer dating Miss Perfect. The fact that he was free to do anything and pursue anyone at his leisure. And the fact that his next pursue-*ee* was her. What the hell had she done!

"Look, I didn't mean to come between you and Matthew. I was tired and moody last night. I took all of my frustrations out on you." She laughed. "I don't know what I was thinking."

"That he intrigues you and excites you? That he makes your heart pound and your palms sweaty. And that you didn't want me anywhere near him?"

Lacey sighed in defeat. Why did it seem that lately everybody could read her emotions like an open book?

"Lacey, Matthew and I have never really been anything more than friends. As you said last night, we were just a convenience for each other. He was looking for companionship in this lonely old town, and I was looking for an excuse to remove Reginald Sterling from my life."

"You and Reginald Sterling?" Lacey could hardly suppress a shudder.

"According to some, we're an *immaculately* matched pair."

Embarrassed, Lacey laughed and shook her head. "Ranting and raving, that's me."

"I have a sister just like you."

"She must drive you crazy."

Amanda smiled again. "She's my best friend."

And in that moment Lacey took a good long look at Amanda Simmons. Since meeting her the night before, she'd given the woman plenty of reasons to despise her. Any lesser person would have held a grudge for the things Lacey had said at dinner. But Amanda still hadn't uttered one single unkind word.

Suddenly Lacey felt ashamed. "Amanda," she said, "I'm sorry." She was surprised how easily those two foreign words slipped off her tongue. She supposed sincerity was the key. And she did mean them. She'd acted terribly toward this kind woman the night before. She only hoped a simple apology would be enough.

Amanda smiled. "I'm so glad we had this talk."

Considering how light she suddenly felt, so was Lacey.

Matthew edged his way out of the church, past a cluster of chattering people, and paused on the church steps. Lacey and Amanda were standing in the churchyard, talking and laughing like two old friends.

It was too strange not to be suspicious. And so he marched over to them, hoping to heaven he wasn't the topic at hand.

He had his answer when he stepped up to them and all the talking and laughing stopped. "Dare I ask what you two are giggling about?"

Lacey smiled at him, and the dazzling effect nearly stopped his heart. The sooner they got that night over with the better. "I don't know, Amanda, dare he?"

"We were discussing your stubbornness, Matthew. And whether or not a good board across the back of the head would do you any good."

"I say it would just break the board," Lacey added.

"While I feel that a chance not taken is an opportunity missed."

Matthew crossed his arms and took in their mischievous grins. "Well, it's nice to see the two of you have found some common ground," he said dryly.

"Ah, here you are, Brady."

Matthew scowled at the familiar voice, and turned to find Reginald Sterling standing behind him in all his Sunday finery. Matthew looked the man over from black buckled shoe to blue satin trousers, from yellow silk vest to white ruffled shirt, and thought he might puke. "Sterling," he greeted.

"I understand your little venture into Fairhaven yesterday produced less than satisfying results. Too bad. You're running out of time."

"Too bad that little outfit you're wearing went out of style before you were born," Lacey remarked.

Reginald Sterling gave her a bland look. "I see your little . . . friend is full of spit and vinegar today."

Lacey took a threatening step forward. "That's right, Mr. Tight—"

Matthew held out his arm and stopped her. The

last thing her blossoming reputation needed was a scene in the churchyard. "One more day is all we're going to need," he assured him.

"We?" the man sniffed. "Don't tell me you've permanently enlisted the help of this woman? I suppose none of us has to ask just exactly what she had to do to change your mind."

"Why, you little weasel of a man," Lacey hissed between gritted teeth, holding onto Matthew's impeding arm. "I'd slap you for that if I could find your cheek beyond that giant nose in the center of your face."

Reginald Sterling rolled his beady eyes, and looked away from her, obviously satisfied that Matthew would hold her back. But it was Matthew he was going to need saving from if the scrawny little bastard didn't watch his step. "I suggest you keep that woman on a sturdy leash, Brady," Reginald remarked. "In my opinion, she is a menace."

"That's funny, Sterling," Matthew shot back. "That's exactly what I was just thinking about you."

"Is a musketeer the only imitation in your wardrobe's repertoire?" Lacey shouted. "Or can we expect Little Lord Fauntelroy next Sunday!"

Matthew smiled. "Now *that* was funny."

Reginald Sterling looked past the two of them and settled his tiny dark eyes on Amanda. "And how do you feel about all this . . . this *shamefulness*?"

"You mean your shamefulness, Reginald?" she replied. "Frankly, I'm appalled."

Reginald paled. "But I haven't . . . he has obviously turned you against me," he blustered. Then recovering his composure, he sneered, "Tell me, Amanda. Will it be a marriage of his convenience? You as his wife, and this trollop as his bed partner?"

"You're dead, mister!" Lacey shouted, finally shoving past Matthew.

But Matthew beat her to the punch—literally. He brought back his fist, and knocked Reginald Sterling back on his proper English ass. The man went sprawling back into the snow.

Matthew shook the pain out of his hand and glanced at Lacey. She was smiling at him. "I couldn't have put that any better myself," she said.

He smiled and offered both women his arms. "Ladies."

Ignoring the crowd that had gathered around, he led the two women toward the row of wagons. Lacey went to speak with the Martins and he watched the enticing sway of her skirt as she walked away.

"The two of you are definitely a matched set," Amanda said to him as he helped her up into the seat of her two-wheeled gig. "I certainly hope that's sinking into your head, Matthew. She's wonderful."

He gave her an impatient look. "The last thing I need is my old flame playing matchmaker for me."

"At least invite her to dinner. Give the two of you some time alone together."

"She's coming over tonight."

"That's wonderful!"

In more ways than Amanda could possibly understand. "Are you making her supper?" she asked carefully.

"I was planning on it, yeah."

"Matthew, be certain to watch the biscuits. You have to take them out when they begin to brown, otherwise you'll have a mess like you did when I—"

"I can handle it," he interrupted.

"Oh, Miss Simmons?" Reverend Conal O'Rourke stepped up to them. "I'm sorry ta interrupt," he said, "but I was, uh, hoping to speak with you about the . . . the . . ." He laughed boyishly. "Goodness, I've completely forgotten what I was gonna speak with ya about."

Matthew gave the reverend an odd look. He'd never known Conal O'Rourke to be at a loss for words.

"That's quite all right, Reverend," Amanda replied meekly. Matthew glanced over at her and was surprised to see a faint blush staining her cheeks. "With such a soul-stirring sermon fresh off your lips—I mean, fresh from your heart, it's not surprising that you're feeling a little absentminded."

"You're very generous," he said, staring at her as if she were the most glorious creature on earth.

"Well, you're very deserving of generosity."

Matthew stared at them in amazement. All these weeks and he'd never noticed. Or he'd been too stubbornly blind to see. Amanda and Conal O'Rourke were in love.

He said good-bye and walked away without either one of them really noticing. He was still so dumbfounded by them, however, that he didn't watch where he was going and bumped right into Lacey.

"What's got you looking so baffled?"

He finally tore his eyes away from the blushing pair, and turned his full attention to the entrancing woman at his side. Not a hard thing to do considering how beautiful she looked that morning. She'd dressed her hair. It was a mass of fiery copper curls pulled back in a waterfall of color down her slim neck. It had taken all his willpower in that church not to lean close and give her ear a nuzzle.

He couldn't get her passionate kisses from the night before out of his mind. He'd slept damn little the night before, especially with her panties tucked beneath his pillow. And he'd found himself in a blind rush to get out the door this morning, afraid he'd arrive too late to sit beside her on a pew.

Lust for the woman was driving him out of his skull. He didn't know what he would have done if he'd arrived and found she'd changed her mind about being with him that night. He needed to be with her, to hold her naked body in his arms again. To feel her tender kisses, her gentle sighs, the sweet rhythm of her body moving with his when they joined at last. As crazy as it seemed, having her was the only way he could think to regain his sanity.

"Matthew?"

He started out of his thoughts, and refocused on her beautiful face. She'd called him Matthew.

"I think Amanda and the reverend have an eye for each other."

Her stare widened, and she looked past him to the couple in question. "Really? . . . He *is* pretty good looking. . . . Yeah." She nodded. "I could see them getting together." Then she looked back at him. "Does the idea bother you?"

He moved closer. "The only thing bothering me right now is you," he answered intently. "Don't be late tonight."

She looked down and fiddled with the cuff on her coat. "Look," she finally said. "Amanda told me that the two of you broke up. And well, I'm sorry if I caused that." She grunted and shook her head. "Imagine that, two apologies in the same morning. Anyway, I just want you to be assured that I'm not interested in some long-term thing, here."

Though that was exactly what Matthew didn't want, the fact that she didn't want it either bothered him just a bit. "One night," he assured her. "One night to get this thing between us over and done with."

The relief that visibly came over her ate at his pride, but he didn't let it show. If she could do this thing without any concerns, any nervousness, or any fears, then he could damn well do the same.

17

Lacey was a bundle of nerves and fear.

She'd spent the day with George and Hazel, and they'd done their best to keep her busy. She'd learned how to crochet, to darn socks, and to build a decent fire in the hearth. But her mind hadn't been on the tasks.

She'd crocheted what looked like a twisted, tangled sort of snake, she'd stabbed herself seven or eight times with the darning needle, and she'd burned her fingers by not blowing out her match soon enough. By the time dusk rolled around, she was wishing she'd scheduled her "appointment" with Matthew for lunch, and just gotten it the hell over with. And maybe then the rather scary notion of birth control would have never occurred to her. But she wasn't about to back out now. No, she'd just have to put her faith in the rhythm method.

Hazel was now fluttering around her like a . . . well, like a mother. "And don't tuck your hair behind your ears," she counseled as Lacey stood on the front porch and waited for George to bring around Big Red. "It makes you look thirteen. Oh, and be sure to eat everything on your plate, Lacey, honey. Men tend to be a tad sensitive about their cookin'."

As if Lacey was going to be able to choke down a single morsel knowing that she was on the menu. "I'll try to remember that," she said.

Hazel beamed and clapped her hands together. "Oh, I am so happy for you and Matthew. I knew somethin' would come of that spark between you two. And now, here ya are, havin' dinner with him— oh, you best watch his hands, Lacey, honey. Matthew's a gentleman, but even the best of men can get carried away if you let 'em."

Lacey smiled painfully. "I'll keep an eye on them." As they're taking off all my clothes, she added tremulously to herself.

George came crunching up through the snow that had fallen gently the previous night, adding to what remained from the storm four days before. Had it really only been four days since she'd arrived? She'd experienced so much, learned so much, it seemed like a lifetime ago.

George patted the animal on the neck and then handed the reins to Lacey. "Try to stay clear of the lake this time," he said teasingly.

"Oh, and Lacey, don't pull away if he tries to kiss ya," Hazel called as Lacey swung into Big Red's saddle.

"Clobber him instead," George added, earning himself a roll of his wife's eyes.

"Well, clobberin' him isn't gonna get the girl anywhere," Hazel replied impatiently. "And one little peck good night certainly isn't gonna hurt anybody."

"I'll see you all later tonight," Lacey said, turning Big Red toward the road.

"Be sure to button that coat up tight," Hazel called. "The last thing we need around here is you catchin' your death of cold."

Lacey smiled and urged Big Red out of the yard. It felt good to have somebody looking out for her for once, and she was smiling as she headed down the road toward town.

Matthew Brady's house was just a mile or so outside of Tranquility, situated at the end of a long drive that was lined with towering Douglas Firs. It was a simple, box-style one-story house, with a rambling front porch and a dormer window looking out from the attic above.

Although it wasn't quite dark yet, two lit lanterns had been hung from the eaves of the porch. Two bright beacons leading her into the spider's lair.

She felt a moment of hesitation as she stared at the daunting front door. You're stepping in way over your head, Lacey girl, she said to herself. But all she planned to do was perform one tiny physical act, nothing millions of people hadn't done before her. She had a mind of her own. She had two fully operating legs. When she was finished, she would stand up and leave and never look back. It was as simple as that.

She dismounted and wrapped Big Red's reins around the porch rail. She climbed the two porch steps and was about to knock when, like a scene out of an old Hitchcock movie, the front door swung open hauntingly.

Taking a deep, calming breath, she stepped inside. She glanced to her right just in time to see Matthew turn into the kitchen and disappear. Frowning in confusion, she looked to her left and saw a modestly decorated living room with a warm fire burning in the hearth. There were candles spread out randomly about the room, creating a warm, vibrant atmosphere, and she was both surprised and touched by the romantic gesture. She took off her coat.

The front door slammed shut, and she let out a startled cry and turned to find Matthew standing behind her, shirtless, and with a plate of food in his hand. "Sorry about the candles. I ran out of kerosene." He took her coat and hung it on a wooden peg by the door. "Here's your dinner."

Her gaze drifted down over the impressive span of his bare chest, down the length of his snug jeans, to his bare feet. He'd apparently begun undressing without her.

"Your dinner," he persisted, as if he were on a tight schedule.

She took the warm plate from his hand, and stared at the food, trying to figure out what it was. It looked like biscuits and gravy. But the thin biscuits were burnt around the edges, and the gravy was lumpy and slightly congealed. Even if she'd had an appetite, which, thank God, she didn't, the food would have been a little too frightening to consume.

"Eat," he coaxed.

She noticed he didn't have a plate for himself. "Where's yours?"

He took her by the arm and led her to the wood frame couch where he determinedly sat her down. "I already ate."

She blinked. "I beg your pardon?"

"I thought I'd get it out of the way."

Get it out of the way? she thought, growing irritated. He glanced impatiently at her plate. "I'd really like to move things along here."

"What am I, a ride at Disneyland?" She tossed the

plate of food onto the couch beside her. "Where I come from, Mr. Don Juan, when two people plan a dinner date they generally eat together."

"We'll be doing plenty of other things together just as soon as you're done eating," he replied curtly.

"Well, if that isn't the most romantic thing I've ever heard. And how am I supposed to choke this fine cuisine down with you towering over me, frothing at the mouth to get my clothes off?"

His jaw clenched. "Romance has nothing to do with tonight. I expected that you'd be just as anxious as I am to get this thing over and done with."

"Oh, you're just turning me into a quivering puddle here, Mr. Brady. Quick say some more. I think I felt my big toe tingle."

He took her by the arm and pulled her up and into his embrace. "If you don't want to eat"—his gaze latched onto her lips—"then we'll move on to dessert."

In that moment Lacey longed for the good old days, when she panicked at his slightest touch and struck out in blind vengeance. Now she was forced to withstand her own body's uncontrollable response to his, and that made it hard to keep her mind focused on being angry.

"I'm really not very hungry," she stated.

"Really?" he said, pulling her closer. "I'm ravenous."

His full, soft lips covered hers in a passionate kiss that quickly took the fight right out of her. It sparked her desire for him, fanning it to a white-hot flame, and she soon forgot about dinner, forgot about his irritating behavior, and sank into his embrace as if it were all she'd ever needed in her life. Their tongues met and mated, thrusted and parried, until she was clinging weakly to his shoulders and longing for so much more.

Finally he broke their mindless embrace, and started raining hot, lingering kisses down her neck. "Where?" he demanded.

"Where?" she whispered back in confusion.

"The couch, the floor, the bed? Where?"

She had to choose? As a person who had never done anything like this before in her life, she wasn't exactly sure how to respond. To the best of her knowledge the bed was the standard site, but the thought of lying snuggled up with him in his own warm covers seemed just a little too intimate.

"The floor," she finally replied, breathless after just a few moments in his arms.

He started lowering her to the rug beneath them.

"I—I mean the couch."

He began backing her up to the sofa.

"Wait—"

"Damn it, Lacey." He stood back from her and pushed his hand through his hair. Then he took a deep breath. "Just relax, okay?" She wondered if he was talking to her or himself. "How about the bed? That would probably be the most comfortable for you."

Lacey shook her head adamantly. "No. Not the bed."

"What's wrong with the bed?"

"Nothing's *wrong* with the bed, it's just . . . it's just *your* bed."

He thought a moment. "You're right. Too personal." He looked down at the rug they were standing on. "Well, the floor's bound to make you sore." He looked over at the sofa. "And the couch is too small."

Lacey couldn't believe she was standing there

quietly as he methodically looked around the room for a place to steal her virginity. No, not steal. She was giving it to him to get rid of it once and for all. No more ice princess. No more vestal virgin.

"I'll be right back," he said. He left the room for the kitchen, and came back a moment later carrying a wooden ladder-back chair with a thick seat cushion. Lacey had no idea what he planned to do with it. Until he sat down, patted his thighs, and told her to climb on board.

"Are you completely insane?" she asked him.

"Do you want to do this thing or not?"

"Well, yes, but not"—she gestured at what he was sitting on— "not like that."

"The bed's too personal, the couch is too small, and the floor's too hard."

"But this way is juuuust right," she mumbled to herself. Somewhere along the line she'd stepped into a twisted version of *Goldilocks and the Three Bears*.

He held out his hand to her, but she was focusing on his muscular thighs straining against the material of his jeans. That was where she was supposed to sit. And that bulging mass in between, the one growing larger by the second . . . well, that was what she was supposed to sit *on*.

"I can't do this," she blurted out.

He held out his hand more insistently. "Yes, you can, Lacey. It's what we both want. Don't let the moment scare you away. Come on. Come here."

Still she hesitated. The idea of climbing up on him as if he were a horse for her to ride was just too damned embarrassing. Her pride just wouldn't let her take a single step in his direction.

"Do I need to come and get you?" he asked in a low voice.

His threat actually sent a little tingle up her spine. Him coming after her would certainly solve the problem of her walking the few feet between them and then straddling his thighs like a lap dancer. And she figured that once he started kissing her again, her embarrassment at being the one "on top" would dissipate in the wake of the desire he brought out in her. But now she had another problem. How did she swallow her pride long enough to answer yes to his question?

Deciding to chance another tactic, she crossed her arms and arched an eyebrow at him. "Are you threatening me, Marshal?"

His answering smile was crooked. Damned sexy. "Would you like me to?"

Another question she wished she could answer but couldn't quite get past her throat.

"Come on, Lacey. We've come too far to back down now. Take your clothes off and sashay on over here."

"Now wait a minute. I am not taking off my clothes. *Waaay* too personal, Sparky."

"You want me to do it again?"

Her face heated. He was right, he had stripped her naked once before. He'd not only touched every square naked inch of her, he'd *seen* every square naked inch of her.

"I'd like to keep this dress," she said with a voice gone suddenly hoarse.

"Fine." He patted his thighs. "We're wasting time."

"You've got some place you need to be?"

"A quick ride to heaven's what I had in mind."

"Well, it isn't going to be starting from that chair."

He braced his hands on his knees and stared impatiently at her. "Why do you have to make everything so goddamned difficult?"

"Because I'm a woman," she retorted.

His lips curved into another crooked grin. "Yes, ma'am." He rose from the chair and padded across the rug toward her. "Yes, ma'am, you are."

He slipped his hand behind her back and kissed her again, long and deep, until she was mindless, dizzy. Then he slid down the front of her, pressing his face into the valley between her breasts, until he could take hold of the hem of her skirt with his hands. When he straightened, gliding smoothly back up her body again, he brought the hem up with him, past her knees, her thighs, and slipped his warm hand beneath her dress.

As he continued to kiss her neck, his warm, questing fingers glided up the curve of her hip and then downward. He cupped the curves of her bare bottom and let out a groan that made her go hot all over: she wasn't wearing any underwear—and not in order to be enticing either. He'd stolen her one and only pair the night before.

She was quickly becoming lost in his sexy voice, his seductive touch. He took her bottom with both hands and slowly lifted her up his body, past the hard bulge hidden by his jeans. "Wrap your legs around me," he commanded.

His mouth had brushed against hers as he'd spoken, and she eagerly stole another kiss from his strong, full lips. He kissed her back, tangling his tongue with hers, and then wrapped her legs around his hips himself.

She held onto his neck as he pulled back from the kiss. "Now what?" she asked breathlessly.

"Now we get this party started."

He held her to him as he backed up to the chair and sat down with her straddling his thighs. She was completely open to him. Vulnerable to his first powerful thrust. And fear and uncertainty found a tiny place in her heart. "You . . . you believe me, don't you? That I haven't done this kind of thing before?"

"I believe you, Lacey," he said, biting gently at her neck.

The answer to that embarrassing question brought Lacey a great deal of relief. So she asked him another. "Will it . . . Will it hurt?"

He hesitated with his answer. "It might," he finally said. "But we'll take it slow."

"No!" She looked into his impassioned eyes and slowly, because they were suddenly shaking so badly, wrapped her legs around the chair. "We'll take it fast," she whispered tremulously. She had to get this over with before she completely chickened out.

He looked at her mouth, her heart skipped a beat, and then he slowly leaned forward and ran his tongue over the length of her bottom lip. The sensation sent a damp warmth between her thighs.

He began kissing her again, and before she knew it she was locking her heels around the back legs of the ladder-back chair. And then he started unbuttoning the front of her dress.

"No clothes off," she reminded him in between his kisses.

"Just a little game of peek-a-boo," he answered, his voice as rough as sandpaper.

She allowed him to unbutton the garment down to her belly, and then slide one edge over until it caught on the hardened tip of her breast. He glided his thumb up the rounded curve of her cleavage, and then eased it beneath the edge of the parted material. Lacey's thighs tightened when the rough pad skidded across her sensitive nipple. She groaned, arched her back, and leaned into him. Then she felt the heat of his mouth where his thumb had been.

"Oh, God," she whispered.

Her dress was pushed down over her shoulders, and both of her breasts were exposed. She didn't care. Anything that would make it easier for him to continue to do to her the things he was doing.

With his arm behind her back he brought her toward him, and suckled her until she was aching deep inside.

"I need to be in you," he whispered urgently. "Right now—no more waiting." He popped open the buttons on the front of his jeans, and his erection, hard, and silky, sprang up between them.

"Tell me what to do," she said as he took hold of her hips and lifted her above his lap.

"Hold on."

He brought her down over him with one strong pull, and the full length of him plunged up inside her, embedding deep and thick. She cried out, not so much from pain but surprise, and he went still beneath her, breathing hard. "Are you all right?" he asked once they'd both regained their senses.

Lacey took a moment to mentally examine her body, more importantly where hers was joined to his. Beside the fact that she was now aching with a sweet, deep longing, she seemed just fine.

But was that it? Was that one strong thrust all there was to the great mysteries between a man and a woman? When another heartbeat passed without him doing anything more, Lacey began to have her suspicions.

"Is that all?" she asked, not able to keep the disappointment from her voice.

"Christ, I hope not," was all he said. He nuzzled

her neck. "Is that all you want?" he added, flickering her bare nipples with his fingers.

She gasped as hot sparks of sensation shot through her breasts. "No. No, I want more."

He began to move within her, and Lacey was filled with the sensation of every nerve ending in her body firing at the same time. She took hold of the back rungs of the chair and began swiveling her hips. It took them a few minutes, but soon she and Matthew were rocking and arching to an erotic rhythm that had them both mindless.

He held onto her hips, tipped his head back over the top rung of the chair, and Lacey watched an erotic play of expressions dance over his face. Frustration, longing, anger, exhilaration, they were all there in one form or another, and she felt an incomparable sense of power that he was feeling all of these things because of her. She leaned over him and let her nipples graze his chest. "Have you had enough, Mr. Brady?"

His eyes snapped open, and then narrowed intently into hers. Before Lacey could stop him, he rose from the chair, still embedded deeply within her, and strode toward the couch.

"But the couch is too small," she protested.

"Not for what I've got in mind." He dropped to his knees on the floor, sitting her down on the edge of the cushions, and took a firm grip on her hips. Then with a wicked, crooked grin, he started thrusting, slow and steady, into her.

These sensations were completely different from the ones before. And Lacey couldn't hold back a cry of shock and delight. An ache was building within her, and she lay back against the couch and allowed him to push her to the point of almost screaming.

When she finally opened her eyes, it was to find him leaning over her, watching her as she had been watching him before with a glint of power in his impassioned stare. "Have *you* had enough, Miss Garder?"

She was so enraptured she could barely speak. "No. Never," she managed to say past the burning pleasure taking over her body. "More!"

"More what?" he demanded in a sexy rasp.

The frustration she was feeling was becoming so great that when she opened her mouth to answer this time a sob came out. "I don't know," she whispered. "I don't, ahhhh, I don't know!"

He took her by the waist and brought her up flush with his chest. "To hell with personal," he stated, kissing her wildly. "I want on top of you, lady. I wanna thrust myself inside you so deep I can't breathe anymore."

He stood with her again, and this time strode to the back of the living room where he kicked open a door. The next thing Lacey knew she was sinking down onto a soft mattress and being pressed into sheets with Matthew's musky male scent clinging to them.

"But—"

"Shhhh," he said, easing his big body down over hers. He sank deep within her again and groaned with pleasure. "Just let me love you, Lacey. Just let me love you."

With steady, measured thrusts, he pushed her to the very verge of some great, mindless precipice, and then helped her over the edge.

And as Lacey's body began to shatter in what seemed like a million fiery stars, something startling happened. It was as though a veil were pulled back just far enough for her to see beneath, a vague fog rolling back from a dark corner of her mind. She knew him. Had known him since the dawn of time. She knew the warm touch of his lips, the strong feel of his arms, the smooth, deep timbre of his voice. They had been made to bring each other joy, comfort, fulfillment.

They were two halves of a perfect whole.

18

Lacey lay on her back in Matthew's bedroom studying the ceiling. The full moon through the open curtains provided enough light for her to see a large, intricately carved rose in the woodwork. Matthew was lying beside her, breathing deep and even, giving her the impression that he was fast asleep. She supposed his fatigue was understandable, after the energy they'd both just spent, but her mind was moving too fast to keep up with, let alone put to sleep.

The experience of being with Matthew had been more than she'd bargained for. Despite her determination to prevent it, he'd gotten under her skin. He'd actually had her believing for a moment that they were spiritually connected in some way—as if that weren't the most ridiculous thing she'd ever considered. She and Matthew Brady were not only complete opposites, they were totally wrong for each other. He was the self-righteous lawman. And she was the free-spirited criminal. Nothing could change the facts. Not even an orgasmically induced delusion.

She should never have let him carry her to his bed. He was all around her now, the sight of him, the feel of him, the smell of him. She could already feel the sensation of an intimate bond forming between them, and she wasn't quite sure how to stop it in its tracks.

The truly frightening thing was, she realized as she listened to his deep, even breathing, a part of her didn't want to stop it.

But that was completely insane. She couldn't let one night of sex—and that's all it had been—distort her thinking. She couldn't let his warmth, the strength of his hands on her body, the magic of his kisses, blind her to the truth: It had been only for the moment.

He'd made love to her only to purge her from his soul as she had done with him. He didn't want her. He didn't need her. He certainly didn't love her. How could he? She was everything he loathed in a woman. What he wanted was evidenced in Amanda Simmons, the woman he'd intended to marry before she'd interfered. What he wanted was kind, gentle, timid, compliant. And Lacey Garder was none of the above.

She closed her eyes and swallowed hard. The wisest thing for her to do now was get up, get dressed, and get out before he woke up and told her to do just that. In fact, he probably wasn't even asleep. He was probably lying there beside her wishing she would take the hint and leave.

Summoning all her courage, Lacey slowly sat up, and eased herself off the side of the bed. She gathered up her clothes from the floor and took them into the front room to dress. The candles he'd lighted were all burned out, and the fire in the hearth was merely smoldering. She was careful not to trip over the ladder-back chair in the center of the room as she finished with the last of the buttons on her dress and walked toward the door for her coat.

The house was eerily quiet as she opened the door and turned back for one last look. And she suddenly realized that she'd lost more than just her virginity here. She'd lost a little piece of her heart. Because deep inside she still wanted Matthew Brady just as desperately as she had before.

She stepped outside and stood on the porch where she slipped on her coat, and took her time buttoning the front placket—as if methodical movement might take her mind off what she'd just done. But it didn't. And neither did her subsequent ride through the cold night air; she was already feeling so numb inside she barely felt the chill.

Ten minutes later the Martins' house finally came into view. Her shelter. Her sanctuary. But now even that frightened her. She'd come to care so much for these people, but soon that would all end. She'd have to leave them too, deny her feelings yet again because nothing on this earth was ever hers to keep. Nothing ever lasted forever. Nothing was ever real.

Realizing this, Lacey stopped the horse beneath her and stared at the house in quiet panic. Inside was everything she'd ever wanted, everything she'd never had. And the pain she experienced at the idea of losing both Matthew and the Martins in just a few short days was almost more than she could bear.

She silently bowed her head, and broke into tears. Her shoulders shook with her sobs as she purged her emotions into the night. She hadn't been allowed to cry as a child, and now she did so as if making up for lost time. She cried until she couldn't breathe, cried until she couldn't see, cried until she couldn't stop.

"That's right, Miss Garder. Let it all out. Pain is a

part of living. It can't hurt you unless you keep it locked up inside where it festers and spoils the soul."

Hiccupping, Lacey blinked the moisture from her eyes and saw the angel lady standing by the fence rail. "How can . . . How can you say that? This hurts. This pain . . . *hurts.*"

"Yes. But it won't destroy you. In fact, it will make you stronger, more capable of dealing with heartache in the future."

"I have . . . no intention of . . . d-dealing with . . . heartache in the future," Lacey said between sobs.

"Without heartache, Miss Garder, there can be no joy."

Lacey wiped at her face and tried to pull herself together by taking a deep breath. She managed to control the hiccupping, but her chin still quivered with unspent emotion. "I feel like a fool," she whispered hoarsely. "I thought I could handle it. I thought I could be with him just once—"

"You are not a fool," the woman insisted. "The bond between you and Mr. Brady is simply stronger than both of your wills combined. Neither one of you could have resisted the attraction for long, Miss Garder. What happened tonight was inevitable."

"I should have known better—"

"You are not listening to me. I said it was inevitable. The two of you are matching pieces, Miss Garder. Two equal halves of one whole."

Lacey's attention caught, and she shot the woman a startled glance. "What did you say?"

"You were made for each other."

"Two halves of a perfect whole," Lacey whispered to herself.

"That's right," the woman replied. "What happened

tonight was, and always has been, meant to be. Matthew Brady is your soul mate. Your one true love."

Lacey stared at her, blinking in shock. All at once she felt like crying again. "You set me up."

"I beg your pardon."

"You could have told me all along who he was, and I could have avoided making such a fool of myself tonight. How could you?" she whispered, feeling horribly betrayed. "If I had known there would be no hope of getting him out of my system, I would never have slept with him."

"Precisely. You would never have let things progress naturally between the two of you. As you have avoided everything in life that might cause you emotional distress, you would have avoided Mr. Brady and what he makes you feel."

"I thought you were supposed to be helping me!"

"I *have* been helping you, Miss Garder. The best way I know how. There are simply some things that it's best you not be made aware of."

Lacey felt shaken and bruised, inside and out, and the last thing she needed was someone telling her it had been for her own good. "What else have you been keeping from me *for my own good*?" she demanded.

When the woman hesitated, Lacey knew there was more. "Tell me."

"I suppose it is time you knew." The woman took a deep breath. "The Martins."

Lacey swallowed. "What about them?"

"They too have a connection to you."

"I don't understand," Lacey said, feeling her chin begin to quiver again.

"You've known them before, before this existence.

You were meant to be born to them here on earth, but then, as you know, a temporal mix-up occurred and you were placed with the wrong mother in the wrong century."

Lacey laughed as new tears filled her eyes. In that moment everything seemed to fall into place: the comfortable way she'd always felt around George and Hazel; the respect she'd had for them from the very beginning; the love she'd come to feel toward them both. The very thought of how wonderful her life could have been if only she'd grown up surrounded by their warmth and guidance brought a newer, deeper ache to her heart.

"They were supposed to be mine?" she whispered.

"And you were supposed to be theirs."

The child they'd never had. "My God," Lacey whispered. "How could this have happened?"

"Mistakes are made, Miss Garder," the woman said gently. "We all make them. The important thing is that we recognize them, forgive ourselves, and then do our best to make recompense."

"And I've never done that, have I," she stated, feeling suddenly so ashamed of herself and all she'd been, all she'd done.

"But you have come so far. In only the last four days. The Martins love you as if you were their own physical daughter. And Mr. Brady—"

"Mr. Brady has had his fill of me, I'm afraid." She laughed bitterly. "I guess that's what I get for giving away the milk for free."

"He cannot get his fill of you. He is your soul mate. He isn't whole, complete, without you."

"But I'm not the person I would have been, should have been, had I been born in the nineteenth century, am I?"

The woman looked away sadly. "Perhaps if you spoke with him—"

"No. It's best for both of us if this ends, here and now."

"Sometimes the avoidance of pain isn't always the best, Miss Garder. Sometimes you must risk anguish for the chance to feel happiness."

For a brief moment Lacey felt an inkling of what it might be like for Matthew Brady to care for her. It was a warm, glorious feeling, one that almost made her want to gamble the heartache and take that chance for happiness. But then it was gone, and her pride was back, squeezing her chest and tightening her throat.

"My soul mate has purged me from his system," she stated. "My other half doesn't want me."

Before she could start crying again, she gave Big Red a nudge with her heels and sent him into the yard. She rode past the house, the one that should have been hers, and thought about the man and the loving parents that by one cruel twist of fate had slipped right through her fingers.

Matthew woke up to an empty bed the next morning—which wouldn't have been so bad if he hadn't been unconsciously reaching for Lacey at the time. He sat up, frowned at the empty room, and realized she was gone. Without a word, she'd left him.

Despite their agreement that this was to be a no-strings-attached moment, her absence left him a little unsettled. He'd made love to her the night before until he didn't have the strength to move. Then he'd fallen asleep with her in his arms and made love to her in his dreams.

And yet she'd had the strength—the will—to sneak out of his bed in the middle of the night.

He lay back on his pillows and remembered how amazed he'd been by her responses to his touches, his kisses. She was incredible, more giving, more uninhibited than he could have ever hoped for. He hadn't thought he'd ever get his fill of her. But of course he had. At least that's what he told himself. That had been the deal after all, one wild, passionate night.

And yet it rankled him that she'd left so easily—without a word. Had he affected her so little? After the night they'd shared, he just couldn't bring himself to believe that. At least his male pride wouldn't let him believe it.

He gritted his teeth, realizing this was classic Lacey Garder. The woman always had to have the last word. Always had to leave him irritated, baffled, intrigued—wanting more. "No," he said out loud.

But even the sound of his own denying voice didn't make the facts any less clear. He still wanted her just as badly as he had before.

He ran his hands through his hair and cursed her under his breath. How in the hell could he have allowed her to do this to him? He wanted her even now, with her scent still on his sheets, with her taste still on his lips, and with her passionate response still a fire in his blood.

But she no longer wanted him. Her absence stated that loud and clear.

The irony of it all left a sick, twisted feeling in the pit of his stomach, and he threw his blankets aside and sat on the edge of his bed. She'd done exactly what he'd intended to do with her; she'd gotten him out of her system.

Bitterness and regret ate at him as he dressed.

He'd told his men that he'd meet them at his office at nine to prepare for the trip to Fairhaven, but he intended to have a few words with Lacey first. He had to know if she'd experienced any of the powerful feelings he'd experienced the night before.

He was on his horse before the sun had crested the top of the snow-covered mountains. The sky was a dark sapphire blue.

Five minutes later Matthew was standing on the Martins' front porch, opening the screen, and knocking on the wooden door. Hazel answered, still in her robe. "Matthew? What the devil are you doing out this early?"

"I need to talk to Lacey."

"She's not awake yet," the woman told him, looking confused at his brisk manner. "But come on in here out of the cold." She stepped aside.

Matthew walked right past her, not missing a step as he made a beeline for Lacey's bedroom.

"Now, hold on! You can't just go bargin' in—"

Matthew stepped into Lacey's room and closed the door behind him, leaning against it in case Hazel decided to pursue him. Lacey was still in bed. But she wasn't asleep. She was sitting up against three or four pillows, with her hair fanned out like copper fire around her shoulders.

Matthew caught his breath at the sight of her. And, without thinking, he respectfully took off his hat. What the hell had she done to him?

"Good morning," she said.

He nodded back, not trusting his voice at the moment.

"I didn't expect you so early."

"I didn't expect you to leave my bed in the middle of the night," he countered.

"Sorry about that. I guess it was a little rude. Have you ever noticed how things just never seem to work out the way you plan?"

He considered her for a moment, thinking something was different about her. But he couldn't quite put his finger on it. "Every now and then," he replied carefully to her question. *As in every day since you arrived,* he added to himself.

"Nothing this week has gone the way I expected," she said, mirroring his own thoughts. "This town is nothing like I expected. The people. The attitudes."

"The attitudes?"

"Toward me in particular." She laughed, but it was almost a sad sound. "These people actually seem to like me."

And then he realized what it was about her that seemed so different. She'd lost her edge, that acidic side of her that generally left a man stinging from head to toe. The bitterness was gone from her eyes, leaving a sad, lonely kind of sparkle. One he ached to reach out to. He'd never wanted to hold a woman so badly in his life.

He cleared his throat. "Listen, Lacey. . . . I came by to . . . to . . . " *To what, genius? To berate her for leaving your bed before you'd given her permission to? Or are you just mad that she had the will to do so? But then maybe . . . just maybe . . . you were dying to see her again before one more second passed.* "Are you all right?" he blurted out. "I mean . . . I thought I'd stop by and . . . well, and make sure—"

"I'm fine." She gave him a faint smile. "And you don't have to feel guilty about last night either. We did what we felt we had to do. And, hey, we're over each other now, right?"

They were? Then why were those words like a dull knife plunging into his heart?

"It's so nice to talk to you without all that sexual tension getting in the way."

"Yeah," he muttered. "Nice."

They sat in silence for a moment, and he tried to look at anything but her. But he couldn't tear his eyes away from her face. That beautiful face.

"Well," he finally said, filling the uncomfortable silence. "I guess I'll be heading into town now to round up my deputies. We'll be leaving in about an hour."

"I'll be ready," she replied.

He put on his hat and turned for the door, his insides feeling like they'd been chewed up and spit out. And then she called his name, and he turned back so fast his hat nearly fell off. "Yes?"

"We'll find that money," she said. "You can bet on that."

"Right," he said.

"And then we can both get back to our lives," she added.

He nodded. "I suppose you'll be leaving soon."

"Once we've got the money I'll be coming back to say good-bye to George and Hazel. Then . . ." She shrugged.

He nodded again.

"Aren't you going to ask me where I'll be going?"

He held her stare for a moment. "It's not any of my business," he finally said. Then he tugged his hat brim and left her room, heading straight for the front door.

"Matthew?" Hazel called from the parlor.

Matthew wasn't in the mood for a chat, he was feeling too beaten up inside, too raw. So he ignored

Hazel and left the house, heading across the porch, and down the steps to his waiting horse.

"Matthew?" Hazel called more adamantly, following him outside. "What the dickens is goin' on between you two?"

He swung up into his saddle and looked at the woman with his heart in his eyes. "Nothing," he said.

But he knew that was a lie. For the first time in his life he'd fallen in love. And it was with a woman who didn't love him back.

He turned his horse and headed for town at a gallop, with the rising sun at his back and the cold morning wind in his face. The sooner they found that money the sooner Lacey could get on with her life. And the sooner he could begin to piece his own back together again.

Lacey didn't want to get out of bed. She didn't want to go through the motions of starting a day that would put her in close proximity to Matthew Brady for hours on end.

Her eyes had to be the diameter of blowholes after all the crying she'd done. And then he'd put her on the verge again, by barging into her room, looking more handsome than she remembered from the night before.

She knew why he'd come. To be sure that it was very clear to her that there were no strings attached to what had happened between them. It had been just as she'd suspected. He'd gotten his fill of her.

And now she had to somehow find the strength to convince herself that she'd gotten her fill of him. But that was like convincing Columbus the earth wasn't round, or a dog that one lick of a bone was plenty. Somehow she would face this crisis as she had all the others in her life, with her head high, her composure cool, and her pride surrounding her like an impenetrable shield.

A soft knock came at her door and Hazel slipped into the bedroom. "Are you all right, Lacey, honey? Matthew just lit outta here like a bat outta hell—"

"He's anxious to round up his men. We're leaving for Fairhaven in a couple of hours."

The woman gave her a scrutinizing look. "You don't look to me like you're up to the trip."

"It doesn't matter," Lacey said, swinging around to sit on the edge of the bed. "I've got to get that money back."

"That money's been awfully important to ya since ya came to town," Hazel said. "Don't suppose you'd care to tell me why?"

"My future depends on its return."

"Your future," the woman repeated.

"I'm on sort of a mission. That's all I can say."

"Well, here's somethin' I can say. I know you plan to leave as soon as that cash is recovered. But I want you to know, *George* and I want you to know, that you will always have a place at our table. There will always be a bed waiting here for ya, Lacey."

Lacey's chin quivered. "Thank you. You and George . . . You and George mean the world to me."

"And ya mean the world to *us*," Hazel blustered, smiling past the dampness rising up in her own eyes. "Now. Matthew's comin' back in just another hour or so, and I know you don't want him seein' you all swollen up and pink from cryin'. So get up and throw some cold water on that pretty face. George and I are headin' in to the restaurant, but I'll be back by three, just in case you get home from Fairhaven early." She cupped Lacey's chin in her hand. "Good luck, Lacey, honey."

Lacey nodded, because she was no longer capable of speech. Her throat had closed off so tightly it ached, and she could only offer Hazel a teary smile as the woman stood and left the room.

She'd need no luck. She'd have Matthew. The other half of her heart and soul.

She sat on the bed, composing herself, until she heard the rattling of harnesses that signified the Martins pulling out of the yard in their wagon. Then she climbed out of bed and dressed, determined to make it through this last final day in Tranquility. It wasn't Matthew's fault that he didn't care for her. And she refused to be bitter and hold it against him. Her feelings were her own problem. She would have to deal with them.

But as she was reaching for her purse the bedroom door slammed open and a bigger problem was suddenly staring her in the face.

Ned and Henry Rawlins had broken out of jail.

19

Matthew felt as if he were about to explode as he rode into town. And the very last thing he expected, or needed, was news that the Rawlins brothers had broken out of jail.

Hell, he should have stayed in California. Drifting wasn't such a bad profession, respectable or not.

His three deputies were waiting outside his office for him when he rode up. They informed him of the situation. Bill looked a little more dopey than usual because he'd been on duty the night before and had been clubbed over the head during the great escape. They also warned Matthew that Reginald Sterling, and the town council minus George Martin, were waiting for him in his office.

The moment Matthew walked in Sterling rose from his chair and opened his mouth to speak. But Matthew held up his hand. "Save it, Sterling. If you want me to catch those two, I don't have time to waste with your bellyaching."

"What I want," the man replied haughtily, "is your badge, Brady."

An odd request considering Matthew didn't wear one.

"You are a travesty to this office, Mr. Brady. A joke! And, as mayor of this town, I demand that you resign immediately."

"What about the rest of you?" Matthew demanded of Zappy Karls, James Kellogg, Willy Black, and Robert Chandler.

"This here looks purty bad, Matthew," Willy Black pointed out.

"We been waitin' damn near a week for you to get that money back," James Kellogg added.

"But you've been far too busy courting damsels, haven't you, Mr. Brady?" Reginald added dryly.

As far as Matthew was concerned that was the last straw. He strode toward the town mayor. "You want my resignation, Sterling? You got it, you pig-faced son of a bitch," he stated, enunciating his words with sharp jabs to Reginald Sterling's chest. "But not before I finish the job I started and bring in every member of that Rawlins family, and return the money to the bank." He'd backed the man against the wall. "Then you can take this job and shove it up your lily-white ass for all I care. . . . Now get the hell out of my office before I lose my temper."

Everyone except his deputies went scampering from the jailhouse. "You don't mean it, do ya?" Larry asked.

"You're not quittin', are ya?" Gene joined in.

Bill was still looking dopey.

"I prefer to think of it as moving on," Matthew said. "A man can only stay in one place for so long."

"But what about Miss Gar—"

Bill got an elbow in his stomach for the trouble of finally opening his mouth, and Gene gave Matthew a weak smile. "He's still reelin' from that whack over the head."

Matthew gave them all a warning glare. "Get saddled up. I'll meet you outside in a minute."

His deputies filed out just as George Martin was coming in. "Matthew, you can't be serious. Tell me you're not resignin'."

Matthew turned for the gun rack. "George, I've had it. I know my father wanted more for me, but, damn it, I'm not the respectable type. No matter how hard I try I just can't squeeze into the mold."

"What the blazes are you talking about?" George demanded.

"I know how much he hated the way I lived. That I went from job to job—"

"Now hold on just one goddamn minute. I don't know who you're talkin' about, but the man I knew was damn proud of his son. He used to tell folks all the time how Matthew had herded cattle. And how Matthew had ridden shotgun on a stage. And how Matthew had dug coal in a mine. Hell, every time somebody would bring up a job the man would go off like a lit fuse talkin' about how Matthew had done that. Plenty of times we damn near shot him—or *ourselves*.

"And, yeah, I suppose an argument can be made for a father not appreciatin' that his son had the roots of a tumbleweed," George continued. "But the thing was, boy, you did those odd jobs so damn well he couldn't be anything but proud. It wasn't laziness, or lack of ambition that drove you on to the next town. It was that you'd done the job, and done the job well, and you were ready for the next challenge."

"Then why? Why the deathbed speech about getting married and finally settling down?"

"He was proud of ya, Matthew, don't you even question that. It was just that he hated to see you never know the challenge of lovin' a good woman, raisin' a passle of kids as admirable and remarkable as yourself. Of buildin' a place you could call home."

Matthew took a deep breath. "You don't know how much I've struggled with this."

"Yes. Yes I do. The most important thing to remember is how much he loved ya, Matthew. And how important to him your happiness was. And hell, if this job makes you unhappy, I'll be the first to shake your hand on your way out of town. But don't quit because of Reginald Sterling. That man seems to keep forgettin' that this town made him mayor because he owns the bank, not because of any fondness on our parts."

Matthew grabbed up a box of shotgun shells and a box of rifle ammunition and shoved them into his saddlebags. "I'm tired of him breathing down my neck."

"Hell, son, this isn't like you. Runnin' off with your tail between your legs. What's really eatin' you? It's not your partin' ways with Miss Simmons is it?"

"How the hell did you know about that?"

"Larry, Bill, and Gene were in the restaurant last night—"

Matthew gritted his teeth. "Larry, Bill, and Gene. I swear those three are worse than a trio of old maids."

"I sorta took it, from the events of last night, that you'd be courtin' Lacey now."

Matthew's mouth went dry. "Events?"

"You did have dinner with her, didn't ya? I mean, she rode off all flighty and nervous, and Hazel was fit to be tied. I swear if I hadn't held the woman back she'd have gone off with Lacey and sat right in between the two of ya all night long."

Matthew rolled his eyes. That would have been interesting. But then if Hazel had come along he wouldn't have taken Lacey Garder to his bed. And he wouldn't be still burning with need for her. *First in their bed, always in your head.* As God was his witness, there wasn't a truer statement on earth.

"Everything go all right between you two?" George asked carefully.

"Why do you ask?" Matthew grumbled, slinging a Winchester over his shoulder.

"Because you look tense enough to split in half."

"If you haven't heard the big news," Matthew said, turning to him, "I had a jailbreak this morning—"

"Reginald told me all about that. And that's not what's eatin' ya." George gave him a speculative look. "You got the look of a wounded bear."

Matthew turned away and grabbed up the shotgun, not interested in filling George in on all the gory details. He was a victim of the heart, wasn't that what they called it? A victim of his own treacherous heart.

"Do me a favor, George," Matthew said as he turned and headed out of the office. "Talk to Zappy about buying the house."

"Matthew, don't you think you're jumpin' the gun just a bit—"

"He was more than happy to buy my father's store," Matthew said. He paused beside his horse and slipped the Winchester into the left saddle scabbard. "Now maybe he'd like a place to live besides a back room."

"I'm sure once you get that money back—"

Matthew slung his saddlebags over his horse's back and tied them down securely. "Just talk to him, George."

"All right, all right. I'll talk to him. If you promise me you'll give this decision some serious thought."

Matthew swung up into his saddle. George was right. There was more to this than a jailbreak, and even Reginald Sterling's constant interference. He supposed he just didn't like the idea of hanging around once Lacey was gone. The tiny town of Tranquility simply wouldn't be the same.

"Promise?" George persisted.

Matthew nodded. "I promise." But he knew rethinking his decision wouldn't do a damn bit of good.

"You still plannin' on takin' Lacey with ya to Fairhaven?" George asked.

"Think I'd survive the day if I left her behind?"

"I think she'd ride after ya. Probably get herself killed in the process."

"My thoughts exactly. We'll be stopping by the house for her."

"If shootin' commences, you'll tell her to keep that pretty little head of hers down?"

Matthew tugged the front of his hat low over his eyes. "Or I'll be sitting on it."

He rode out of town with his three deputies following close behind, kicking up dirty snow and mud behind them. It was time for him to face Lacey again. And this time he wouldn't be wearing his heart on his sleeve.

Matthew and his posse road into the Martins' front yard fifteen minutes later. He told his men to wait while he climbed the porch steps and knocked on the wooden door. He was feeling nervous as hell.

No one answered his knock, so he knocked again, louder this time. Still no answer.

Finally he pushed open the door and poked his head inside the entryway. "Miss Garder?" he called. "Are you ready to go?"

The house was so silent, a tiny chill itched its way up his spine to his scalp. He pushed all the way inside and glanced into the empty parlor. Then he headed for Lacey's room. The door was standing half open. The room was empty.

"Lacey?" he shouted in the entryway.

Maybe she'd heard them ride up and went out to the barn for Big Red, he thought logically. He walked down the hallway, through the kitchen, and out the back door. That's when he saw hoof prints and churned up snow, and slowly eased his gun out of his holster.

He turned his attention to the barn. "Lacey?" he called again. "If you're in the barn come on out here where I can see you."

The loft door rattled in the breeze. But other than that, nothing moved.

His three deputies came riding around the side of the house. "Something up, boss?" Larry asked.

"Bill, you and Gene head around the back of the barn. Watch the windows."

Without a single question, the two men rode off to do as their boss ordered.

"Where's Miss Garder?" Larry asked.

"Hopefully," Matthew said, beginning to move cautiously toward the barn, "in there."

But she wasn't in the barn. And neither was Big Red.

"Did she leave without us, do ya think?" Gene asked as he and Bill joined them in the barn.

"No," Matthew replied. It had been too important to her that they do this thing together.

He walked back to the back of the house and stared down at the hoof prints in the snow.

"Looks like two horses," Larry said.

Matthew nodded. They all followed the tracks to the yard between the barn and house.

"And then three horses ride off from here," Gene stated.

"It's the Rawlins brothers, isn't it?" Bill asked. "They got her, didn't they?"

Hearing his suspicions spoken out loud sent a tremor of fear and rage sweeping through Matthew. He reholstered his gun, and clenched his fists at his sides as he headed back to his horse around front. It was the Rawlins brothers all right and if they'd pulled out one coppery strand of hair on her head . . . he'd tear them to pieces with his bare hands.

Lacey's hands were cold and numb. And the tight rope binding them together wasn't helping any. She'd been kidnapped, plain and simple, and was now at the mercy of two unpredictable men who were good and pissed.

They knew she'd tricked them into telling her how to find their sister; they'd taken great joy in telling her that as they'd thrown her into Big Red's saddle and tied her hands to the pommel. And they'd also described with great detail exactly what they intended to do to her once they reached Fairhaven and found the hotel where their sister was hiding out.

At least she wasn't a virgin, Lacey thought to herself as they passed the fork in the road that had caused her so much trouble two days before. As if either man stood a chance of surviving a rape against her. They were bigger, stronger—smelling and otherwise—and chances were she wouldn't be able to fight them off. But she'd get even. Sooner or later they'd turn their backs and get a good taste of just how bitterly vengeful Lacey Garder could be.

For now, she had to concentrate on simply staying in the saddle as Big Red was forced to maneuver down a steep incline that was shaded by stout evergreens and slick with snow and ice. They were moving at breakneck speed, and she had heard the men mention that they would reach Fairhaven in less than an hour.

Her purse was lopped over her neck and under her arm, sadly out of reach of her bound hands. But tucked inside was the only useful thing she'd brought with her to the nineteenth century: a small canister of pepper spray.

"I still don't see how we're gonna keep that marshal from followin' us," Ned said. He was the one holding Big Red's reins, and towing Lacey along behind them. "Look at all the tracks we're makin'."

"Don't worry about it," Henry answered. "We'll be on a ship for Mexico by nightfall. He'll never find us, or that money."

"Our friend sure is gonna be hot around the frilly collar about that."

Henry chuckled. "He should have known better than to try and lord it over a Rawlins. As far as I'm concerned, the money's ours. We earned every penny. Ain't that right, Miss sweet thing?"

"Go to hell," Lacey sneered.

"Aw, now that just plain ain't neighborly. I'm gonna have a whole lotta fun teachin' you some proper womanly manners."

Ned snickered. "Among other things. Shall we flip a coin over her and see who goes first?"

"Hell no," Henry drawled, giving Lacey a lecherous leer over his beefy shoulder. "The lady likes it double, remember? We'll be taking our turns at the same time."

Lacey thought she might gag. But she knew better than to show them one ounce of fear—even though she was beginning to feel it down to her toes. She kept trying to work her hands free of the rope, but all that was getting her were sore arms and chewed-up wrists.

"I bet she's got skin like roses," Ned remarked.

"The kind that'll hold teeth marks," his brother added.

"I'm gonna bite my name across her belly."

"I've got other places in mind."

Dream on, Lacey thought rancorously. She'd kill *herself* first.

They passed a road with a carved wooden sign that read Geneva two miles, and rode right on past. Big Red slipped on a patch of ice, lost his footing, and snorted disconcertingly. Lacey was staying in the saddle by sheer strength of will. The same thing that would decide whether or not she survived this situation.

When they rode into Fairhaven it was still early in the morning. Lacey had been moved from Big Red to Ned's horse. She was sitting in front of Ned in the saddle, with a gun planted in her ribs, as they rode down a side street and headed for what Henry called the old coal mines. It took only two hotels before they found the right one. Lorraine was hiding out in a seedy, two-story shack on the farthest side of town.

And then Lacey was dragged up the stairs, with no one in the lobby paying much attention, and shoved through a door with the number five written in black paint so worn you could barely read it.

"Honey, we're home!" Henry bellowed.

A small, fragile-looking young girl rose from a filthy cot against the far wall.

"Fetch us some grub, Lorraine," Ned commanded as he shoved Lacey farther into the dismal room. "We ain't had nothing to eat all mornin'."

Lacey blinked at the girl. *This* was the fearsome Lorraine Rawlins? She wasn't much bigger than Lacey, and didn't look a day over sixteen. The girl's reputation obviously had been greatly exaggerated.

"Glad to see you two could finally make it," the girl muttered softly.

"And don't give us any lip either," Henry warned. He took off his heavy coat and threw it on a worn brown sofa with the stuffing coming out along the edges. Then he turned to Lacey, and she flinched inwardly at his intentful grin.

"Who's this?" Lorraine asked as she handed her brothers a plate of bread and stale-looking cheese. "I gotta feed her too?"

"Naw," Henry told her. "We got somethin' else in mind to give her."

Lorraine looked at Lacey and their eyes met. The girl was dirty, dressed in rags, and her black hair was cropped short and in rats, but she had the most striking green eyes Lacey had ever seen.

"You must be the dreaded Lorraine," Lacey said. "The fearsome, merciless bank robber."

"My brothers are showin' me the ropes," she replied, but without much enthusiasm.

Suddenly a big beefy hand shot out and cuffed the girl on the side of the head. "Fetch us somethin' to drink, Rainey," Henry ordered.

"We got any of that whiskey left?" Ned asked.

"Not whiskey, you idiot. We can't afford to get drunk when we're on the run."

"You drank it all before the robbery," Lorraine Rawlins retorted with a spark in her green eyes.

Henry turned a vicious glare on the girl. "You implyin' somethin', little sister?"

"I think she's implyin' that we got drunk before the robbery," Ned remarked.

Henry shot out another hand, this time catching Lorraine on the side of the jaw. Lacey had seen enough. She turned to Henry Rawlins and gave him a good, swift kick in the shin. Which earned her a slap alongside the head that knocked her to the floor.

"I think," Henry said, angrily beginning to undo the buttons on the front of his pants, "that it's time I began your lessons."

"There's a ship leaving at noon," his sister blurted out.

"What?" Ned asked her.

"I . . . I check with the front desk every mornin', just in case it's the day you two break outta jail. And I checked this mornin' and there's a ship leaving for Mexico at twelve o'clock noon today."

"Well, that's perfect!" Ned exclaimed.

Henry was still glowering at Lacey, however. "Yeah. Perfect. Where's that money?" he demanded from his sister.

"Over here," she told him, walking toward the cot. She lifted up the mattress and pulled out two canvas bags. "I figured I should hide it."

Ned stepped eagerly around Lacey and snatched the bags from his sister's hands. "We're rich," he said. "Rich!"

"Take out enough for four ship fares."

"Four?" Ned asked.

Henry kept his green eyes level on Lacey. "Four. Miss Garder would just hate to be left behind." He gave her a kick in the hip that jarred her teeth. "Wouldn't you?"

"Desperately," she answered tightly.

"Tie her up in that chair over there," he ordered Ned.

Lacey was hauled to her feet by the rope binding her hands, and she clamped her lips to keep from crying out from the pain of the hemp rubbing against her raw wrists. She was dropped into a wooden chair, and tied tightly to it with another long piece of rough rope.

"We'll be back," Henry said, as he and his brother headed for the door. "You keep an eye on her," he warned his sister.

"Yeah," Ned added, grinning. "She's gonna be our entertainment on our long trip south."

As soon as the door closed Lacey let out a huge sigh of relief. She now had some time to think of a way out of the mess she'd found herself in.

And the first place she was going to look for help was from the young woman who was now sitting quietly on the cot across the room.

"I can't believe you're their sister," Lacey said.

"Neither can I," was the mumbled reply.

Lacey felt a surge of hope. It was apparent that there was no love lost between this girl and her brothers. "I don't suppose you'd—"

"Don't even ask it, lady," the girl shot out.

Lacey blinked in surprise at the girl's sudden rancor.

"I'm not as stupid as they think. Or as you think. So don't bother tryin' to talk your way out of those ropes."

"I was only going to say—"

"I know what you were gonna say," the girl interrupted again and stood up from the cot. "You were gonna say, gee, Rainey, they treat you so shabby, why not stick it to 'em by lettin' me go free. That about cover it?"

The girl was quicker than Lacey had given her credit for, probably than anyone had given her credit for, so she wasn't going to waste her time lying to her. "That about covers it. Can't blame a girl for trying."

"No," she shot back snidely. "I s'pose you can't."

Hell, with her brothers gone Lorraine Rawlins was a veritable spitfire. "This a pretty common thing then? Them kidnapping women and you playing watchdog for them?"

That question appeared to make the girl a little uncomfortable. "They've never done it before now."

"I hear they've never robbed a bank before, either. Getting a little full of themselves, are they? What's next? Rape and murder? And them dragging you right along with them the whole way."

"Henry says a good livin' could be made robbin' banks."

"He's right. But trust me. It's not worth it. You're always moving, always looking over your shoulder, never trusting anybody, and being trusted even less. You'll have no home, no friends, no family—"

"*They're* my family."

"I wouldn't go around bragging about that to too many people, Lorraine. They're not exactly well liked if you know what I mean."

"They're feared," she stated.

"Even by their sister."

The girl shot her an angry, haunted look. "I do what I'm told and I do just fine."

Although she'd been young at the time, Lacey
remembered that feeling well. Thinking that everything mean and brutal that she got she deserved, and
everything kind that was withheld from her she
didn't. "You're not just fine, Lorraine. Those two
men treat you no better than a dog. You intend to live
your life this way?"

"I got no choice."

"Your life is full of choices!" Lacey shouted
angrily. Lorraine flinched, and even took a step back
from her.

"I'm sorry," Lacey said, toning her voice down.
"This is sort of a sore subject for me. You see, I've
been in your shoes, Lorraine. I've done things I'm
ashamed of while telling myself I had no choice. The
truth was, I was just too afraid to do what I knew was
right."

"You're just sayin' that so I'll let you go."

"Yes, I want you to let me go. But I'm saying this
so you'll stop and think about what you're doing with
your life before it's too late, before you get so deep
into this mess with your brothers that you have no
way out. Leave them while you have the chance."

The girl snorted. "And where would I go?"

"Well, there has to be some government agency,
some juvenile shelter—"

"You mean an orphanage? Where they'd work me
to death, feed me bread and water, and stuff me into
a room full of other misbegottens like myself? Or
were you meaning that I should live on the streets.
Find my meals in garbage bins. Sell my body to keep
clothes on my back and shoes on my feet?"

"Those can't be your only choices."

"Just where exactly are you *from*, lady? Without a
family I got nothin'."

And that's when Lacey got an idea and broke into a smile. "I know where you can find one."

"Huh?"

"A family. I know where you can find a family that would give you all the love, warmth, and support you could possibly want or need. All you have to do is trust me enough to untie me from this chair."

20

It was almost high noon, a time when shadows melted into their benefactors. And that's exactly how Matthew felt, as if he were a shadow that had blended into nothing.

He'd ridden to Fairhaven at breakneck speed without saying a single word to any of his deputies. The Rawlins brothers had at least an hour's headstart on him and they didn't have a moment to waste. By the time they'd reached the city limits just over an hour later he was panicked, frustrated, and angry as hell. He was going to kill Ned and Henry Rawlins.

He and his deputies spent the next two hours scouring the city, every hotel, every saloon, every bordello, anywhere three pieces of Rawlins trash might hide. They had no luck, and as each precious minute ticked away, Matthew became more and more agitated. By now they could have met up with Lorraine and ridden off in any direction with Lacey. But he swore to himself that he'd never stop looking for her.

He reined in his horse in front of the Broadway Grocer and took a deep, steadying breath. They were never going to get anywhere as long as they were pounding down the streets like a pack of blood-hounds. "We need to split up," he said to his deputies. This was the most he'd spoken to them since they'd left the Martin farm, and the men looked at him in surprise.

"You mean inta fours?" Gene asked.

"No, inta sixes," Larry retorted, swatting Gene with his hat. "Shut up and listen to the man."

"We'll each take one of the main streets," Matthew continued. "If you see anything, fire your gun in the air and the rest of us will come running."

"Did ya get that, Bill?" Larry asked. "He said inta the *air*. Not inta the horse of the man beside ya."

"Aw, hell, Larry, I apologized for that weeks ago."

Matthew shook his head as the three men rode off in separate directions. It was going to take an act of God for any of those three to find a thing.

He turned left at the next street and rode a straight line down Broadway. He kept his pace unhurried, and his manner uncaring, but secretly perused every person he passed. His gut told him they were still here, somewhere in town. But they had to be on the move or he and his men would have found them in one of the countless hotels they'd ransacked.

He came to the end of the street and craned his neck to check down the long alleyway. It led to a dead end. He swore under his breath, and stopped his horse to recollect himself. "She's going to be all right," he whispered to himself. "God, help me find her."

Why hadn't he taken her advice and brought her to Fairhaven days ago? Then they would have found the money and she'd now be safe at the Martins' where she belonged. No. She'd be gone, disappeared out of his life as quickly as she'd appeared.

A sudden shout echoed toward him, the unmistakable cry of a man in pain. And nobody could inflict injury on a man with more precision than Lacey Garder.

Matthew dug his heels into his horse's flanks and went charging back up the street. He turned right, then right again, and headed down Green Street. When he came to an alley on his left, the sight that greeted him made him heave a gigantic sigh of relief. Lacey and a young girl were cornered by the Rawlins brothers, and the two women were actually holding their own; Ned was looking wary, and Henry was grabbing his groin, looking decidedly nauseous.

Matthew leaped down from his horse and strode toward the group. "You bastard sons-a-bitches," he muttered to himself. He didn't unholster his gun, knowing that the only way to rid himself of this blood lust was some good physical exertion.

Lacey saw him first. "Matthew!" she cried in surprise—and what he hoped was happiness. Matthew only looked at her long enough to see that she was all right. Then he focused on killing himself a Rawlins.

He'd never been so scared in his life as he'd been the moment he'd realized what had happened to her. He'd been eaten up so badly inside for the past four hours, he doubted there was anything left of him under his skin. And now somebody was going to pay.

Henry being the bigger of the two men, Matthew headed straight for him. Ned tried to step into his path, but Matthew took care of him with just one punch to the stomach. Without missing a beat, his left fist then connected hard with Henry's jaw, jarring from Henry's hand the gun he'd managed to get halfway out of its holster. Henry fought back wildly, swinging blindly at Matthew with both fists. But

Matthew was quicker, and Henry never touched him.

By the time the outlaw was finally doubled over, his face bloody and his breath raspy, Matthew was beginning to run out of murderous steam. "If you touched her," he said, breathing hard, "I swear I'll finish the job."

"Matthew, look out!"

He turned, reaching for his gun, but it was all just a second too late. Something hard hit him on the back of the head. Pain shot through his skull and he dropped to his knees, but knowing Lacey needed him helped him manage to stay conscious.

Meanwhile Henry had recovered somewhat, and was now heading for him.

"Hey, Godzilla?" Lacey called. Henry paused and looked her way, his face a bloody mess. And Lacey stepped forward with a small black canister in her hand and sprayed something into his eyes. Henry screamed, as if he'd been doused in acid, and dropped to his knees.

Matthew tried to stand, but the world was tilting too far to his left. Lacey rushed to his side as Ned hurried toward his brother. "Matthew? Are you all right?"

Henry was being helped to his feet and Matthew struggled to stand once again. He couldn't let them get away. But the gentle pressure of Lacey's hand on his shoulder was all it took to stop him from wasting his depleting energy. He wasn't capable of pursuing the men now, so he consoled himself with the knowledge that Lacey was at least safe.

She cringed over his wound. Apparently it wasn't a pretty sight. "We need to get you to a doctor."

"There's one just down the street," the girl standing next to her said.

Their voices were becoming nothing but echoes, as if they were speaking from the bottom of a well.

"Help me get him to his feet," Lacey said.

Matthew's head throbbed as Lacey and her friend helped him stand. His knees were wobbly as they began to slowly walk him to the mouth of the alleyway. He stared at her profile, trying hard to focus on it. "I came to save you," he said, sounding drunk even to his own ears.

She smiled at him and it made his heart leap. "I know you did. Thank you."

He turned and smiled at the scruffy-looking girl supporting his left side. "She said thank you."

"Here's the doctor's place," the girl said.

Matthew squinted up at a clean, white-painted building front, but then he had to close his eyes and rest from the effort.

"Just a few more steps," Lacey said.

He turned and looked at her again, his gaze wobbling as his attention drifted down to her lips. "Can I have a kiss?"

She frowned at him, but then broke into an easy smile. "He knocked the sense right out of you, didn't he?"

"Hell no," he replied, his words sounding sluggish. "I'm . . . I'm just . . . fine . . . ."

And that's the last thing he remembered before crumbling to the ground at her feet.

Five stitches. That's what it took to sew the one-inch gash in Matthew Brady's head. Ned Rawlins had hit him with a brick, proving once and for all that Matthew's skull wasn't as hard as a rock.

Now he was lying on the bed in one of the hotel rooms his three faithful deputies had rented for the night, sleeping off a dose of morphine the doctor had given him. Lacey had taken off his bloodstained shirt— the man bled like a stuck pig—leaving him bare from the waist up. That had been her first mistake. Her second was in thinking she could spend the night caring for him and not feel the overpowering urge to touch him, to soothe him, to reassure him that everything was going to work out fine now for him and his town.

She was sitting beside the bed, smoothing the hair back from his forehead. He was still sleeping off the effects of the morphine, and they were all hoping he wouldn't be cross-eyed for the rest of his life. It was now almost eight o'clock. The sun had long since set. Gene, Bill, and Larry had been out all day searching for Ned and Henry. But Lacey was sure that the brothers had sailed on that ship bound for Mexico and were long gone.

A soft knock came at the door and she was surprised by her sudden burst of panic. She supposed her kidnapping and subsequent escape had affected her more than she realized. She picked up Matthew's heavy Colt .45 from the nightstand, and called out, "Who's there?"

"It's Rainey."

She heaved a heavy sigh of relief and set the gun back down. She walked across the room and unlocked the door.

"He still out?" Rainey asked, walking into the room.

"Like a blown fuse."

"Huh?"

"Nothing." Lacey suddenly felt very tired. "Did you get something to eat for dinner?"

"Yeah. I got a little somethin' in the restaurant downstairs and charged it to the room—he sure is a looker, isn't he," she added matter of factly, as she moved to the side of Matthew's bed.

"Isn't he," Lacey agreed, staring openly at him.

"Here." Lorraine held out a small box. "I brought you up somethin'. Figured you could use a good meal yourself. I'll just set it over here on the dresser. Say, you don't think he'd mind if I ordered up a bath and charged it to the room, do ya?"

Lacey looked the girl up and down, not bothering to hide her distaste at the dirty clothes she was wearing or her ratty black hair. "I say take the chance," she advised.

Rainey looked down at herself. "Yeah, I guess I could use a good scrubbin'."

A groan came from the bed, and Matthew Brady slowly cracked open his eyes. "Who's got the hammer?" he asked hoarsely.

Lacey moved closer to him, thinking he might be delirious. "What hammer?"

"The one pounding on my head. Jesus, did I get hit by a delivery wagon?"

She smiled in relief. "A brick. You've got five stitches in the back of your head."

He felt his wound with gentle fingers, and then opened his eyes all the way. He looked at Lacey, his eyes hard and fathomless, and then his whole face softened as he broke into a chagrined smile. "Did I save you . . . or did you save me?"

"From where I was standin' it looked like a little bit of both," Lorraine remarked.

His attention turned to the girl standing at the foot of his bed. "Who's this?"

"This," Lacey said, "is Lorraine Rawlins."

Matthew's expression hardened with confusion and suspicion. "You're joking."

"I don't think he likes me," Lorraine commented.

"Be glad he's not shoving his gun in your face," Lacey replied. "No joke, Matthew. Her brothers forced her to be a part of the robbery, and I'm sure they're responsible for her much exaggerated reputation. She helped me escape them, and is now gladly turning over the money they stole."

"It didn't look to me like you escaped."

"We did, but they found us before we could get out of the city. We're lucky you came along when you did," she added softly.

Matthew's gaze collided with hers, and he moved his fingers to cover where her hand was resting on the mattress. His warmth infused her, skittering up her arm, making her feel safe and secure. But when he looked back at Lorraine the suspicion returned to his eyes. "You've given me quite a chase, Miss Rawlins."

"Folks tend to do that when their lives are at stake," Lorraine said.

"I wouldn't have hurt you."

"Well, it wasn't you I was worried about."

"Rainey was afraid of her brothers," Lacey explained. "You know how sweet and gentle they can be."

His attention snapped back to Lacey. "They didn't hurt you, did they?" He struggled to sit up. "If they did so help me I'll—"

"Down, killer," she said, pressing his shoulders back to the bed, although it did give her a little thrill to have him acting so protective. "Except for some nasty rope burns, I'm fine."

"A little high-strung, isn't he?" Lorraine remarked.

Matthew closed his eyes and relaxed back into the pillow beneath his head. "Christ, she sounds just like you."

"Well, I'm headin' for that bath," Lorraine said, turning for the door. "You two have a nice night." Her ebony eyebrows lifted suggestively. "Or a frenzied one."

"Must be a student of yours," Matthew mumbled as Lorraine left the room and shut the door.

"Do you think the Martins will like her?"

He opened his eyes. "What do the Martins have to do with it?"

"That's where I'm taking her. To the Martins'."

Matthew squeezed her fingers. "That's a noble gesture."

"It is? Hey, I don't think I've ever done one of those before."

"You're easing the Martins' loneliness, and helping Lorraine at the same time. Hell, it's a great idea."

"But do you think they'll like her? She's a little scruffy looking—"

"I think they'll love her." His gaze settled on her lips in that same disconcerting way that always made her pulse race. "She only has to open her mouth and you come spouting out."

Lacey frowned. "I can't tell if that's a compliment or a set-down."

"And it's probably better that way."

Her frowned deepened. He was talking in circles and she wondered if he'd been affected by that hit over the head more than she'd first imagined. "How's that hammering?"

"Hmmm?"

"In your head?"

"Oh." He suddenly cringed. "You know, it's starting

to hurt like the devil. Maybe you better have a look at it."

Concern etching her face, she leaned over him hoping he hadn't torn out a stitch, and, without warning, he caught hold of her arm and pulled her down on top of him. She let out a cry of surprise as her breasts flattened against his hard chest and her gaze slammed into his. She wasn't at all sure what to make of this sudden move on his part. "I . . . um . . . Is it feeling better then?"

"Remarkably," he whispered as he leaned up and gave her a full, lingering kiss.

"Then me checking it was just a scam?"

"Absolutely," he replied between tastes of her luscious lips.

"Then it doesn't hurt at all?"

"The pain's moved a little lower, Lacey." He looked intently into her eyes. "I was hoping you might want to do something about that."

Lacey didn't have to be a rocket scientist to know what he was talking about. "You mean you want to . . . again?"

"Just one more moment, Lacey," he whispered. "Just one more time."

His mouth covered hers in a hungry embrace that left her breathless and wanting more. So much more. Her dress went up around her hips. Her drawers were pulled down around her knees, then her ankles, until they were tossed onto the floor. He undid the front of his pants, straddled her over him, and embedded himself inside her before she had a chance to even wonder why he was so interested in making love to her again. And by then she couldn't have cared less what his reasons were.

She gripped his sleek, muscular shoulders, kissing

his neck as he kissed hers, and savored the feel of him beneath her, around her, inside her. Soon they were moving as one to the erotic rhythm they'd perfected only the night before, both gasping for breath, both straining to feel every sensation, every pleasure, to give to the other as well as to receive.

It wasn't long before Lacey's body broke free, shattering and clenching all around him, urging him to join her in a journey to the stars. He pulsed within her, holding her close and whispering her name on a passionate, raspy sigh.

And when it was all over, when they were both too dazed to think straight, he curled her up into him, wrapped his arms securely around her back, and tucked her head beneath his chin. "Don't try sneaking out on me again, or I'll be forced to tie you to the bedpost."

Lacey smiled. "I've got enough rope burns to last me a lifetime, thanks."

He made a soft, sympathetic sound in the back of his throat and brought one of her wrists up to look at in the lamplight. There was an angry-looking red ring around it, and it was still slightly raw even though the doctor had given her some ointment to take the sting out of it.

And then Matthew did the tenderest thing; he opened her fingers and placed a soft kiss on her palm. The act brought tears to her eyes. It was good to know that at least he'd come to like her a little bit. And yet it made her so sad to know that he would never feel as deeply for her as she'd come to feel for him.

"I'm sorry you had to go through this," he said.

"It's not your fault."

"If I hadn't been so stubborn, if I'd taken you with me the first time I came here—"

She pressed her fingers against his lips. "Shhhh."

He kissed them, and then kissed her warmly, tenderly. It was all too much emotion for Lacey to bear and she let out a nervous laugh. "I think we should get some sleep. You should be well rested when you ride into Tranquility and throw that stolen money into Reginald Sterling's face."

He went still. "And you should be well rested when you say good-bye to everybody."

She nodded, rigidly. That was something she wasn't prepared to think about just yet. "The important thing is the town is saved and so is your job."

"I'm quitting."

She blinked. "What?"

"The town of Tranquility has lost its appeal. I figure now that the money's recovered, I'll be moving on."

She pulled back from him in shock. "You can't do that! When I think of all the trouble I went through to save you that stupid—I won't let you do it!"

He pushed his hand through the side of her hair and gripped her head. "You can't stop me from leaving any more than I can stop you."

He was absolutely right. And she groaned in frustration. She flopped over onto her back and folded her arms across her chest. "You're so damned pigheaded, stubborn," she grumbled under her breath, "I'm surprised that brick survived."

"What was that?" He moved closer to her and threw his heavy leg over hers.

"I didn't say a thing," she replied innocently.

"Oh, I heard something. By any chance was it the sound of the pot calling the kettle black?"

"The whole damn world knows I'm not half as stubborn as you, Matthew Brady."

He chuckled in her ear as he nibbled on the delicate lobe. "Said by the woman who risked life and limb to ride to Fairhaven all by herself."

"Said by the man who refused under the best advice to take her to Fairhaven with him."

"The best advice?" he echoed, moving his enticing nibbles down to the arch of her neck.

"Mine," she returned.

"And you're not short in the ego department, either." He got a sharp elbow in his ribs for that remark.

"Said by a man who never takes anyone else's advice."

"Said by a woman who always thinks *hers* should be taken."

"You're really beginning to irritate me, Brady."

"Then shut up and kiss me, Lacey."

She turned and glared at his infuriatingly sexy grin. "You'd like that, wouldn't you?"

"Oh, yes. Very much."

"You'd like me to forfeit this argument by falling helplessly into your strong arms?"

He glanced down at his bulging bicep. "You really think they're strong?"

"Amazingly."

"Then fall away."

She gave him one last final glare before turning toward him.

He wrapped his arms around her and pulled her to his chest. "Will you answer me one question?" he asked, his mouth hovering next to hers.

She wanted his kiss as badly as a thirsty man wanted water. "Anything," she whispered back.

"I won't stumble across a jail with you in it someday, will I?"

She smiled at him, knowing the truth of what she was about to say. "I've decided to mend my wayward ways."

"Ummm. But not *too* much I hope." Before she knew it he was kissing her again.

"Shall we go another round?" he whispered against her lips a few moments later. He was already unbuttoning the front of her dress.

"One more for the road," she whispered back, desire already coiled tightly in her belly.

"I want you bare this time."

"Turnabout's fair play."

And before long they were both lying naked in each other's arms, chasing yet again that one elusive moment.

21

"What's up between you two?"

Lacey managed to tear her eyes away from Matthew's broad back long enough to give Lorraine a sharp look. "Nothing," she replied in a hushed voice.

"Nothing? Then why do you keep starin' at him like he's the last man on the face of the earth?"

Lacey reined her horse next to Lorraine's and forced the girl to stop. "Could you possibly keep your voice down?" she asked sharply.

"Well, somebody oughta let him know how ya feel."

"I don't want him to know."

Lorraine gave her a baffled look. "Does he hit ya?"

"No, he doesn't—"

"Then he sleeps with other women."

"No, he—"

"Then he must smell bad or somethin', 'cause it sure isn't that handsome face of his."

"He doesn't feel the same way about me."

A light of understanding came into the girl's bright green eyes. "Ohhh. Well, now that's peculiar," she added, staring after Matthew. "He sure seemed to like you well enough this mornin'."

Lorraine rode on leaving Lacey to stare after her in shock. Now what the hell had Matthew done to give Lorraine that idea? He'd barely said two words to anybody all morning.

He and Lacey had fallen asleep in each other's arms the night before, and she'd slept better than she had in her life. After making love with him twice, even she'd started believing that maybe he was feeling more toward her than he was letting on.

But when she woke up, he was already dressed and packing up his saddlebags. Her hopes were even further crushed when he told her he wanted to get back to town early enough for her to leave while it was still daylight. It had been Deputy Larry who'd helped her up into Big Red's saddle. And Deputy Bill who'd offered her a biscuit to eat on the road.

One last fling was all Matthew had wanted from her. That was about all women like her were for in the good old nineteenth century.

She urged her horse up next to Lorraine's again. "What gives you that idea?"

"What idea?"

Lacey glanced at the four men riding ahead of them to be sure none of them were overhearing. "That he liked me well enough this morning."

"The way he kept starin' at ya when you weren't lookin'."

"*What* way?"

"The same way you been lookin' at him all mornin'." That was impossible. Lacey didn't believe it—*couldn't* believe it. She actually considered riding right up next to him and demanding to know how he felt about her, but that action was only bound to get her pride damaged even more than it already was. She could always have Lorraine ride up and ask him. . . . Gee, that would be about as subtle as a Mack truck.

No, Lorraine was mistaken. She'd misread a glance, or most likely a glare. What did a sixteen-year-old girl know about love and the way a man and woman looked at each other anyway?

Lacey once again resigned herself to love unrequited, and refocused her attention on the slushy road. She'd completed her mission and had earned herself a place in the nineteenth century. But not a place in Matthew Brady's heart.

They rode into Tranquility just before noon, and had a crowd gathered around them by the time they reined up in front of Hazel's restaurant. The entire afternoon clientele came out and was gathered on the front walk to greet them. Lacey was pulled off her horse by George, who gave her a tight, warm hug, then handed her over to Hazel for more of the same. Lacey had never felt so missed or so welcomed.

"Where's the brothers?" Paul Smith shouted up at Matthew from the crowd.

"I'm sorry to say they got away."

"Well. I see you've failed again, Marshal," Reginald Sterling remarked, stepping out of the restaurant. "Or should I say *ex*-marshal."

In a moment of unbridled glory, Matthew hefted up his saddlebags and threw them at Reginald Sterling's feet. "There's your money back, Sterling. You can take whatever's missing out of my final paycheck."

"Final paycheck?" Paul Smith repeated.

"You're leaving us?" Reed Baxter called out.

"The good marshal has been kind enough to tender his resignation."

"But he found the money!" Nettie O'Rourke shouted.

"Well, yes," Reginald went on, "but, as you can see, he's failed to even capture the three ne'er-do-wells who stole it in the first place."

Damn that Reginald Sterling, Lacey thought. She'd never known a man who so desperately deserved a good solid kick in the teeth.

"Your name wouldn't be *Reginald* Sterling would it?"

All eyes turned to Lorraine, who was hanging back from the crowd. The girl nudged her horse forward a few paces, her eyes narrowed on the town's mayor.

"A high-falutin' Englishman?"

Reginald gave the girl a disdainful up-down look, even though she looked worlds better since her bath the night before. "And who might you be?" he asked.

"I asked you first, mister. Is Reginald Sterling your name?"

The man rolled his eyes. "Yes. *I* am Reginald Sterling, mayor of Tranquility, owner of the city bank."

"Well, I'll be damned," Lorraine replied.

"What is it?" Lacey asked.

"It's him. Reginald Sterling. The man who talked Ned and Henry into robbin' the bank in the first place. You're the *mayor*?"

Reginald Sterling's face went snow-white pale above his scarlet red cravat. "Who is this little misbegotten?" he demanded.

"This little misbegotten," Lacey told him, "is Lorraine Rawlins, Ned and Henry's sister."

The crowd fell deathly silent and stared first at Lorraine, and then at Reginald Sterling. "Well, she's obviously a low-down crook and liar just like her brothers," Reginald stated, his voice high and shaking.

"I don't lie, mister," Lorraine retorted angrily. "And I doubt I'm as low-down as a man who'd steal from his own bank just to make the town marshal look bad."

The crowd let out a collective gasp and looked at Matthew, whose eyes narrowed ruthlessly. "So now it all begins to make sense," he said.

"Don't be ridiculous," Reginald blustered. Despite the chill in the air, sweat was breaking out on his high brow. "None of it makes sense."

Matthew swung down from his horse. "The bank left open. The safe unlocked. Your overprotective act when Lacey went in to talk to Ned and Henry. You were afraid they'd rat on you, weren't you, Sterling?"

Reginald was backing toward the restaurant doors. "Never. I would never—"

"All this just to get me out of town and out of Amanda's life."

"Come to think of it," Bill said, "he was the last person to visit Ned and Henry last night before they broke out."

Reginald let out a nervous laugh, and then turned suddenly in an attempt to dash to safety inside the restaurant. But he ran right into George Martin's broad chest. Matthew stepped up onto the boardwalk and took Reginald by the back of his black velvet jacket. Then he hauled him into the street toward his dismounting deputies. "Reginald Sterling, you're under arrest. Larry, Gene, Bill. Take Reggie here and show him to our best accommodations."

"But you quit!" Reginald shouted as the three deputies pulled him across the street. "You resigned! *He resiiiigned!*"

The crowd stood in quiet shock as their mayor and banker was led away to jail. But then Hazel threw up her arms. "Well, shoot me in the foot!" she cried. "This town's got its money back, and we're about to have an election for a new mayor! I say we throw ourselves a party!"

The crowd let out a cheer and stampeded into the restaurant, chanting, "Apple pie, apple pie, apple pie."

Matthew was smiling as he turned away from them and headed toward Lacey. He looked like he had something on his mind, but then Paul Smith came storming back outside and took him by the arm. "Get on in here, Marshal! We gotta know how you saved the damsel and rescued the money, for cryin' out loud!"

He gave her a regretful look as he was hauled inside amidst the roar of fifty or so rowdy men.

"Looks like Marshal Matt has saved the day," Nettie stated.

"Hot damn, I'm so proud of that boy," Hazel said. She dabbed at her eyes with the hem of her apron. "And you," she added, looking at Lacey with great big teary eyes, "you are the bravest, most wonderful young lady I know."

"Now, honey bunch," George said, patting his wife on the back, "don't cry all over the girl."

"I'm sorry, Lacey. I'm just gonna miss ya so much when ya leave."

And then Lorraine spoke up. "Why would she leave?"

They all turned to look at the girl, who, once again, was hanging back a few feet. The Martins both smiled at her, and she stared back at them with wide, mistrustful eyes.

"George and Hazel Martin, Nettie, this is Lorraine Rawlins," Lacey said.

"Pleased to mee'cha," the girl said moodily. Then she glared at Lacey. "You didn't tell me you was leavin'."

"Rainey is fresh out of family," Lacey explained, her throat getting tighter by the second. She'd never before been surrounded by an entire group of people who didn't want her to go. "And I was hoping maybe you and George could put her up for a while since I'll be leaving and you'll have that spare room—"

"Spare room or not, Lorraine is welcome to stay with us as long as she likes," Hazel assured her.

"Absolutely," George agreed.

"You see, Rainey," Lacy said. "I told you everything would be fine."

"You never told me you were gonna ride off and leave me here with a pack of strangers. I thought you said you were like me and didn't have family."

"*We* are Lacey's family," Hazel spoke up. "And she won't stay gone. She'll be back for birthdays, and holidays, and all kinds of special occasions. Isn't that right, Lacey."

Lacey nodded because she was too choked up to speak. For so many years she'd had no place to spend Christmas. No one to sing her happy birthday. Now she had the Martins. They were her family.

"Let's all head inside and get this party rollin'," George said. "I wanna hear Matthew's story too, by God."

Nettie smiled at Lorraine and motioned for the girl to precede her inside. George followed, but Hazel hung back with Lacey. "Are you comin'?" Hazel asked.

"Just give me a minute," Lacey whispered in a tear-choked voice.

Hazel nodded and went inside, and Lacey turned toward the street as her tears began to fall. Emotion was overwhelming her, tightening her chest and making it hard to breathe.

"Congratulations, Miss Garder."

She looked up to find her spiritual guide standing there in front of her and quickly dried her eyes. "You're surprised I pulled it off, aren't you?"

"No. I wouldn't have risked my reputation, my career, if I believed you would fail. I'm so proud of you, Miss Garder. You've blossomed into the woman you were always meant to be."

Lacey laughed. "For all you know I could leave this town only to rob the next."

"You've learned too much about kindness and responsibility to do something like that. That ice around your heart is finally melted."

A sob broke from Lacey's throat. "Leaving me raw and unprotected."

"Leaving you human. Capable of expressing all kinds of emotions. Not just pain and sorrow, but happiness and love."

"I do love the Martins."

"And perhaps maybe even someone else?"

New tears burned her eyes. "Perhaps."

"Tell me something, Miss Garder, what is your one true wish?"

"Wish?"

She sniffled and dried her eyes once again. The thought occurred to her that maybe the woman was giving her a break, maybe she'd reconsidered her earlier stipulations and would now send Lacey back to the twentieth century without depositing her back in jail. But in a burst of realization Lacey knew that that wasn't what she wanted. *This* was her home. Here in

Tranquility with the Martins. With Nettie. With Amanda. Even with the lumberjacks who pinched her and begged her to marry them. It would all be so perfect if only . . . if only . . .

"What is it, Miss Garder?"

"It's just impossible," she whispered.

"Sometimes," the guide said carefully, "just saying things out loud can have an amazing effect. How about if you try that?"

Lacey laughed. "Like wishing on a star?"

"Exactly."

She looked up at the clear blue sky and felt the winter chill brush against her damp cheeks. If only it could be that easy. "I wish . . . I wish Matthew Brady loved me half as much as I love him."

She opened her eyes and discovered that the guide had vanished. And then she felt a pair of strong hands on her shoulders, and a pair of full, warm lips kissing the arch of her neck above the collar of her coat. "I've never known anybody who wished upon stars in the middle of the day."

Matthew. She'd known it the moment he'd touched her. Her heart soared and her pride squeezed knowing that he'd heard her utter her deepest desire.

She wanted to turn and curl herself into his strong, secure arms. And she wanted to push away from him and run, protect her vulnerable heart before he had a chance to break it in two. These inner dilemmas kept her from doing anything but stand there as he kissed his way to her ear.

"I do love you, Lacey," she heard him whisper. And she thought she'd burst with the joy of hearing it. "I do."

She turned in his arms and saw the truth reflected in his eyes. "But I'm nothing like Amanda. I'm not dainty and perfect, or gentle or respectable."

He was kissing her face, brushing away her tears with his lips. "You're strong, and brave, and perfect and beautiful. God, Lacey, I'll die without you. Say you'll stay."

"But you're leaving."

He took her face in his hands and peered into her eyes. "Only if you are."

And in that moment Lacey finally knew what utter and unabashed love was. She tossed her pride to the wind, and threw her arms around his neck. "Say you love me again," she demanded.

He laughed at her. "I love you again."

"And promise that you'll never be stubborn again as long as we live."

He frowned playfully at her. "What about those nights when I ask you to join me on a chair and you're too shy to take me up on the offer?"

She angled her mouth toward his. "We can make a few exceptions—"

"You two finished out here, yet?" George called.

Matthew swung Lacey around and they both stared at the crowd converged in the doorway and staring out the windows. "She spoken for now?" Paul Smith demanded, elbowing his way to the front of the crowd.

"She is," Matthew replied, sweeping Lacey up into his arms. "I catch any of you sawdust boys taking baths and begging her to marry you again, you'll be spending some long hard time in my jail."

"Then you're stayin'?" George asked.

Matthew looked at Lacey, and she knew the choice was hers. Just as she knew that if she chose to leave, he'd be coming with her. She smiled at him, and he grinned back. "We're staying!" he shouted.

And the entire town of Tranquility let out a deafening cheer of delight as Matthew and Lacey sealed their mutual decision with a long, passionate kiss.

"Now that," Stella said, "is a happy ending. I must say I'm going to miss this job."

Nelson was pursing his lips again. "Yes, well, congratulations, old girl, it looks as though you've cinched that promotion. Now, if you'll excuse me, I need to check in with my office—"

"Not so fast," Stella interrupted. "You know, Nelson, with my promotion a position has opened up for a new spiritual guide."

"Really? Well, I'm sure you'll find someone in no time—"

"I've already spoken with Maximillian and we both agree. *You* will fill that position."

Nelson's jaw dropped open. "But I don't know the first thing—"

"About compassion? Not to worry, Nelson, I will be showing you the ropes personally." She broke into a smile. "Perhaps I'll even buy you a little hat with Mr. Destiny inscribed on the front. Now, come along, I have just the woman in mind for you."

"*Woman?*" Nelson called, following along after her. "Couldn't we start out with a cat or a dog? A hamster might be nice. They're cute. Don't get out much—and they don't *live* long. . . ."

Let HarperMonogram
Sweep You Away

❧❧❧❧

MRS. MIRACLE by Debbie Macomber
Bestselling Author
Seth Webster, a widower with two young children, finds the answer to his prayers when a very special housekeeper arrives. Her wisdom is priceless, but it is the woman she finds for Seth who is truly heaven sent.

DESTINY'S EMBRACE by Suzanne Elizabeth
Award-winning Time Travel Series
Winsome criminal Lacey Garder faces imprisonment, until her guardian angel sends her back in time to 1879. Rugged Marshal Matthew Brady is the law in Tranquility, Washington Territory, and he soon finds Lacey guilty of love in the first degree.

SECOND CHANCES by Sharon Sala
Romantic Times Award-winning Author
Matt Holt had disappeared out of Billie Jean Walker's life once before, but fate has brought them together again. Now Matt is determined to grab a second chance at love—especially the kind that comes once in lifetime.

FOREVER AND ALWAYS by Donna Grove
Emily Winters must enlist the help of handsome reporter Ross Gallagher to rebuild her father's Pennsylvania printing business after the Civil War. But will working closely with the man she's always loved distract her from her goals?

And in case you missed last month's selections...

DANCING MOON by Barbara Samuel
Fleeing from her cruel husband, Tess Fallon finds herself on the Santa Fe trail and at the mercy of Joaquin Morales. He brands her with his kiss, but they must conquer the threats of the past before embracing the paradise found in each other's arms.

BURNING LOVE by Nan Ryan
Winner of the *Romantic Times* Lifetime Achievement Award
While traveling across the Arabian desert, American socialite
Temple Longworth is captured by a handsome sheik.
Imprisoned in *El Süf*'s lush oasis, Temple struggles not to lose
her heart to a man whose touch promises ecstasy.

A LITTLE PEACE AND QUIET by Modean Moon
Bestselling Author
A handsome stranger is drawn to a Victorian house—and the
attractive woman who is restoring it. When an evil presence is
unleashed, David and Anne risk falling under its spell unless
they can join together to create a powerful love.

ALMOST A LADY by Barbara Ankrum
Lawman Luke Turner is caught in the middle of a Colorado
snowstorm, handcuffed to beautiful pickpocket Maddy
Barnes. While stranded in a hostile town, the unlikely couple
discovers more trouble than they ever bargained for—and
heavenly pleasures neither can deny.

Harper Monogram